For Florence and Theodore

DECEMBER 1ST

I

KATE

Kate thrust her hands deep into the pockets of the battered Barbour jacket that had once been Adam's. Her face was stinging from the cold and rain, and the wind whipped her hair about her face. *A good day for a funeral,* she thought.

There was a small, huddled group of mourners gathered in the garden. Her children, Max and Emmie, faces serious underneath their rain hoods. Fergus, her neighbour, his wife Natalie, and their son James. They all looked solemn, or maybe just cold.

Kate saw her mother walking towards her across the communal garden; a neat, purposeful figure wearing an old mac and clutching an enormous black umbrella. The wind caught it and dragged Jean along, so that she hopped the last few steps towards Kate.

'Bloody thing,' said Jean, wrestling the umbrella into submission. 'How are you, darling?'

'Hi, Mum,' Kate said, ducking to kiss Jean's wet cheek. She was a full head taller than her mother. As always, Jean smelled of Elizabeth Arden perfume and soap.

'Appropriate weather for a funeral, at any rate,' Jean said, waving to the children. 'We do seem to be making a habit of this, don't we?'

Kate shivered. To lose your father and husband in the space of two years was no ordinary bad luck. It was a special, uniquely brutal sort of bad luck. And then, yesterday, Emmie had found Hamish the hamster, cold and stiff in his cage.

It wouldn't be Christmas without a death in the family, Kate thought grimly. Emmie was clutching the damp shoebox with Hamish's body inside.

'How are the kids holding up?' Jean asked.

'Not too bad,' said Kate. 'Considering . . . everything.'

Jean squeezed her arm. 'They're tough nuts, both of them. They get that from you. Alice and I are both softies.'

Kate remembered the shock, somewhere in her self-absorbed teens, of realising that her mother was beautiful. Before that, she had always just been *Mum*. Jean and her sister Alice were both dainty, dark-haired, elfin; all soft curves, small wrists, dimples and rosy cheeks. Kate was tall and blonde, like her father Gerard, and had inherited his thick, dark brows and long limbs.

The only thing she had inherited from her mother was her temper. Jean's rages, like sudden squalls on a sunny day, were legendary in their family, but they seemed to have petered out with age. 'I got sick of being so angry all the time,' Jean had told Kate once. 'Life is hard enough.'

Fergus stepped forward. He was a tall man with a comforting presence who was paid huge sums of money to give motivational speeches to companies. The funeral had been his idea, so Kate had asked him to officiate. 'Your funeral,' she had told him when he groaned. 'Besides, you know you love making a speech.'

'If everyone is here now,' Fergus said, 'I thought we might begin.'

Kate nodded, stamping her feet. *Make it snappy*, she thought. This was the sort of cold, driving wet rain which Edinburgh specialised in at this time of year. Only yesterday, the garden had been filled with crisp, clear winter sunshine.

The first day of December. On this day one year ago, Kate had got the Call, her phone buzzing in her jeans pocket as she had cycled through the Meadows.

And the year before that, only a few days later, Jean had rung, telling her that her dad had been rushed into hospital.

Christmas was cursed in this family, Kate thought.

'We are here,' Fergus said, in sonorous tones, 'to lay to rest Hamish the hamster. Max, would you like to say a few words?'

Max pushed his rain-splattered glasses further up his nose. He had volunteered to speak, which had pleased Kate as he had become uncharacteristically shy since starting school.

'Hamish was not just a hamster,' he said. 'He was a member of our family. For a pet, he was quite low maintenance. We didn't need to walk him or have him groomed. All we really needed to do was love him.'

Kate felt a wave of guilt. Her first emotion on discovering Hamish's death had been relief that she would never again have to clear out that revolting cage. She had always wanted a dog, but Adam had put his foot down and Hamish was the compromise.

Emmie came forward, carrying the shoebox. Fergus knelt with her as they laid the box into a freshly dug hole in the ground that was a bit larger than Kate had envisioned. She cast a nervous glance behind her, wondering whether any of the neighbours were watching. She had a feeling that some of them wouldn't be best pleased with the ceremony, particularly not Mr Watson at number 36, for whom the communal garden was a source of pride.

The earth was laid over the box and neatly patted down with Emmie's little blue spade.

'All right everyone, let's go inside and get warm,' Kate said. 'I think we should raise a glass in Hamish's memory.'

Back inside Kate's flat, everything felt more cheerful. Wet coats were hung on radiators, filling the air with the smell of damp wool, and boots stacked by the door. Jean ruffled her dark curls.

'Crisps and wine in the kitchen,' said Kate, shaking out her own wet hair. It had once been honey-blonde but now, with her roots grown out and grey hairs growing in, it was more of a muddy sort of brown.

'I have to say,' said Jean, leading her down the hallway, 'you are getting very good at wakes.'

'I should be,' said Kate, 'I've had a lot of practice.'

Sometimes, when Kate woke in the mornings, there would be a moment when she would forget. That was the worst. The at-once horrible and blissful moment in which you forgot your life had changed at all.

Her father, Gerard Whyte, had died at Christmas two years ago, an infection swiftly curtailing his cancer. And then, on the 1st of December last year, her husband Adam Patterson, thirty-nine years old, had run a red light and been killed instantly.

'I can't believe it,' Kate had told the police. 'He was such a careful driver.'

Because Adam *had* been careful. He was all five-year plans and budget projections, while Kate was impulse and snap decisions, last-minute holidays and figure-it-out-later. It was the source of most of their arguments, his forethought running up against her impetuosity, but it had also, Kate thought, made them a team.

Adam had encouraged Kate to leave Domus – the interior design house where she had happily spent a decade working with her adored boss, Madeleine Hawes – to set up her own company. Kate had taken the plunge, rented office space for Whyte Designs, hired a small but brilliant team, and gradually built a client list.

Her clean, minimalist style and ability to transform

spaces on a shoestring started to get attention. She began to feature on the front of industry magazines; was asked to speak at conferences; got a few big commissions for local celebrities.

Adam had suggested they sell their tiny flat and buy a bigger one: a sprawling, rundown, four-bedroom flat in Marchmont with a barely functioning boiler and faulty wiring. It would be Kate's dream project; she could use it to showcase her skills, and then they would sell it for a profit.

Kate had felt uneasy about the idea. 'I'm worried about the kids, living with all that dust,' she had said, knowing that wasn't quite the problem but unsure what was. 'Plus, we can't afford a four-bed flat in Marchmont, even in this state.'

But Adam had been confident. 'If it gets really bad, we'll rent somewhere for a few months,' he had said. 'Stop worrying.'

When Adam told you there was nothing to worry about, you believed him.

They had sold their flat, put most of their stuff in storage, moved in. And then a week later, Adam had died, and it turned out that their savings, the stocks and shares and bonds that Kate had never bothered to understand, didn't actually exist. The problem with being a vague, creative type married to a financial wizard, Kate realised, is that you don't know to look behind the curtain.

She had let her team go, with a month's pay and no explanations. It was a dark secret Kate had carried alone this past year. She couldn't bear the thought of telling Jean or Alice.

And now there they were, her and Max and Emmie, in purgatory. She could neither afford to do the flat up nor sell it. Instead, they waited – in a flat with holes in the walls and dust on the floor, picking their way over cables and brushing their teeth with water the colour of weak tea.

Kate had come to hate the flat: the mess, the bills stacking up, the clouds of dust that would rise up whenever she sat down on the sofa. Once she would have rolled her sleeves up and got stuck in, made the best of the situation, but now she felt paralysed by the immensity of the task.

Now, Kate stood in the doorway of the kitchen, watching Fergus doing a magic trick with a napkin and a fork for the kids, Nat rolling her eyes and pouring wine. A funeral for Hamish was exactly the sort of whimsy that Adam would have hated. But Emmie and Max were laughing now, for the first time in days. The miserable flat seemed warmer and cosier, full of people. Fergus always knew best.

He and Nat had started as playground acquaintances but had swiftly become her best friends, particularly in the last few years. They had a knack of checking in without being irritating or invasive.

'Now you see it,' said Fergus, holding the napkin steady. He waited a beat, then whipped it away. 'Now you don't.'

Emmie shrieked and clapped. 'Again,' she said. 'I want to see how you did it.'

'It's magic,' said Fergus mysteriously. 'Appearances can be deceptive.'

A lump swelled in Kate's throat. Suddenly the dusty kitchen – full of her best friends and her children, drinking, talking and laughing – felt claustrophobic. That was the thing about grief: half the time it came out of nowhere and knocked you off your feet.

She slipped unnoticed out of the kitchen and went into the bathroom. There was no lock on the door, but she propped a stool underneath it and sat on the toilet seat, head in hands, breathing through the pain, trying to slow her racing heart. What a mess she had made of things, she thought. Or rather, what a mess she and Adam had made between them.

Another Christmas, looming on the horizon. Like a ticking clock, waiting, with none of the joy and warmth the day should offer.

Her father had died on Christmas Eve. The next day had been a nightmare. Exhausted from a night in the hospital, trying to explain death to the children, that Grandpa wasn't going to be here anymore. Jean, pale and stoic. Plastering on a smile for hastily wrapped presents and cooking a lunch none of them could eat.

And then last Christmas, only weeks after Adam's death. All of them still stunned, the children pale and irritable, quick to tantrums and tears. Max sobbing because Kate had bought the wrong Lego set. A mockery of Christmas, tainted forever with grief and confusion.

The children had fallen asleep on the sofa in front of the television and Kate had carried them to bed. 'Is this Christmas?' Max had asked sleepily.

She would do things differently this year. She had to.

There was a knock on the door. One of the kids, needing the toilet.

'Come in,' called Kate, stretching out her leg and kicking the stool away.

It wasn't one of the kids; it was Nat, holding two glasses of wine. 'Are you okay?' she said, coming in and shutting the door behind her.

'I'm okay,' Kate said, straightening up and pushing back her hair. 'It just hits me sometimes; how strange it is that we're living our lives without him. This pet funeral is the sort of thing that Adam would have hated. His mum used to flush their goldfish down the toilet.' She gave a shaky laugh. 'I'm worried about Christmas. Last year was so shit. I wish Adam was here to talk to about stuff.'

Nat perched on the edge of the bath and handed Kate a

glass of wine. 'Is there anything I can help with?' she said. 'You can talk to me about stuff, you know.'

'I know,' said Kate. Her fear was becoming the sort of whingeing, clinging friend Nat and Fergus would dread being around. 'It's just the usual stuff: Max finding it hard to make friends and Emmie stuck with bloody Lydia.'

On the first day of primary school, a small, determined girl called Lydia had approached Emmie and told her that they were 'best friends forever'. They'd been stuck with her ever since. She ruled Emmie's life with an iron fist, dictating every-thing from what Emmie was allowed to eat at lunch to who she was allowed to speak to during the day. Kate didn't think the friendship made Emmie happy, and she didn't think the teacher liked it much either, but there wasn't much she could do about it except grit her teeth and hope it fizzled out.

'It's a lot to deal with on your own,' said Nat sympathetically.

'It's been a year,' said Kate. 'I can't be a helpless widow for ever. I need to—'

There was another knock on the door. Kate sighed. 'Come in,' she called, resignedly.

It was Jean, looking flushed and holding a near-empty glass of wine. Her mother had a low tolerance for alcohol. 'Emmie is looking pale,' she said, without preamble. 'Is she getting enough vitamin D? We only see the sun about once a year in this country.' She sat on the side of the bath along-side Nat and fixed Kate with her candid, grey-eyed stare. 'Are you all right, sweetheart?'

The tenderness in her voice brought the lump back to Kate's throat. She could feel the tears starting. 'I miss Adam,' wailed Kate, slumping forward into Jean's lap.

Kate heard Jean murmur to Nat, 'I've got this now, love,' and then the sound of the door shutting behind her friend.

They sat in silence for a while, while Jean stroked Kate's hair and Kate wept noiselessly. 'I'm making your trousers all wet,' she said at last.

'That doesn't matter,' Jean said soothingly. She leant over and tore off a handful of toilet paper. 'Here.'

Kate sat up and mopped at her eyes. 'I just hate this time of year. It's so . . . relentlessly jolly. School fetes and the PTA and happy families getting their Christmas trees. I'm a mess. I can't even face school pickup. Fergus gets the kids every afternoon. The last time I got them, the teacher did a double take.' She took a deep, shuddering breath. 'I hate Christmas.'

'You can't hate Christmas,' said Jean, sounding shocked. 'It was always our favourite time of year.'

'I do,' Kate insisted stubbornly. 'First Dad, then Adam, and now Hamish. This family has a . . . a Christmas curse.'

'Enough of that,' said Jean firmly. 'You know,' she said, eyeing Kate speculatively, 'you could consider coming to grief group with me.'

'Not that again,' said Kate. 'It's never going to happen. I hate joining things.'

Kate had been pleased when Jean had started going out again after her father's death, but now the sheer volume of activities, along with the roster of new friends, was making Kate dizzy. There was tennis on a Monday and ceramics on a Tuesday and a patisserie course on a Wednesday. She had started making sourdough and jam and had bought a set of calligraphy pens.

It made Kate wonder how much it was a front for unresolved grief. The flat in which they'd grown up remained exactly the same, as though her father had merely popped out to get milk. His shirts hanging in the wardrobe, his paperwork stacked and neatly filed in his old roll-top desk, his reading glasses and the book he'd been reading open on his bedside table along with his beloved, battered wrist-watch. It wasn't healthy.

Then, last year, Jean had announced she'd been attending a group for the bereaved. 'Like a book group, but with more crying,' she had said. 'You should come along, Kate.' It sounded like Kate's idea of hell.

'They're a lovely bunch of people,' Jean said now. 'I think you might find it helpful. Ada thinks so.'

Ada was the organiser of the grief group and seemed to have a lot of opinions. Kate had never met her, but was deeply mistrustful of her.

Kate shook her head. 'Couldn't even if I wanted to. No babysitter,' she said.

'Fergus and Nat have said they'll help,' said Jean.

Kate narrowed her eyes. 'You've mentioned it to them?'

'Come on, darling,' said Jean. 'You need to . . . buck up a bit. You can't write off this time of year – think of the children. Give them a Christmas to remember.'

'You're one to talk,' said Kate sullenly. 'You're living in a shrine to Dad. How many times have I offered to help you sort through his stuff?' Jean was silent. 'Tell you what,' said Kate, inspiration striking. 'I'll make you a deal. You go through Dad's things and clear them out, and I'll come to this grief group.'

Jean looked uncertain. 'I don't know,' she said.

'It's been two years, Mum. You need to face up to it,' said Kate firmly. If Jean could dish out tough love, then so could she. She held out her hand to Jean. 'Do we have a deal?'

'All right,' said Jean slowly, putting her hand in Kate's. Kate noted the contrast between her mother's elegant oval nails, painted a soft pink, and her own square, bitten ones. 'Deal.'

'I can't believe you sold me out,' Kate said, following Nat, Fergus and James down the hall. The wake was over. She took James's jacket from the peg and helped him into it. 'The last thing I want to do is go to this group. Can you imagine? Everyone sitting there, crying . . .'

Nat smiled at her, tugging on her hat. 'Sorry. Actually, I'm not sorry. You're awesome. I want you to be happy, or at least a bit happier. This might help.'

Nat was a bit like a terrier, Kate had always thought. If she decided you were worth bothering with, you had a friend for life.

Nat was a lecturer in feminist theory at the university, had a regular column in the *Herald*, and was always on the news to talk about 'anything that involves women,' as she put it. She avoided school pickup as determinedly as Kate did. 'I can give a lecture to 200 people or be interviewed on live TV about the pay gap,' she had said, 'but I can't face the playground. Isn't that pathetic?'

Kate knew what Nat meant. Running the gauntlet that was the playground at home time was the closest thing to being back at school yourself. That had to change. Jean was right.

'Grief group. I can just imagine it,' Kate muttered. 'A community centre somewhere. Bad coffee and stale biscuits.' She gave James a hug. He was a little carbon copy of Fergus, complete with the same curly red hair and quietly amused expression. 'Thanks for coming. It wouldn't be a Patterson–Whyte family funeral without you guys. See you at the next one.'

'Don't joke,' said Nat, laying a small hand on her arm. 'You are definitely due some good luck now. I'm sorry for your loss, by the way. Poor Hamish.'

'Hamish was a nightmare,' said Kate.

'Still, it's hard for the kids. Fergus is like you, desperate to get a dog, but I keep saying I can't face the inevitable heartbreak when something happens to it.'

Fergus rolled his eyes, wrapping his scarf around his neck. 'I keep saying by that logic, we'd never do anything. Never have kids, never leave the house, never get in a car . . .' He stopped and flushed. 'Sorry, Kate,' he muttered. 'What an idiot.'

'It's okay!' Kate said quickly. The worst thing about people putting their foot in it was their own discomfort. 'I'll see you tomorrow.'

'Am I picking up your two at home time?' said Fergus, still pink with embarrassment.

'No thank you,' Kate said firmly. 'I'm turning over a new leaf. I'll be there.'

Kate shut the door behind them and leaned against it for a moment, her eyes closed. She could hear her mother's warm laugh, her children's chatter. She opened her eyes and they fell on the stack of bills on the upturned crate that functioned as their hall table.

Tomorrow was a fresh start. Kate would shake off the apathy that had dogged her all year. Shower and dress nicely every morning for school. Deal with the mounting stack of bills. Talk to the bank about a loan. Get the flat on the market. Go through her contacts and try to resurrect her failing career.

The children would go into school tomorrow with healthy snacks, full water bottles, clean uniforms. She would help them with their homework and avoid the PTA, run by a ferocious woman called Veronica. And, for the sake of the children, she would embrace Christmas cheer. Give them a Christmas to remember. Buy a wreath and a turkey and make paper snowflakes. She would do it if it killed her.

And if that wasn't Christmas spirit, Kate thought triumphantly, then she didn't know what was.

2

JEAN

Jean watched with pleasure as the pale morning sunshine began to filter through the slats of the blinds, throwing columns of light onto the floor. She loved her flat – not that it was *her* flat, not really. It was the family home. But now it felt like hers.

She was all alone. She still slept on the left-hand side of the bed though, leaving the right untouched. How long, she wondered, before she reclaimed the whole bed? She imagined taking up all that space, star-fishing out with abandon.

'Just hog the bed now,' Kate had said once. 'There have to be some advantages to this nightmare. Having the bed to myself is one of them. You should try it, Mum.'

Tentatively, Jean stretched out a hand towards the cool pillow next to her. Occupied by Gerard for over forty years, the only absences when he went away for work. His glasses were still in the drawer of the bedside table. The book he had been reading, the corner of a page neatly turned down. He might have just gone out.

Jean took another sip of her coffee. For over forty years, Jean had woken to the smell of coffee. Long before the trendy coffee bars had invaded Morningside, with their flat whites and oat milk cortados, Gerard would buy little paper-wrapped packages of coffee beans and bring them home where he would grind them himself with a little wooden machine. The whole house would smell of freshly ground coffee by 7 a.m.

Kate and Alice had clubbed together a few years ago and bought Gerard a state-of-the-art coffee grinder, smarter and more efficient, but it had remained in its box. 'Can't teach an old dog new tricks,' he had said ruefully. 'Besides, I like taking my time.'

Now, Jean had to make her own coffee in the mornings. Padding down the worn, carpeted stairs in her bare feet, making her way through the darkened flat, switching on the kitchen light, listening to the news as the coffee bubbled on the stove. She bought ground coffee these days. It didn't taste quite the same.

Sometimes the idea that Gerard was gone seemed ridiculous. He was as reliable and constant as the grandfather clock in their downstairs hallway. Good in a crisis. Big, capable, weathered hands; hands made for scooping up the children, for undoing jars and fixing furniture, for digging in the earth.

'A real man,' her mother Nina had said approvingly, when she had met him for the first time. 'He knows where he's going.'

Her father, Gianni, the owner of a local ice-cream parlour and caffe, had been less sure. 'Restless,' he had said. 'Wants a lot, that boy.'

And Gerard had wanted a lot. Worked his way up the shipyard business. Headed up the company. Hired more staff. Moved them from the tiny cottage in Ayrshire to a two-bedroom flat in Glasgow, then later to a four-bedroom one in Edinburgh.

Private school for the girls. Holidays abroad. Everything they could want, the girls had. Treasured Alice, the youngest, who was scared of dogs and loud noises and parties. And Kate, smart, popular, quick to anger, scared of nothing. Always running late and forgetting things, but so funny and carelessly pretty that no one minded. Good at horse-riding and games, she had moved through life with enviable ease. Even meeting Adam in her first week at university had seemed entirely in character. Kate had led the definition of a charmed life – until two years ago. Now, as she drank her coffee, Jean worried about her daughter. She had dark circles under her eyes. If Jean mentioned her job, Kate's gaze skittered away and she would mumble something vague about an upcoming project that never seemed to materialise. The flat was a state, and the kids were unhappy. It was to be expected, but Jean wished there was something she could do.

Jean should bring them some dinner tonight, she thought. Feed them all up a bit. She could make her baked pasta with sausage that the kids loved. She would enjoy doing some proper cooking for a change. It was a waste cooking for one.

Jean stretched her arms over her head, easing the knot in her shoulders, then pulled back the covers and swung her legs onto the polished floorboards. Her gaze landed on Gerard's dressing gown hanging on the back of the door and she remembered the deal she had struck with her daughter to clear out Gerard's things.

Inside the wardrobe, Gerard's shirts hung, neatly ironed. His shoes, polished. A frisson of fear went through Jean, sharp as a knife. What was she so scared of?

If only she knew. That was the problem.

Still, at least she had persuaded Kate to come with her to grief group. She would meet everyone, get to know them all. And perhaps, then, Jean's news would come as less of a shock.

3

KATE

Sweat ran down Kate's back as she sped the last few steps into the playground, dragging a child by each hand. Mud splashed up her trousers. Glancing at the playground clock she saw with relief that they were on time.

'Thank god,' she muttered.

'Did we make it?' Max said anxiously.

'We made it,' said Kate, wiping her forehead with the heel of her hand. A combination of drizzle and sweat made her blouse cling damply to her body. She realised she was clenching her jaw, which her dentist had told her to stop doing. 'I told you not to worry.'

'Are you okay, Mum?' said Max. 'You're all pink.'

'Fine,' she wheezed. She really had to start exercising again, she thought. She should get her bike out of the shed and start cycling into town.

Emmie was already scanning the playground for Lydia. 'See you later, Mum,' she said, accepting a kiss. 'Is Fergus picking us up?'

'No, I am,' said Kate firmly, pushing back her daughter's thick fringe and tucking her hair behind her ears. She needed to book in haircuts for them. *Add it to the list*, she thought.

'If you say so,' Emmie said, her tone faintly disbelieving.

She squeezed Kate's hand and ran off, little legs flashing quickly across the playground.

Kate crouched down in front of Max, who was staring at the school building with apprehensive eyes. He was young for his year and still looked so much smaller than the other children. He had hated the big, noisy playground from the very first day. Her little chatterbox had become a quiet, anxious child overnight, scared of monsters under the bed and big kids in the playground.

'Hey,' she said softly, touching his perfect cheek. 'Buddy. You'll be fine today, all right?' He lifted his chin in a courageous gesture that tugged at her heart. 'Here's your snack,' she said, holding out an apple that had definitely seen better days.

He sighed and shoved it into his rucksack. 'Please go to the shops, Mum,' he said.

'I will,' she replied, wondering whether there would be time today. She had her first client meeting in months, a caffe refurb in town, and she didn't want to blow it. She kissed him on the head. 'See you later.'

On the way to the gate she saw Veronica Peterson approaching, clad in her usual immaculate athleisure, flanked by her sidekicks, Tamara and Lois. The holy trinity of the PTA.

'Kate,' Veronica said, raising her voice in an authoritative way that stopped Kate in her tracks. 'Glad I caught you. Bit of a surprise to see you here so early.'

'Veronica, Tamara, Lois, hi.' Kate swung her shoulder bag purposefully onto her arm. 'I'm actually in a bit of a rush.'

'The juggle is real,' Veronica said, her smile revealing gleaming white teeth. 'I know what it's like for us career women.'

'Of course you do,' Kate said. All those granola bowls woudn't photograph themselves.

Veronica ran a hugely successful Instagram home account on which she shared photographs of her adorable children, Sienna and Hugo, and her vast, beautiful home. She posted recipes for vegan brownies made with grated courgette, and ideas for Montessori play. She was married to a handsome trainer called Craig, who worked for Celtic FC.

The Petersons threw glamorous Christmas parties to raise money for the PTA, parties with champagne and canapés and waiters. They were the celebrity couple of Lyndoch Primary.

One of Kate's dark secrets was that she was Veronica's biggest fan. She had been obsessed since the kids had started at the school and had seen Veronica's followers climb from a few hundred to twenty thousand on the back of a viral avocado-mousse recipe. She read every post and watched Veronica's tutorials on five-minute-school-run makeup and bedtime skincare routine. She dreamed of recreating Veronica's sleek outfits from her own haphazard wardrobe. Veronica both fascinated and terrified her.

Tamara and Lois were lesser evils. Kate and Adam had nicknamed them the Flying Monkeys. Veronica was the wicked witch.

For several years Veronica had run the PTA alongside a sweet, bewildered-looking mother from the year above. Then last term there had been some sort of disagreement and Veronica had seized power in a coup. Half the PTA had left in protest and she ruled the remaining half with an iron fist.

'Look who it is,' said Tamara, nudging Lois. Kate glanced in the direction of her gaze. A man was crouched down in front of a boy about Emmie's age. Kate could only see a broad back in an ugly brown cord blazer and a head of dark hair.

'Who's that?' Kate said. 'I don't recognise him.'

'He's the reason we're all early for drop off,' said Lois, and giggled.

'Lois. Please,' said Veronica, frowning at her. 'Don't be disgusting.'

Lois subsided, looking chastened. Kate watched as the man kissed his son on the cheek, ruffled his hair, and sent him running into the school. Kate noticed the boy was wearing shining red patent leather shoes with his grey uniform.

'That's Matthias Devaux and the kid is Olivier,' said Veronica. 'He started last term. I can't believe you haven't noticed. He's in Emmie's *class*, Kate.' She smiled humourlessly. 'Although he's always on time, so you might not have run into him.'

The man stood then, unfolding himself, and Kate realised he was not only broad but very tall. He had the look of a rumpled professor, with glasses, superior expression and dishevelled dark hair.

'Goodness,' Kate said faintly. 'Good-looking, isn't he?'

'French, I think,' said Tamara, her flinty blue eyes following the man as he walked back across the playground, oblivious to the scrutiny. 'The mother lives in Europe, the dad has main custody. That's just odd, isn't it?'

'Whatever,' said Veronica, dismissing the topic. Her raptor-like gaze snapped back to Kate, who regretted not taking the opportunity to escape while they were all distracted. 'Kate, I need to talk to you, it's important.'

'I really am going to be late for work,' Kate pleaded. 'I've got a meeting in town.'

'I'll walk with you to the bus stop,' said Veronica. She took hold of Kate's arm and marched her towards the gate. 'Although you really should *walk* into town, Kate.' She tapped her Fitbit. 'Get your steps in.'

Veronica glanced back over her shoulder at Lois and Tamara, who were trotting after them, ponytails bouncing. 'Why don't you two go ahead to the caffe and get a table,' she called over her shoulder. 'I'll have an oat milk flat white and a chia bowl.'

Lois and Tamara nodded obediently and turned off towards the caffe. Kate and Veronica continued to walk towards the bus stop. Veronica's grip was firm on Kate's arm. Kate felt like she had been taken hostage.

'You look smart today, Kate, for you,' Veronica said. 'Big client?'

'A caffe refurbishment,' Kate said. 'Lovely heritage spot.'

The caffe was actually a dingy diner on the edges of central Edinburgh that had been shut down for health code violations. The owner, a man called Marco, had decided to 'spruce things up a bit' and for some reason he had contacted Kate.

'That's good news,' said Veronica. 'You could use some luck, things have been a bit stagnant on the work front, haven't they? Now, I'll come straight to the point. Christmas is the busiest time of year and the PTA is running low on numbers.'

'Oh no, why?' Kate said, walking faster.

Veronica easily kept pace with her long, lycra-clad legs. 'There were some creative disagreements,' she said. 'The Christmas schedule was intimidating for some people. But I'm bringing in fresh blood. Forget bake sales, we're thinking big. The Christmas party, the fete. Lois's husband Dan is doing us a new website. It's looking like we might get a celebrity appearance at the fete.'

'Really? Who?' asked Kate, mildly intrigued.

Veronica winked. 'Wouldn't you like to find out? It's fun. We have a glass of wine, put the world to rights, or at least Lyndoch Primary. It's great for making friends. Like one, big, happy family. I heard that Max has been *struggling* a bit, socially . . .'

The bus stop was in sight. Kate made a last valiant attempt at resistance. 'You don't want me, Veronica. I don't bake, I don't craft. I have zero skills to bring to the table.'

'Nonsense. You're so stylish, Kate. I need someone with artistic flair. We're going to make this Christmas the best yet.'

'I don't like Christmas,' Kate muttered.

Veronica stopped abruptly on the pavement. 'Shit. I forgot I need to let the cleaner in. I've got a photoshoot later.' She smoothed back a strand of dark, shining hair and pointed a finger at Kate. 'Kate, the PTA needs *you* this Christmas. We'll pick this up at home time.'

'I'm working late,' Kate said, thinking fast. 'Fergus is doing pickup.'

'You're so lucky to have that arrangement with Fergus, aren't you?' Veronica said. She laughed musically; Kate wasn't altogether sure that it was a nice laugh. 'He's virtually on call! What *do* you do to men, Kate?'

'No idea,' Kate said, gritting her teeth and sending a mental apology to her dentist. 'Let's text!'

She sped to the bus stop, where a little queue had formed. As she waited, Kate pulled out her phone and texted Fergus. She couldn't admit the truth – that she didn't want to face Veronica twice in one day – so she told a white lie.

'I know I said I was turning over a new leaf, but I have a ton of work on. Would you mind getting the kids after all? I'll make it up to you.'

She didn't have to wait very long for a reply.

'No problem.'

Reliable, helpful Fergus. He never seemed to mind. He even seemed to like the playground. 'Most of them are nice,' he would say. 'You're making them out to be way scarier than they are.'

Kate boarded the bus, swiping her card and squeezing into a seat beside an old woman with several bags of shopping. Glancing at her phone, she saw that Jean had texted her.

'So excited you're coming along to group tomorrow!' she had written, followed by a succession of emojis, a sprinkling of hearts, a dancing woman and, for some reason, an elephant. Kate smiled.

Kate stared out of the window at the driving rain, her reflection fractured and blurred beyond recognition. Once, she would have flipped open her mirror, adjusted her makeup, and been satisfied with what she saw. Thick mane of blonde hair, long black lashes, perfect skin even as a teenager, eyes that changed with the light from green to grey to blue. Now she had wrinkles at the corners of her eyes and mouth, dark circles under her eyes, and her skin was grey with fatigue. She couldn't remember the last time she'd had a haircut.

Give them a Christmas to remember. Stockings, turkey, Christmas music. Bowls full of nuts. Orange slices dried in the oven and strung from ribbon. The things the children had made, misshapen lumps of hardened dough, covered in glitter, brought home from the nursery over the years.

Then and there, on the crowded number 15 bus with its fogged-up windows and smell of damp wool, Kate made a vow. The children would not have to face a third terrible Christmas in a row. This year, Christmas in the Whyte household would be different.

This year, it would be perfect.

4

Caffe Firenze was a dingy diner on a busy main road, with boarded up windows and a public health warning taped to the front door.

The owner greeted her in a filthy apron, yawning. He smelt of cigarettes and frying fat and was holding a mug of tea.

'Marco,' he said, sticking out his hand. 'You came, then.'

'Of course,' said Kate, trying to sound enthusiastic. 'I'd love to hear a bit more about the place. It's very ...' She glanced around at the ripped leather booths and pools of unidentified liquid on the floor. 'Very atmospheric. You can tell there's real heritage here.'

He shrugged. 'I'd say so. Been in my family for years, but my dad always had very set ideas, shall we say. It's an Italian thing.'

'I'm Italian, on my mum's side,' said Kate, trying to ingratiate herself. 'My grandparents had a place a bit like this out of the city. A caffe and ice-cream parlour.'

If she'd hoped that would endear Marco to her, she was wrong. He gave her an unimpressed look. 'Well, let's just say my dad doesn't like change. He's finally retired though, so I get a say at last. We were shut down last year. Health and

27

safety. I'm taking the opportunity to get a different vibe going in here. Maybe a bit more, I don't know . . .'

'Cosy?' said Kate, looking around at the cracked windows and chipped tables and trying to think of anything Caffe Firenze currently wasn't. A cold draught swept in from the street and she shivered. 'Welcoming?'

He nodded, swigging his tea. 'Aye. Change things up a bit, you know, but keep the good bits. Lots of the business will be old-timers. We're getting a new chef, modern Italian, young guy.'

'How did you find me?' Kate asked. Maybe her ancient website was bringing in some business at last.

'I googled interior designers in Edinburgh and the first seven said no.'

Great, Kate thought. 'There's loads of potential here,' she said, determined to keep things upbeat. 'It's a wonderful space.' She ran a finger tentatively along the wood panelling, leaving her finger sticky and grey with dirt. 'These original features are fantastic. I'll put together a proposal and send you a breakdown of the budget and fee, then you can see if you want to proceed. I'll need to take some initial photos . . .'

'Go ahead,' Marco said, waving his hand. 'I'll be out back when you're done.'

He ambled off. Kate rolled up her sleeves and got to work. Her phone rang just as she was crouching on the floor trying to peel back the filthy lino to see what was beneath. She pulled it out and glanced at the screen. Jean.

'Hi, Mum,' Kate said, wedging her phone beneath her ear. She thought she saw something dark moving underneath the fryer and hastily shuffled back. 'What's up?'

Jean's warm, lilting voice came tinnily down the phone. 'Hello, darling. How are the babies?'

'Fine,' said Kate. 'We made it to school on time, so Max was happy. He's that anxious about being late. Anxious about everything, these days.' She chewed her knuckle. 'Do you think that's because of what happened with Adam?'

'Who knows?' said Jean. 'I was scared of my own shadow as a child. And look at me now!'

Kate grinned, thinking of her small, fierce mother. 'Not much rattles you,' she agreed.

'He'll be fine,' said Jean reassuringly. 'It's not long to go before Christmas and then it's a new year and he'll make some friends, I'm sure of it. I thought I'd come round tonight, bring dinner? I know how rushed you are, with work. All your glamorous meetings.'

Yeah right, Kate thought, surveying the dismal caffe. She mentally reviewed the contents of her freezer at home. There were definitely some fish fingers in there, she thought. Time to stand on her own two feet.

'Thanks, Mum, but there's no need. I've got something for the kids ready.'

'All right then, I'll leave you to it,' Jean said. And then, rather shyly, 'I'm so excited you're coming to group! You will love the gang. I can't wait for you to meet . . . well, to meet them all.'

The gang. Kate shuddered, imagining the circle of sad widows, weeping into their cups of bad coffee.

'I can't wait, Mum. See you then.'

Kate hung up the phone and looked around at the caffe. A tap dripped into a rusted sink.

'I've finished up now,' she called through the door. Silence from Marco. 'Will I send that brief over later?'

A grunt which she assumed was assent.

Sighing, Kate left the caffe, jerking the door shut behind her with difficulty. She would walk home, she thought, get

29

in those steps like Veronica said. She had only walked a few feet though, when she heard a voice calling her name.

A familiar voice, low and musical, with the slightest hint of a European accent. Madeleine Hawes, her old boss at Domus. Her heart sank.

'Kate!' Kate turned slowly. As usual, Madeleine looked perfect. Her heart sank even lower.

Madeleine was German-born but had lived in Scotland since she was eighteen, when she had come over to study architecture. She had elegantly cropped grey hair and wore expensive clothes – navy cashmere sweaters and loose, immaculately tailored trousers and white trainers that never seemed to get muddy no matter the weather. She was dry and funny and warm all at once. Smart without ever showing off, generous with her knowledge and experience, always encouraging. Kate worshipped her.

When Kate had nervously told Madeleine she was going to strike out alone, Madeleine had sent her on her way with goodwill and hope, and a beautiful, monogrammed leather diary.

'For your exciting new projects,' Madeleine had said, enveloping Kate in a hug and a cloud of Chanel. 'I can't wait to see you poach all our clients. Keep us on our toes, Kate Whyte.'

Kate hadn't seen Madeleine since the wet December afternoon of Adam's funeral. At least then, she'd had an excuse for her dishevelled appearance.

Madeleine looked as composed as ever now, in a crisp shirt and cream coat. Only Madeleine could pull off an all-white outfit in rain-swept Edinburgh.

'Madeleine,' Kate said. She took several long strides away from Caffe Firenze, hoping to disassociate herself from it with all speed.

'Kate, darling! I thought that was you. Come here.'

Madeleine drew Kate into a warm, fragrant embrace. Kate fought the urge to throw herself upon that elegant neck and beg for help. *Rescue me*, she thought. Take me back to Domus, with my comfortable salary and interesting projects and choice of delicious lunches every day.

'How are you?' Kate said into Madeleine's shoulder. 'How's the team?'

'Oh, you know,' said Madeleine, pulling back to examine Kate. Her brown eyes took in Kate's shapeless sweater and the dust on her trousers from crawling around on the floor of Caffe Firenze. Unobtrusively, she lifted a piece of lint from Kate's sleeve. 'Lucas in accounts had his baby, it's a girl, *very* sweet, he looks exhausted. The rest of us are exactly the same as always. Busy, of course. We're doing the new block of flats by the canal, it's been a nightmare with the council, you know how it is.'

'Sounds stressful,' said Kate enviously.

'Kate darling, I've been meaning to ring you for months now. I don't want you to think I'm one of those fair-weather friends who drop away when something bad happens. But here we are and it's been ages. How *are* you?'

'Um.' Kate struggled to think of an honest answer. 'The kids are well.'

'How's the renovation going?' said Madeleine.

'Going well,' said Kate. *So much for honesty*, she thought. 'And work generally couldn't be better. Lots of exciting stuff in the, um, pipeline.'

'Great,' said Madeleine slowly. There was a little furrow between her eyes. 'Because if you ever need anything, you know where I am. I would be happy to help.' She took a step closer. 'I would absolutely hate the idea that you were struggling in any way . . .'

'No, it's all good!' Kate said. She could see a bus approaching the nearby stop and she flagged it down. 'That's my bus, I must dash. I'll call you!'

'Please do,' said Madeleine.

Through the window, she mimed a phone sign at Madeleine with her fingers as the bus peeled away from the kerb.

Forget the ten thousand steps, she thought, sinking into a seat. Preserving her dignity was worth so much more.

5

JEAN

Today was the day.

Jean had set aside the whole morning to go through Gerard's things. A deal was a deal, and Kate was keeping her side by coming to grief group.

Jean made herself a cup of tea while she thought about where to start. Not the study, she thought, a wave of panic hitting her; she simply couldn't. The bedroom, maybe?

She carried her tea upstairs and surveyed the room. She would start with his wardrobe. How bad could that be?

Opening Gerard's side of the wardrobe, though, she was struck anew by the smell. Creed and mothballs and something else, something sturdy and outdoorsy and indefinably Gerard.

His shirts and trousers were hung neatly. Always frugal, he kept his clothes until they wore through. He wouldn't want anything to go to waste now.

She began to lift down the hangers. The good clothes she put in a pile for charity, the others in a pile for the recycling point. She set aside his thick cream Arran jumper that she had always borrowed on holiday, along with his wedding suit and his gardening shirt, worn almost transparent. The girls might like her to keep those.

As she worked and the minutes passed, she realised that she did, indeed, feel lighter. It wasn't as bad as she had expected. Each item brought fond memories. A pair of faded cords reminded her of Gerard sitting on the back step in the evening, smoking his pipe. A tweed suit brought to mind an image of the kids running to him as he came down the road, home from work, jacket slung over his shoulder, tie loosened.

His dressing gown hung on the door and she lifted it down, burying her face into it, smelling Gerard's morning smell. It was a good dressing gown, thick plaid, almost new – Ally and Kate had bought it for him shortly after his diagnosis. Lots of wear in it yet. Someone would use it.

In the end she had a large pile for the charity shop and a smaller pile to keep. Emboldened by her success, Jean turned to Gerard's bedside drawer. The watch, glinting dully in the morning light, went into the pile for keeping. Max might like to wear it one day. One of his briarwood pipes, several of which were knocking around the house, went in too. There was his medication, neatly arranged. She would have to take that all to the hospital, Jean thought, to dispose of. And then, as she was lifting the stack of boxes out, something drifted to the floor. A polaroid.

She stooped and picked it up. A group standing in front of a building in what looked like Edinburgh Old Town, grinning. A tall man in a cream suit and T-shirt, and two girls, wearing baggy jumpers and jeans and Doc Marten boots. And, standing slightly apart, in jeans and with his shirt sleeves rolled up, was Gerard.

He wore what Jean thought of as his 'photograph expression', wary and amused. His hair was pushed back and he was squinting against the sun. It bleached his face, bringing his sharp cheekbones and heavy brows into relief.

It was unlike Gerard to keep an old photograph. He was so unsentimental. Jean was the one always hoarding children's exercise books and drawings. Not that Kate or Alice ever seemed to want to see them.

The girls might like to see this picture of their father, though, young, handsome, standing in the sunshine, in his jeans and battered trainers. From a time before he was just Dad.

Jean turned the photo over. Scrawled on the back in biro were the words EDINBURGH FRINGE 1980.

A memory stirred, one that Jean would have liked to tamp down. Gerard had worked in the theatre one summer, as a props and odd-job man, before he'd got the job at the shipyard. Building sets. He had worked at the Fringe in the summer of 1980, just before Kate was born. Hung out with a lot of posh students, he had told her. Not much to write home about.

But that had been the summer that—

Jean sat back on her heels. She didn't want to remember that summer, not one bit.

She had put it carefully away in her mind, in a sealed box. Something best forgotten. For both of them, she had thought.

And yet – in the drawer beside his bed, tucked neatly away out of sight – Gerard had kept this photo.

6

Fergus

KATE

Kate arrived at Fergus and Nat's a little after six. Fergus opened the door wearing an apron spattered with red sauce.

'Kids are doing their homework in front of the telly I'm afraid,' he said. His face was shining from the heat of the kitchen and his red hair stood up. 'Come through, have a glass of wine. I've got a bolognese on.'

Fergus and Natalie's home was exactly what Kate thought a home should be – not elegant but comfortable, filled with scruffy furniture and clutter, and the smell of something always on the stove.

The kids were curled up on the sofa. James was wearing a tiger costume. Emmie, looking surely more grown up than she had even this morning, was absorbed in her reading book, her lips moving as she sounded out words, dark brows lowered in concentration. Max was staring at the TV and barely glanced at Kate as she came in. A plate with the remains of sliced vegetables was on the table in front of them.

'Hi kids!' said Kate chirpily. 'How was school?'

A chorus of grunts was the only response. Kate knew by now that information about the children's day had to be extracted carefully, like panning for gold.

She followed Fergus into the kitchen. It was peaceful in here too – the sauce bubbling away on the stove and a glass of wine on the side, music playing from the radio, a spill of school paperwork and drawings on the table.

'Are they eating *carrot sticks*?' she asked Fergus, eyeing her children through the interconnecting door. He poured her a glass of wine and she took it gratefully. 'How do you do it? I can never get Max to eat a vegetable!'

He shrugged. 'Kids always behave better at other people's houses,' he said, slicing a cucumber. 'They get enough junk during the day. Those school lunches are terrible.' He looked at her slyly. 'Perhaps I could lobby the PTA, I hear you're their latest recruit.'

Fergus always seemed to know the playground gossip while remaining too pure to gossip himself.

'Not yet I'm not,' said Kate. 'Listen, if I'm going to this grief group with Mum then I might need to take you or Nat up on your offer to babysit.'

'Of course,' Fergus said. 'I'm pleased you're going. I think it'll be good for you.'

'Mmm.' She took a sip of her wine. Fergus and Nat always had good wine, like proper grown ups. Kate usually bought the most reduced bottle she could find in the Tesco near the flat.

'I could repay the favour,' she said, 'and you and Nat could go out. If James doesn't mind sleeping over in our death trap of a flat.'

Fergus's big, gentle face lit up. 'Actually, next Friday is our anniversary and I wanted to surprise Nat. Is that any good?'

'You're on.'

Kate counted on her fingers. 'It's your sixth, right? That's sugar.' A memory flashed into her mind, unbidden, of Adam presenting her with a little sugar mouse and a bouquet of red roses. *Sweets to the sweet.*

'I bet Adam got you something good, didn't he?' said Fergus. 'He always pulled the stops out, a real romantic. Put the rest of us to shame.'

'He certainly knew how to make a grand gesture,' Kate said. To change the subject, she said, 'Have you met this French dad at school?' She picked a piece of red pepper from the salad and ate it. 'The PTA mums are all over him.'

'Of course,' said Fergus. 'He looks like central casting for a hot French dad. Nat said it might be enough to tempt her into doing the school run.'

'You should befriend him,' Kate urged. 'Find out his story. He looks mysterious, like he has a secret sadness.'

Fergus snorted. 'Probably because he's ended up at Lyndoch Primary.'

Kate glanced at the clock. Dinner time. The thought of taking the kids away from this cosy scene, back to the flat where she had been working for most of the afternoon, littered with cups of cold tea and dirty plates, made her stomach clench. 'Time to go,' she said.

'You're welcome to stay for dinner,' Fergus said. 'We've got loads.'

'Thanks, but no,' Kate said, finishing her wine. 'This term, I'm standing on my own two feet.' If she repeated it enough times, she thought, it might become true.

'You can let us help, Kate,' Fergus said. 'Me and Nat. It's no bother.'

That was what Jean had said; she must radiate desperation. 'You guys help me enough,' Kate said firmly. 'I'm not going to be one of those emotional vampires.' She called into the other room. 'Come on you two. Let's go. Fish fingers and chips at home. Say thank you to Fergus for having you.'

Emmie and Max put their shoes on, groaning. They didn't want to leave either, Kate thought, and why would they.

'They had chips for lunch,' Fergus said, following her into the hall.

'I'll throw in some peas.'

Across the square and back in their flat, Kate flung on all the functioning lights to try and make it less bleak, turned on the oven and tipped fish fingers and chips onto a tray. There were less in the packet than she had thought. She slung knives and forks onto the table with a clatter. The room still had a bare, spartan feel. There was no point in getting their furniture out of storage when there was so much dust and debris everywhere. It felt as though they were camping in their own lives.

Emmie was sitting at the table, drawing, and Max was laying out his train track. Kate wondered sometimes whether he was a bit old now for trains – all the kids at school seemed to be into *Pokemon* and *Star Wars* – but Jean had told her not to fuss. 'Very calming, laying down all that track,' she had said.

'Mummy,' said Emmie, swivelling around in her chair. She had felt-tip ink on her fingers and glitter on one cheek. 'Can I tell you something?'

'You sure can,' said Kate, ripping open a bag of frozen peas with her teeth and pouring them into a saucepan, setting it on the hob.

'I made a new friend,' said Emmie, bouncing on her heels.

'That's great!' said Kate. Any change in Emmie's current friendship scenario could only be an improvement. 'Who is she?'

'It's a boy,' Emmie corrected. 'He's called,' Emmie drew out the syllables, 'Ol-iv-ee-ayy.'

'Olivier,' Kate said thoughtfully. She rattled some frozen peas into a bowl – she and Emmie liked to eat them raw, another thing her dentist wouldn't like – and sat down next to her daughter. 'I think I saw his dad this morning. Is he French?'

'He's not French, he's from Belgium,' said Emmie, catching a pea that had rolled onto the table and popping it into her mouth. She began to tick a series of facts off on her fingers. 'Olivier moved here last term from Belgium. His mummy and daddy don't live together. He gets a packed lunch because his daddy says the school food is *crap*. He was wearing shiny red shoes, not black school shoes.'

'Interesting,' Kate said. 'Didn't Lydia mind you playing with someone else?'

'Lydia wasn't there,' said Emmie, eating some more peas. 'She's off sick.'

On holiday, more like, Kate thought. That family had a carefree attitude towards term dates. They might be back any day now, though. She would have to act fast.

'You and Olivier should have a playdate,' she said. 'Tomorrow, if he's free.'

Emmie eyed her suspiciously. 'Whenever I want a play-date with Lydia you say you're too busy.'

'Oh, well,' Kate said evasively. 'It would be nice to … welcome them to the neighbourhood, if they're new. If I see Olivier's daddy in the playground tomorrow morning, why don't I ask him about it?'

'Yay,' said Emmie, eating another handful of peas. 'Thanks, Mummy.'

Beaming, Kate stood and caught the pan of peas from boiling over. Arranging playdates *and* a potential new job. Her fresh start was going very well indeed.

7

Jean had fallen in love with Gerard Whyte the moment she had seen him, one late summer afternoon, walking across a football pitch.

She had been sitting on a bench by the pitch with two of her friends, Michelle and Fiona, doing their homework and watching the boys. Jean had only been feigning interest in the boys till that point; she had grown up with plenty of extended family and an older brother. To her, boys were just other children – maybe a bit smellier and more annoying, but that was all.

'Ah, there's Gerard Whyte,' her friend Michelle had said, swinging her legs. 'He's fit.'

'Yeah, he's fit,' said Fiona, eyeing him critically. 'Definitely.'

Jean had watched Gerard walking towards his mates, ball under his arm. He had looked serious, stern even, with his thick eyebrows. Older.

'His mum moved them out last year,' whispered Michelle. 'They might be getting divorced.' As Jean watched, one of his friends called to Gerard and he broke into the best smile Jean had ever seen. That was it – she was head over heels. There wasn't one feature of his face that she would have improved upon.

Jean thought of that day as the start of her study of Gerard Whyte. His likes and dislikes. His friends and family.

43

Michelle was right – his parents were getting divorced, which made him a bit of a novelty. She knew when he played football and that he was on free school meals. One thrilling day she was standing behind him at Mario's and watched him order a bag of chips.

It never occurred to her, over all those days and weeks and months and years of observing Gerard Whyte, that he might have noticed her back.

That summer's day, waiting for the number 15 bus. Knowing that he was there, but too scared to look right at him.

Jean Capaldi, I thought that was you.

8

KATE

'Ten to!' Kate said triumphantly, glancing at her watch. 'The first bell hasn't even rung yet. We're early. *And* I brought snacks.'

'Real snacks?' asked Max. 'Quavers? Hula-hoops?'

'Raisins.'

'God, Mum.' He took the little cardboard box. 'I suppose it's better than nothing, but that's not really food.' He ran into school. *Please*, thought Kate, *let someone talk to him today*.

'He's right. There's no nutrition in a raisin.'

The low voice, heavily accented, came from beside Kate. Her gaze snapped up to see the new dad, Belgian not French, towering over her.

'A raisin is a fruit,' Kate said defensively, standing and dusting off her jeans. Even at her full height, she still had to tilt her head to look him in the eye, which was unusual for her. 'Or at least it was once.'

'That's him, Mummy,' Emmie said excitedly, tugging at Kate's arm. 'That's my friend, Olivier and his daddy.'

Olivier Devaux was standing beside his father. The boy had dark hair, brown skin, and enormous dark eyes. He was wearing his shiny red shoes and wearing a unicorn backpack with a fluffy unicorn keyring attached.

45

His father was dressed in the same ugly corduroy jacket as the other day, collar turned up against the wind which whipped through the playground. He looked like he should be in a caffe, smoking a Gitanes over an espresso, instead of standing outside Lyndoch Primary on a wet December morning.

'Hi,' Kate said, pasting on her friendliest smile. She was aware that the PTA posse were watching, presumably lip-reading their exchange. 'I'm Emmie's mum, Kate. I don't think we've met. I'm usually running a bit late in the mornings.'

He held out a hand. 'I am Matthias.'

'Emmie was full of chat about Olivier yesterday,' Kate said. 'I was thinking we might arrange a playdate.'

'Sure, we could do that,' he said. He glanced at the playground clock, Kate's nemesis. 'Olivier, I think it is time to go in. You don't want to be late.'

'I'll go with you,' said Emmie. 'Olivier gets nervous,' she explained to Kate.

'Bye, Papa.' The boy lifted his face to be kissed and then let Emmie take his hand and lead him into school.

Kate was too busy beaming with pride at Emmie's kindness to notice that Matthias was already walking towards the gate. She turned and trotted after him.

'About that playdate. How about this afternoon?' said Kate. She reached the gate ahead of him, neatly blocking his path. Veronica's tactics were rubbing off on her.

'Today?' he said, looking taken aback.

'No time like the present,' Kate said. Lydia could come back any day now.

'Today could work,' he said slowly. 'My schedule is quite relaxed at the moment. I am a musician.' *Of course you are*, thought Kate.

'Why don't you and Olivier walk back with us after school?' she said. 'Give me your number, just in case.'

Matthias recited it obediently and she keyed it into her phone.

'Does it rain every day here?' he asked, looking around the playground. 'Also, why are there no plants?'

Kate followed his gaze around the playground, which admittedly looked rather bleak today. A child's abandoned sweater lay in a puddle and crisp packets blew in the wind. As if on cue, the rain picked up.

'Not every day,' said Kate, pulling up her hood. 'It's a good school,' she added. 'Their teacher is great. There's an organic vegetable garden.'

'The lunches are terrible,' he said, turning up the collar of his coat still further. 'See you later.'

He walked up the path, a tall, bulky figure next to the stragglers and latecomers running the other way. He had an abrupt manner, she thought. Almost rude. Or was it just French?

Veronica appeared at her elbow, wearing yoga trousers and a padded jacket and clutching an eco cup. She wore fluffy grey earmuffs over her sleek, dark ponytail.

'Goodness Kate, that's efficient, even for you,' she said, smirking. 'Another willing slave to add to your list?'

'It's just a playdate,' muttered Kate. She opened the gate and began walking.

Veronica loped beside her, gazelle-like. 'Well, go on. We're all dying to know. What's he like?'

Kate thought. 'He seems quite ... blunt,' she said at last. 'Doesn't like the rain. Isn't happy about the lunches.'

'How dare he!' said Veronica indignantly. 'Although, I'm with him on the lunches. Zero nutrition. As soon as we get Christmas out of the way, I'm going to lobby hard for parental menu approval. That reminds me, I've got something for you.' She began to rummage through her tan shoulder bag.

'Nice bag,' said Kate, eyeing it enviously. 'New, is it?'

'Yeah, it's a brand I'm working with, Parisian, vegan leather, room for the kitchen sink,' Veronica said absentmindedly. She held out a bottle of cloudy liquid. 'Here. This will change your life, Kate.'

Kate took the bottle and peered at the label. 'What is it?'

'Probiotic,' Veronica said. 'I did a partnership with the company last month. Maybe you saw it on my feed?'

'I must have missed that one,' lied Kate.

'Anyway, now I have stacks of the stuff and it's the nuts. Healthy gut, healthy mind. Honestly, you should speak to my nutritionist, I'll set it up for you. You used to be so *glowing*.'

'Thanks,' said Kate, sourly. She stuffed the bottle into her own worn backpack. She and Veronica reached the street.

'How's Max's reading coming along, by the way?' asked Veronica. 'Still P2 level? Hugo is reading at P3 now.'

'Um.' Kate realised she had no idea how Max's reading was getting on because he always did his homework with Fergus. 'It's going okay I think.'

'I watched a fascinating documentary on how to encourage kids to learn intuitively, it's on Netflix, I'll text you.' Veronica fluttered her fingers at her. 'Tell me *everything* about your playdate. Take your probiotics. And Kate?'

'Yes?' Kate paused, hand poised on the gate.

Veronica winked. 'Don't think I've forgotten about the PTA.'

9

JEAN

Jean had been waiting for the bus when Gerard Whyte came and sat down next to her. She went to secretarial college four days a week. University wasn't an option for her; her brother Luca was going to Manchester to study medicine.

She had been angry about that for a full month after the exams. She had done well, better even than expected, with grades like that she could have gone nearly anywhere. Luca hadn't done as well, but he still got to go.

Jean had been so angry that she had taken all her textbooks out to the back garden and burned them. Her father had watched her wearily from the porch.

'We could have passed those on, Jeanie,' he had said, when the books were reduced – after a surprisingly long time – to smouldering ash. 'Someone else could have used them. What good did that do?'

Now, a month later, Jean wasn't angry any more. She liked secretarial college, and lots of her friends were kicking around still. She had time for cooking and helping her parents out in the caffe which brought in some extra cash in tips. She had a boyfriend, Tony, who her parents liked. Life was good.

It was a hot day in August. The teacher got nasty when they were late, and Jean had been looking anxiously at her watch when Gerard Whyte had come and sat next to her.

At first, she wasn't sure it was really him. She had thought she'd seen him before – in a queue, on the street, sitting at one of the desks in the library. It was never him, though, just some other tall, blond boy. Now, she stared at his battered trainers and they waited for the bus in silence.

It wasn't until the bus pulled into view that she had risked a glance at him. And then, to her amazement, he spoke to her. He said, 'Jean Capaldi, I thought that was you.'

10

KATE

Kate couldn't get the front door open.

'This happens when it rains,' she said, jamming first her hip and then her shoulder against the door. 'I think the wood's a bit warped . . .'

'Would you like me to try?' Matthias asked, stepping forward. He looked as though he could rip the entire door off its hinges with a flick of his wrist.

'Nope, just a little push should do it.' Kate smashed her shoulder heavily against the door, wincing in pain and sending flakes of paint onto the floor. 'There! Go on in.'

'Come on,' said Emmie, taking charge. 'You come into our room, Olivier. Careful of the wires and that broken floorboard. Keep your shoes on, there's splinters.'

The children disappeared off into their bedroom, shutting the door behind them. There was a silence, in which Kate watched Matthias take in the gutted flat. It wasn't often that she had people round, other than Nat and Fergus who were tactful enough not to mention the dire state of affairs. Through Matthias's judgemental eyes, it looked even worse than usual.

'We're in the middle of a refurb,' she said, kicking the door viciously shut behind her. 'My husband and I were going to do it up last year and sell it, but then he died.'

Matthias blinked at her. 'I'm sorry,' he said.

'Oh, it's fine,' said Kate. 'Not fine of course, but you know. It was a car accident, which was weird because he was a super careful driver, we used to make fun of him for it.' She was babbling, she thought. His calm self-possession made her nervous. 'Anyway, come on through.'

Matthias walked ahead of her down the hallway. There was dust on the back of his jacket.

'We're used to it now,' Kate said, ushering him into the kitchen. 'It's a bit like camping.'

'Camping is just for a weekend,' Matthias said. He looked around. 'You could buy some plants, maybe. That would help.'

'I'll get right on it,' said Kate. 'Thanks for the design tips.'

She put the kettle on, reached up for the tea cannister – the dust had penetrated every cupboard, each drawer – and realised it was empty.

'Sorry,' she said. 'No tea. I need to go to the shops.'

'That is okay,' he said. He carefully dusted off the seat of a chair with a dishcloth before sitting down.

'Coffee, then? It's the one thing I always have a lot of,' she said.

'No thank you,' he said, glancing at his watch. 'It's after three.'

Kate spooned coffee into the cafetiere and flipped on the kettle. 'And that means no coffee?'

'Not if I want to sleep. You won't sleep either, if you drink all that.'

Kate reached for the kettle and poured water onto the grounds. 'Coffee doesn't affect me at all,' she said firmly. She hadn't slept a full night through for months. 'Is there anything you *would* like? What about a biscuit?'

He took a stale Oreo cookie from the tin she held out. She watched as he examined it and then laid it down on the table.

'I suppose you bake?' she said.

'My mother taught me and now I bake with Olivier.'

Kate imagined him and Olivier, wearing identical white aprons, calmly stirring biscuit batter to the sounds of jazz music. A tray of golden-brown biscuits, perfectly round, coming out of the oven. Olivier would probably also help with the washing up afterwards.

'That's nice,' she said, weakly. Her phone rang. 'I'll get this if you don't mind,' she said. 'It might be work.'

To her surprise, it was indeed Marco. 'Hiya, Kath. I took a look at your proposal.'

'Great,' she said, injecting as much professionalism into her tone as she could. 'What do you think?'

'Some of the ideas are nice, I like the layout. But honestly? My dad's loosening up a bit, but I'll lose him altogether with a concrete floor and all that. It's a caff, not some hipster bar. The old timers won't know what to think.'

'That's no problem at all,' said Kate quickly. 'It's just a starting point. I can send you some alternatives. We can get it right.'

There was a pause. 'If you think so,' said Marco doubtfully.

'I'm positive.' She lowered her voice. 'At this point in a project I would usually be on retainer.'

'Aye, let's get this proposal agreed first, yeah? Speak later, Kath.'

He hung up. Kate glared at her phone.

'All okay?' said Matthias.

'Yeah, it's a client,' Kate said. 'Currently my only client. He wants some . . . revisions before I invoice.'

'What is it that you do?' Matthias asked.

'I'm an interior designer.' The words fell into silence as she watched Matthias slowly take in the plaster hanging off the walls, the sheet of plastic that hung over a hole in the far wall.

'An interior designer?' he said. 'So, this is just a work in progress?'

'That's right,' she said.

Work in progress. Story of her life.

Later that night, after Matthias and Olivier had gone, Kate bathed and fed the children and put Max to bed.

She turned on his nightlight, tucking him in with all his stuffed animals. Once she and Adam had argued over whose turn it was to put chatterbox Max to bed, knowing it would be a long haul but now Kate felt acutely the preciousness of this moment. Adam would never again touch Max's smooth, flushed cheek, stroke his hair still damp from the bath, embark on the endless litany of lullabies, answer any of the impossible questions Max always had bubbling on the tip of his tongue.

A familiar lump rose in Kate's throat. Sometimes missing and hating Adam went hand in hand. How dare he leave them all, and in such a mess? How dare he be so careless?

'Mummy,' called Emmie down the hall. Kate looked up to see her standing in the doorway, wearing unicorn pyjamas and fluffy slippers. 'Can I look at the pictures of you and Daddy?'

She meant the photo albums stacked in the study.

'Of course, baby,' Kate said, although her heart sank. She went and fetched the albums and brought them through to the sitting room, where Emmie was waiting expectantly on the sofa. A miniature Adam, with her dark, curling hair and navy eyes.

'I want to look at the ones of you and Daddy at university,' Emmie said. 'And the wedding ones. The cake and the dress and the flowers and the veil . . .'

Kate set a heavy album in Emmie's lap and edged towards the kitchen. 'You make a start, I'm just going to get that washing out.'

Emmie tugged at her arm. 'No, stay Mummy. I need you to tell me the stories,' she said.

Kate sighed. Looking at these photos was like peeling off a scab, with excruciating slowness.

She sat down next to Emmie and tucked her legs under her.

'That was when you first met Daddy,' Emmie said, pointing.

A picture of Kate and Adam on their first day at university in London, grinning uncertainly at the camera with a group of newfound mates. So young, both of them. All the girls had fancied Adam. And he had chosen her, Kate Whyte, the scruffy art student with her paint-smeared sweatshirts and ripped tights and green hair. 'You two are like our king and queen,' her best friend Gina had told her once.

'And this is you at a *house party*,' continued Emmie, her finger moving over the page. Her and Gina, cheeks squished together, grinning like idiots at the camera, covered in paint.

'We'd drunk too much beer,' said Kate. Emmie squealed in glee, and Kate laughed. She must call Gina in London, it had been months, and Gina's calls had tailed off. Grief made people nervous; a cliché, but it was true. She turned the page.

'Daddy asked you to marry him,' Emmie said, clasping her hands, gazing rapt at a picture of Kate and Adam on the lawn of the elegant country hotel where he had proposed.

A walk in the rain. The clouds parting and a beam of sunshine, Adam dropping down on one knee, ring in his pocket, sandwiches and champagne in a picnic basket for after. Always, with Adam, the grand gesture.

Kate could still recall the rush of pleasure when Adam had produced that little box and she had seen the beautiful ring glinting there in cushioned splendour. She hadn't been surprised – she wasn't stupid, she had suspected from the moment he had booked the hotel for Valentine's Day – but she had felt . . . satisfaction. Her life was moving forward according to plan. Perfect.

She held out her hand now, looking at her engagement ring. The ring sat a little tighter these days, and the diamond needed cleaning. It was dull. She had taken it off once as an experiment, but her fingers kept worrying at the space where it had been.

'And then,' Emmie breathed, turning the page. 'You got married.'

This was the apotheosis, as far as Emmie was concerned, of her mother's life.

Kate laughed and kissed her daughter's head. 'You were the surprise guest.'

There was Kate, radiant in her simple wedding dress, an embryonic Emmie snug in her belly, golden hair shining in the sunshine, red lips parted in a smile. Nose wrinkling over a single, celebratory glass of champagne. Adam, tanned, dark hair cropped neatly for the big day, more handsome than ever in his blue suit. His hand on her belly, beaming with pride.

Her parents, dancing together, laughing. Jean looking like an ethereal pixie in a chic green suit, tucked into the crook of Gerard's arm as though she was always meant to belong there. Adam's mother, smiling more timidly under an enormous hat. She had died not a year later.

'And it was a happy day?' Emmie said, prompting her mother. She knew this script off by heart.

'And it was a happy day,' repeated Kate obediently. She knew the script too. 'The happiest day of my life.'

Emmie chewed her finger, frowning. 'What about when I was born? Wasn't that the happiest day? And when Max was born too, I guess,' she added grudgingly.

Kate laughed. 'Those days too. Lots of happiest days.' She glanced at her watch. 'It's getting late, and you've got school in the morning. Go on and brush your teeth.'

Emmie groaned dramatically and ran off to the bathroom. Kate looked again at their wedding photo. She laid a finger on her younger self, face alight with possibility and excitement. Only seven years ago – it felt like another lifetime.

Adam, standing proudly beside his new wife, surrounded by friends and family; he had no idea what was to come, how suddenly the shining life spread out before him would be cut short.

'The happiest day of my life,' Kate whispered.

II

JEAN

Gianni Capaldi wasn't happy that Jean was seeing Gerard Whyte. 'He's a good lad,' he said. 'But you're both awful young, Jeannie.'

Gerard's parents were no happier about her. Gerard never said, but he didn't have to. Jean was sure that her being Italian came into it.

'What shall we do about them?' she had asked Gerard one day. They were lying in the Botanic gardens on a thick blanket, wrapped in sweaters, her head on his chest. It was January and the wind was bitter, but they could spend hours here without anyone knowing. When Jean wanted to annoy her father, she would get Ger to come by the caffe and they would share a nougat and a coke. Their kisses afterwards tasted sweet and sticky.

Gerard remained almost disappointingly calm. 'They'll come round,' he said, easily. She could feel his heart beating hard and strong in his chest. 'When we explain we're getting married, they'll not fuss.'

She raised herself up on one elbow. 'We're getting married, are we now?' she said.

He smiled and ran his hand through her curls. She rested her cheek in the curve of his hand, calloused from his summer working on the building site.

'How about a summer wedding?' he said.

'Not *this* summer?' she said.

'Aye.' He grinned at her. 'I've been saving up.'

Just like that, they were engaged, and there was nothing that anyone could do about it. Gianni looked rather grey when they told him, but he accepted it with good enough grace. Jean had a feeling that her mum had seen it coming and told him to behave himself.

Nina said nothing till one day when she and Jean were working a shift at the caffe. She was arm-deep in washing up and Jean was drying.

'I don't understand the hurry, Jeanie,' Nina said. 'Get engaged by all means. You can have a long engagement and still go to secretarial college. See a bit of life. There's no rush. Is there?' Her gaze, sharp and knowing, made Jean flush. Her mother had an uncanny sixth sense.

'No reason at all,' she had said. 'Except that we want to.'

Nina had shrugged. 'Not much to say to that then, is there.' She smiled, and Jean thought how beautiful she looked, movie-star beautiful, there among the dishes with hands swollen from the hot water. 'But remember, you don't get just one shot at life these days. This doesn't work out, kid or no kid, you can walk away, whatever your father says.'

'Okay Mum,' Jean had said, grinning. Because who on earth went into a marriage at eighteen and madly in love thinking that one day they might need to leave it.

12

KATE

Kate woke, heart beating hard, and lay there for a minute in the panicked aftermath of her dream. The smell of frying bacon and coffee drifted up from downstairs. Jean must have let herself in to see to the kids and their iron levels. Pale blue daylight filtered through the curtain. It was late.

It was always the same dream. Adam needed to tell her something very urgent, but he never managed it.

There was a thick pane of glass in the way. Kate could see Adam's mouth moving, but she couldn't hear the words. His expression was familiar, a mixture of frustration and tolerant affection. *Come on, Kate. It's simple. You just have to pay attention.*

Pulling on tracksuit bottoms and a thick cardigan, Kate dragged herself downstairs and into the kitchen, following the cooking smells. The kitchen was a beacon of warmth. Jean was at the stove, cooking, and the kids were sitting at the table, glasses of milk in front of them. *Good Morning Scotland* was on the radio. Max was laboriously peeling a tangerine, his tongue protruding through his teeth. Kate marvelled at the cheerful atmosphere Jean managed to create even in their makeshift kitchen.

'Mummy,' Max called.

Emmie said sternly, 'Granny said not to wake you. You were meant to sleep in.'

'I'd have got you in a minute,' said Jean. She was wearing a cashmere sweater in a forest green, cropped trousers and trainers. 'I've got my golf class this morning round the corner, so I thought I'd stop by. I've put a few bits in the fridge. It was looking a bit peaky.' That was Jean being tactful. 'Coffee?'

'Yes please,' said Kate gratefully. She slumped into a chair, pushing her tangled hair out of her eyes. 'I didn't know you played golf, Mum. Yet another activity?'

Jean was busily buttering morning rolls with blackened tops, the children's favourite. 'I signed up a few weeks ago,' she said, eyes on the bread. 'A lot of walking, apparently it keeps you fit. Do you want some breakfast? I made enough.'

'No thanks,' said Kate. It smelled amazing, but Veronica was probably sitting down to a beetroot smoothie at this very moment.

Jean proffered a little white cardboard box. 'Cannoli?'

'Go on then.' Kate bit into a cannoli, crumbly pastry falling apart on her tongue. It was her favourite sort, filled with a sharp, sweet lemon-cream. Jonny at the deli had a soft spot for Jean, as most men in the area did, and was always popping in an extra pastry or chocolate.

Jean put plates of crispy bacon, rolls and fried eggs down in front of the children, who fell on the food with elbows flying, as though they hadn't eaten in weeks.

'I do feed them you know, Mum,' said Kate, half amused and half embarrassed.

'Of course you do, love, but at this time of year it's such a treat to have something hot,' said Jean. She sat opposite Kate and poured out the coffee. 'Spoiling children is what grannies are for. I heard you're seeing Alice for lunch this week?'

Kate nodded, still chewing her pastry. She had been cancelling and rescheduling her sister for weeks now. Her little sister lived in a picture-perfect cottage in a village outside the city with her taciturn engineer boyfriend Mark and a flock of chickens, an idyllic life that threw into sharp relief how chaotic Kate's was. 'Can't wait,' she said. 'She and Mark just got back from a romantic weekend away. I want to know if he's put a ring on it yet.'

'Oh, you,' said Jean, shaking her head. 'Leave your sister be. She's happy and god knows marriage isn't everything.'

'It is if you want it, though,' Kate said stubbornly.

'Happiness looks different to everyone,' Jean said. She took a sip of her coffee. 'Are you excited about group tonight?'

'What?' Kate yawned so hard she thought her jaw might dislocate. 'Oh, the grief group, yes.'

'I really think you'll love it,' Jean said, looking at Kate over the rim of her coffee cup. 'If you give it a chance. The people are ever so nice.' She took a deep breath. 'I've been seeing them a bit, you know, socially. I'd like to introduce you—'

'Speaking of which,' said Kate, 'how's your side of the bargain going?'

'I sorted through Dad's wardrobe,' said Jean proudly.

'Well done, Mum,' said Kate. 'What about the study next? I never knew anyone for filing every last receipt as though it was crucial paperwork. You can shred the lot of them, I'd have thought.'

'I might leave the study till last,' said Jean, staring into her coffee. 'Do the shed or something.' She sounded nervous, and Kate laid a hand on hers.

'It'll be okay, Mum, I promise,' she said softly. 'You might as well get it out of the way. Do you want me to come round and help?'

'No!' said Jean quickly. 'You've got enough on. It's best if I do this myself.'

'All right.' Kate sat back. She looked more closely at her mother. Jean's skin was glowing, almost luminous, her cheeks were pink, and her hair thick and shiny, gleaming chestnut and silver in the weak sunshine. 'You look well, Mum,' she said enviously. 'In fact, you look amazing.'

Jean laughed, went even pinker, and drained her coffee cup. 'It's this unexpected sunshine. It makes everything look better, even this old face.' She pulled back her sleeve to glance at her watch. 'I should get to my golf.'

'Okay, have fun. Thanks for breakfast.'

Jean kissed the children and bustled off, her loafers tapping smartly down the hall. Kate heard the front door shut.

She lifted a spoon to examine her own haggard face. In its warped reflection, she saw flecks of yesterday's mascara down one cheek, hair ratty, skin sallow and dry. If Jean was looking more radiant by the day, Kate was deteriorating at an accelerated rate.

'Do I have to go to school?' asked Max. 'Couldn't you teach me here?'

'You wouldn't learn much, I'm afraid,' said Kate sympathetically, setting down the spoon. 'Besides, Mummy needs to work. It will get better, I promise.' She had been saying that for months now.

'Mummy,' said Emmie, wiping crumbs from her mouth with the back of her hand, 'can we have another playdate with Olivier? He's come up with the idea for the Christmas play and I have the main part. Pirate queen.'

'Pirate queen?' said Kate. 'What sort of Christmas play is this?'

'He came to *our* house,' said Emmie. 'I want to see his. They're lighting advent candles. They do Christmas early because of where they come from.'

Kate hesitated. It would be nice for the kids to do something Christmassy. But making conversation with Matthias had been like chatting to a rock.

'All right,' she said, at last. 'I'll ask his dad. Go on now and get dressed.'

As Emmie went off to get ready for school and Max finished his bacon, Kate's gaze fell on the bottle of probiotic Veronica had given her. She picked it up and read the label. *Healthier microbiome, healthier you.* She poured some into her empty coffee cup, sniffed it suspiciously, then downed it in one.

At this point, she would try anything.

Drop-off went without a hitch. The kids were in a good mood after their nutritious breakfast and the sun was shining. Kate saw Matthias walking just ahead on the path.

As though he sensed her, though, he turned. 'Hello,' he said. His expression was as inscrutable as ever. 'Thanks for yesterday. Olivier had a good time. He doesn't always hit it off with other children straight away.'

'Then other children don't have any taste,' Kate said. She felt obscurely protective of Olivier. Matthias was dressed smartly today, in a navy suit. 'Where are you off to?'

'I am working. I've got a job with the orchestra.'

'Where's your instrument?'

'In the van,' he said.

'Kate.' Veronica jogged lightly up behind them. 'PTA. I'm not taking no for an answer. You'll learn this about me

– I never give up, not when I want something. Do it for Christmas and if you hate it, you can quit in January.'

Veronica's eyes were glittering with fervour. *Why resist,* Kate thought wearily. Veronica would never stop. She was the Terminator of Edinburgh.

'Fine,' Kate relented. 'You win. I'll do it. Sign me up.'

'Yesss,' said Veronica, punching the air. 'Kate, I'm *so* pleased. You are exactly the sort of creative type we want on board. We've got our reliable members. What we need are a few wild cards like you.'

'Thanks,' muttered Kate. 'I think.'

'The first meeting is Monday at two, okay? We usually aim to keep them out of working hours but as you can imagine, things are stepping up a gear so close to Christmas. I'll text you a reminder now I know you're not a details person, Kate.' She glanced at her Apple watch. 'I've got to go, I'll be late for spin, but I'll see you later.'

She jogged off, ponytail swinging as she ran.

Kate sighed heavily. Matthias was still standing there, and Kate saw the merest trace of amusement on his face. 'The PTA?' he said.

Kate scowled. 'I've been meaning to sign up.'

'No,' he said softly.

'What?' she said, startled.

'*No.* That's all you had to say. One little word. You should try it some time.'

The last threads of Kate's fraying temper snapped. 'It's all right for you,' she snapped. 'You're a man, and if someone asks you to do something – which they hardly ever will, because you're a man – the bar for what you're capable of is set so low that you can just say *no,* and no one will think you're a crap parent. And even if they *do* think that, you won't care what they think. Because you're a man.'

He blinked at her. 'You may have a point there,' he said.

She forced herself to take a deep breath. It came out more like a grunt.

'I do have a point,' she said. She lowered her voice. 'But I'm sorry I shouted. I was actually going to ask if we could organise a playdate for Friday? The children are keen.'

'We can do Friday,' he said. 'The children can light an advent candle, if they would like.'

'Great, see you then,' said Kate. 'Have a good day.'

Bloody Christmas, she thought, marching against the wind to the bus stop. PTA Christmas fair, Christmas party, advent candles. It was starting to feel like a Christmas conspiracy.

And, in the midst of it all, Kate had never felt less festive.

'But why didn't you just say no?' said Alice. 'I can't imagine anyone less suited to the PTA than you.'

'You wouldn't understand, Ally,' Kate said loftily. 'This sort of thing gets complicated when there are children involved.'

Alice snorted. 'If you say so. Sounds like you were too scared of this Veronica woman.'

They were sitting in their favourite caffe in Stockbridge with cinnamon buns and coffee, black for Kate, and salted caramel latte with whipped cream for Alice.

Alice had come up for the day to do some shopping. She looked her usual tranquil self. She was wearing a black tea dress sprigged with tiny flowers with elaborately puffed sleeves, thick grey tights and boots, and the same rosy-pink lipstick she'd worn since university. Her nails were painted pale pink and she wore her thick, shining chestnut brown hair long with a fringe. She had looked pretty much the same at age four; Kate could imagine her looking the same at eighty. It was both reassuring and worrying.

Once, when Alice had been visiting Kate at university, a drunken ex had approached them in a pub. 'Sisters, hmm?' he had said. 'Makes sense. You,' he had levelled a wavering finger at Kate, 'are the one men will want to sleep with. But you,' he'd swivelled to Alice, 'are the one they'll fall for.' It had stayed with Kate in the way off-handed, cruel comments had a way of doing.

'How's Mark?' she asked now. She had never quite hit it off with Mark. He was polite at family gatherings, and clearly adored Alice, but was monosyllabic to the point of rudeness. Shy, Jean insisted. 'He's good,' said Alice. 'We're both working flat out on the house. We sanded the original floorboards downstairs. I need to get your advice on the paint for the bedrooms. Nothing like what you could pull off,' she added. 'But I'm pleased with it.'

A piece of dough stuck in Kate's throat and she took a gulp of water. The thought of freshly sanded floorboards gave her an actual pang of longing.

'It'll be ready in time for Christmas,' Alice went on happily, stirring whipped cream into her drink. 'You and the kids and Mum can just show up. You won't have to do a thing, you can just relax.'

Kate forced down the cake and cleared her throat. 'Actually, I think you should all come to ours for Christmas,' she said.

There was a pause, in which Alice stared and Kate tried to work out where that had come from.

'Really?' Alice said, not bothering to hide her incredulity. '*You* want to do Christmas? But you don't cook. And your flat isn't . . .' Kate could see her casting around for a diplomatic phrase. 'It's not quite ready, is it?'

'I'll have it sorted by then,' Kate said airily. 'Besides, we have an oven and what else do you need?'

'Chairs?' said Alice. 'Running water? More than four plates?'

'That's all in hand,' Kate said. 'We've got plenty of room.' That much at least was true, she thought.

'Well, all right,' said Alice placidly. 'If you're sure, then we'd love to.'

'Great,' said Kate, already bitterly regretting her suggestion. To change the subject, she said, 'Have you spoken to Mum? I've agreed to go to her bloody grief group tonight on the condition she sorts through Dad's stuff.'

'Kate,' Alice tutted. 'You shouldn't bully her. She'll do it when she's ready.'

'It's been two years,' said Kate. 'She's throwing herself into all these golf lessons and life-drawing classes, but until she starts getting rid of Dad's things, she'll never move on.'

Alice shook her head. 'I'm not sure that'll ever happen,' she said. 'They loved each other so much.'

'I know,' said Kate, sighing. Her parents were the great romance she and Alice had always aspired to. 'Together at eighteen and as in love then as the day he died. Remember the way he would look at Mum, as though he couldn't believe his luck. That's a tough act to live up to.'

'You and Adam managed it, though,' said Alice. 'Perfect couple. No wonder me and Mark aren't going to get married. Why bother when the standards are so high?'

'Don't know about that,' said Kate, feeling herself flushing. 'Speaking of romance, you don't think Mum would ever date again, do you? Only she's looking . . . different these days. Really well and glowing. She's always busy and sort of distracted.'

'Oh no,' said Alice, sounding shocked. 'Date again, after Dad? She never would.'

'No,' agreed Kate, relieved at the disbelief in her sister's voice. The very thought of their mum falling in love again, after losing the grand love of her life, was madness. 'Of course she wouldn't. What a ridiculous idea.'

'Ridiculous,' said Alice.

13

JEAN

Jean waited outside the building for Kate. She thought that
would make it less intimidating for Kate. Not that Kate was
easily intimidated.

She could see Kate now, trudging through the puddles,
head bent against the wind and rain, shielded by a lopsided
umbrella with its spokes hanging loose. Jean would have to
buy her a new one, she thought. She could drop it round
one morning, just pop it by the front door. Kate was so
prickly these days about accepting help, but surely she
would take the gift of a decent umbrella.

Even damp and frowning crossly, the sight of her daughter
made Jean's heart stop. Having children was like a love affair
that never ended. Kate was beautiful, a sort of casual, dishevelled beauty that withstood unkempt hair and sleepless nights.
All the boys were mad for Kate at art college. Although today,
she did wish Kate had worn something other than that old
jacket of Adam's and what looked like a jumper with holes in it.

Jean waved and Kate lifted a hand in greeting.

'There you are! I'm so glad you came.' Jean spoke breath-
lessly. She was more nervous than she'd thought. 'I was half
expecting you to cancel, what with this weather.'

'I nearly did.' Kate stared up at the building. 'I'm dreading this. Talking to complete strangers about what happened.'

'A stranger is just a friend you haven't met,' said Jean, and Kate groaned.

'Come on.' She began to tug Kate towards the entrance. 'Give it a chance.'

'Fine,' said Kate. 'But remember, this is on the condition you start on the study next, okay? Keep going while you're on a roll.'

The room was oppressively hot, and people were sitting in chairs arranged in a circle. They looked up as they walked in.

Jean led Kate over by the hand. 'Kate, this is Maggie, Ada and Frances. Ladies, this is my daughter, Kate,' she said.

The women smiled and said hello.

'And this,' said Jean, trying to keep the tremulous note out of her voice, 'is Rory.'

Jean watched as Rory stood up and put out his hand. 'Pleased to meet you, Kate,' he said.

'And you,' Kate said, sounding anything but. Jean sighed. She was reminded suddenly of Kate's teenage years, when they would haul her from her bedroom, surly and scowling, to say hello to guests.

Jean nudged her as they sat down on uncomfortable chairs. 'Don't be rude,' she hissed. 'Remember, we have a deal.'

Ada poured them out cups of coffee. Kate took a sip and winced.

'Have a biscuit, love,' said Maggie, holding out the plate of custard creams, and Kate shook her head.

'No thanks,' she said.

'It's tough isn't it, to eat when you're grieving,' said Maggie sympathetically.'

'I'm just not hungry,' Kate said firmly. 'Big lunch. Nothing to do with grief.'

'I always went the other way. It started with bread and butter,' Maggie said dreamily. She had a round, hopeful face that was flushed with the heat of the room. 'And then biscuits – I could eat a whole packet and have my tea after. I'm trying to rein it in now.'

'Diets are a con,' said Frances. 'A capitalist pyramid scheme. All you need is nutritious, homemade, *vegan* food . . .'

Jean caught Kate giving the faintest eye roll. Fortunately, Ada tapped her teaspoon against her mug. 'Order,' she called, smiling. 'We don't want our newest recruit to think all we do is chat now, do we?'

Jean watched as Kate took in Ada, her ruddy, beaming face and headful of thick, red hair, greying slightly in places, the layers of jauntily coloured homemade knitwear, purple nails and clacking bangles.

'Firstly . . . welcome, Kate,' said Ada. 'Let's give her a round of applause for coming, especially on this dreadful night. We all know that making yourself vulnerable emotionally is not easy. Well done, Kate.'

There was a smattering of polite applause. 'Perhaps we should all go around and introduce ourselves for our newcomer. I'm Ada,' Ada pointed to her name tag and laughed. 'As you can see! My son died last year of a stroke.'

Maggie swallowed her biscuit and wiped crumbs from her mouth. 'Maggie – and my girlfriend Milly died two years ago. She had an asthma attack.'

Toying with one of her many silver rings, Frances said, 'I'm Frances. My sister Georgie died six months ago. She'd been sick her whole life.'

They all turned to look at Kate.

'Husband, Adam, last year – car crash. Father, two years ago, cancer.' Kate sounded almost triumphant, Jean thought.

As though she was trumping the rest of them in the grief stakes. 'Oh, and we lost our family pet a week ago. I think that's everyone who's died recently.'

'Lovely, thank you,' said Ada, as cheerily as if she were chairing a knitting circle. 'Rory, it's your turn to speak today, isn't it?' She added to Kate, 'I don't know if Jean said, but we've been bringing in things which remind us of our lost ones. Sort of like show-and-tell but with death.'

Kate glared at Jean. 'No, she didn't mention that,' she said.

'It's okay,' Jean said soothingly, reaching over and taking her hand. 'You don't have to speak unless you want to. Give it a few weeks and then you can decide.'

Rory cleared his throat. His voice was low and his speech slow and deliberate. His dark eyes looked somewhere into the middle distance when he spoke.

'My wife Jenny died thirty years ago,' he said. 'Cancer got her. We met when we were fourteen, can you believe, and married when we were nineteen. Who does that these days? The kids thought coming to this group would help, apparently it's good to talk.' He held up a battered book. *Classic Scottish Cookery*. 'This was her favourite cookbook. Her Ma gave it her on her wedding day and told her to keep me happy with it.' There was laughter from the group, except Kate who remained stony-faced. 'She did that,' Rory said fondly.

'Her mince and tatties were to die for. When she got sick, the first thing she did was give me cookery lessons. Don't want you and the kids going hungry, she said. Brown the mince first, Rory, don't be afraid to let it catch and make sure you get meat with a bit of fat on it, it's where the flavour is. Thirty years and I can still hear her.' He ran a weathered hand fondly across the cover. 'Those boys could cook themselves a square meal by the time they were ten and that's more than I can say for others their age.'

They all passed around the book, turned the grease-stained pages. Some had pencil scribbles in the margin. One, for red lentils and sausages, was circled alongside the words, NED'S BIRTHDAY SUPPER. Drop scones. Shortbread. Something called coffee kisses.

'Did Jenny ever leave the kitchen?' Kate muttered to Jean as she turned the pages.

'Oh, hush,' said Jean, glancing anxiously at Rory.

'This looks nice, doesn't it?' said Maggie, holding up a page. 'Dundee cake. Haven't had that in years. Mind if I take a photo, Rory?'

'I need a drink,' said Kate, grumpily.

She and Jean were outside, doing up their coats. The rain had died down but the wind was worse than before. Rubbish whirled about the street.

'Shhh,' said Jean. Ada came bustling past them, doing up her coat, a red felted affair with toggles.

'Terrible out here, isn't it?' she said. She tugged on a green woollen hat covered in sequins. Jean wondered whether the Christmassy colour scheme was deliberate. 'How did you find your first group, Kate dear?'

Kate bit her lip, clearly torn between truth and diplomacy. 'I know I'm new here,' she said at last, 'but it feels a bit ... reductive. Poor Jenny was more than some recipes.'

'Aye of course she was,' said Ada equably. 'It's one way of remembering though. A way for Rory to talk about her.' She pulled on a pair of fluffy green gloves. 'We're all taking it one day at a time, Kate.' She squinted into the street. 'See you next time. If we don't get blown away!'

Her hearty laugh rang out as she stepped out into the wind.

'I suppose she's right,' said Kate grudgingly, watching Ada go, holding on to her hat. 'People are entitled to remember the good times, too. Even if it's mince and tatties.'

'Exactly!' said Jean. 'You and Adam had so many good times. Wouldn't it be nice to remember them?'

'Yeah,' Kate said shortly. 'I suppose it would. Shall we get going?'

As they walked, Jean watched Kate's stern, beautiful profile. Something was wrong with her daughter; she just didn't know what. But if Jean had learnt anything, it was that nothing was ever as simple as it seemed.

Jean let herself back into the flat. After the bustle of the tram and the street, the crowds of people beginning their Christmas shopping in earnest, it seemed oddly quiet. She still had to catch herself from calling out to Gerard.

'Hullo, are you in?' she would call, and he would call back, 'Through here, love.'

The silence that greeted her now was surprising each time.

Jean wiped her boots, put them carefully away and hung up her coat. Things were certainly *tidier* without a husband and children in the flat. After a lifetime of people trooping in and out, muddy boots by the door, phones ringing, weekends crammed with kids' parties and music lessons, school trips, gym kits slung on the stairs – now, Jean was alone for the first time.

Sometimes the loneliness was so loud and so terrible it filled the flat. Sometimes, like now, it had a frisson of pleasure. If Jean put down a sweater, no one would move it. There was no one to cook for or clean up after. Just her.

There was a pile of post on the hall table and she scooped it up. She walked into the kitchen, opened the fridge, and surveyed the contents. For the first time in her life, she didn't have to cook. It felt like too much effort. She couldn't bring herself to buy a microwave yet, even though those meals for one in the supermarket looked awfully convenient.

She put on the radio to drown out the silence and poured a glass of red wine, just a small one. She took out some cheese from the fridge, wrapped in wax paper and opened a jar of shiny green olives, with difficulty, because the lid was stiff – one of those things she would have handed to Gerard. She remembered with pleasure that there was some chocolate mousse for after. Not quite as good as a husband, chocolate mousse, but up there. She smiled. It was the sort of joke Gerard might have made.

Jean sat at the kitchen table, scarred and grooved from many evenings of children eating their dinner and doing their homework, and ate her olives and cheese. The sound of the radio and the red wine and the darkness beyond her French windows made her feel calm. Something that was almost contentment settled over her. Nagging away underneath it all, though, was the worry.

She would have to tell Kate soon, and she wasn't sure how she would take it. Alice, she was less worried about.

Alice was slow to anger and quick to forgive. Kate was another story. She had Jean's fierce, unpredictable temper. In the grip of a rage, Kate had done all sorts of things. Walked out of an exam. Shaved her head after a break-up. The flat had once rung with the sound of angry footsteps and slamming doors.

She would have to tell her soon, Jean thought. Just not quite yet.

14

KATE

Matthias's flat in Marchmont was set back down a little cobbled lane, up a steep flight of stairs to the second floor. The door was painted olive green, and there was a Christmas wreath on the door.

'Here we go,' Matthias said. He unlocked the door and held it open. The kids went in first and Olivier led them down the corridor to what she assumed must be his room.

'Nice flat,' Kate said, looking around at a pristine hallway. It smelled comforting, of baking and clean washing and pine. Wholesome. She wasn't sure what she had expected – something more obviously masculine and functional, perhaps, all grey surfaces and hard edges.

Kate tugged off her filthy boots and put them on the rack next to Olivier's red patent leather ones. Each pair was stacked neatly.

She followed Matthias down the hallway. It was *really* nice, she thought, making mental notes for Veronica. All simple wooden furniture and plants. Scrupulously clean. Warm. The smell of pine was coming from branches which decorated every surface. The whole flat looked Christmassy.

There were candles, twinkling fairy lights, and angels made from brown paper. Kate thought guiltily of their own decorations, still in the attic.

Matthias went ahead into the sitting room, and soon the sound of jazz music floated through the flat. Kate hung back slightly to peer into the bathroom as she walked past. More plants. A big block of Provencal soap and a wide porcelain tub. Kate couldn't remember the last time she had taken a proper bath in a big tub.

She glanced back to see Matthias watching her from the hallway.

'It is like you are taking notes,' he said.

'It's . . . different to what I expected,' she said.

'What *did* you expect?'

'Oh. I don't know, really,' she said lamely. 'But I approve, it's lovely.'

He held up a stovetop coffee maker. 'Coffee, I assume?'

'Yes please,' Kate said. There was a beautifully decorated tree in the sitting room, covered in glass baubles.

In the kitchen, Kate sat carefully on what she recognised as an expensive mid-century dining chair. There was a vase of red tulips on the table, a planter with herbs on the windowsill, a calendar neatly marked and not a crumb in sight. 'I *am* taking notes, by the way. Everyone is super curious about you. For obvious reasons – single dad, jazz musician, French . . .'

'I am from Belgium,' he said. He lit the gas under the coffee maker. 'And I play classical music with an orchestra. The cello.'

'One out of three isn't bad,' Kate said, grinning.

He reached past her for a coffee cup. 'What did your husband do?' he asked.

'Adam was a lawyer.'

The coffee machine whistled. He poured her coffee black.

'Do you have milk?' Kate asked, feeling horribly unso-phisticated. He poured some in, and Kate blew across the surface, watching the clouds settle. She took a sip.

'This is good coffee,' she said, with feeling. 'And you are separated from your wife?' she asked. She could be blunt, if he was.

'Olivier's mum and I were not married.' He sat down opposite her with a cup of herbal tea. He stirred his tea, and then set down the spoon neatly in a saucer. 'Lily is a musician too. She travels a lot.'

Olivier appeared in the doorway, followed by Emmie and Max. 'Can we have some snacks?' he asked.

Matthias turned and his sombre face filled with warmth. 'Of course.' He stood and put some biscuits on a plate. 'How are you all getting on?' he asked.

'Good,' said Olivier. He glanced at Kate. 'Kate, I love your hair. What colour is it? It's not quite yellow, is it?'

'Oh . . .' said Kate, flustered. She touched her hair. 'Once upon a time it was. But I'd need to go to the hairdresser to make it really yellow again. Now it's just sort of . . . mouse.'

'It's pretty,' said Olivier generously. 'You can see all different colours, can't you Papa?'

Matthias looked at Kate, his dark gaze considering. 'You can.'

Out of nowhere Kate felt an unexpected shiver down her spine. A flutter in the pit of her stomach. Where on earth had that come from? She had clearly spent too much time on her own. She took a quick swallow of coffee and scalded her mouth.

'I can't believe you have your tree already.'

'But it's December,' said Matthias, sounding surprised. 'That's when you get a tree in this country, no?'

'I guess,' Kate said resentfully. 'If you're organised.'

'We should go and get you one,' Matthias said. 'Next weekend.' Kate opened her mouth to protest and he held up a hand. 'I have the van,' he said.

'Papa,' said Olivier, 'you said we could light the advent candle tonight with Max and Emmie.'

'Of course,' said Matthias, standing. He flipped off the lights, plunging the room into gloomy afternoon shadows. Then he lifted down a wreath, set with four candles. 'We light a candle every week in the run-up to Christmas. There are four candles, and Olivier did the first one last week. That leaves one for you, Max, and one for you, Emmie.'

'What about Mummy?' asked Max.

'And one for Kate,' said Matthias. 'Max, you're the youngest. You should go first.'

Max was nervous around fire but, guided by Matthias, he carefully struck the match and held the wavering flame to the candle. It gleamed brightly in the darkened room.

'It's pretty, isn't it Mummy?' said Emmie, her face shining in the candlelight.

'It really is,' admitted Kate.

'Beautiful,' Matthias said. His dark eyes met hers, and again Kate felt that inexplicable little tremor, somewhere in the pit of her stomach, darting like the candle flame in the dark.

15

JEAN

Jean stood apprehensively in the doorway of the study, clutching a bin liner. It was dark in the room, curtains drawn. It smelled close, too. She had avoided the room since Gerard had died, although her cleaner gave it a cursory dust and vacuum every fortnight.

Her palms were sweating slightly, and she wiped them on her trousers. Taking a deep breath, she turned on the light.

It had been in the study that it had happened. That dreadful day when Gerard had stood up from his desk and said he didn't think he was well enough to work after all. Everything had changed that day.

Jean walked around the room, taking it all in. The old, roll-top desk. The key that hung from a piece of string on the nail above it. The desk chair, the lamp. The fireplace swept of ash and the mantle above it, with its parade of children's wonky clay sculptures – incense burners, candlesticks – which Kate and Ally had proudly brought home from school over the years.

The grandchildren's drawings, pinned to a cork board. Photographs of his family, in heavy silver frames. One of Gerard and Jean on their wedding day, both of them smiling stiffly at the camera. An awkward day, with neither set of parents being more than polite. The relief when they had got to their little bed and breakfast by the coast and Jean had kicked off her uncomfortable shoes, knowing that they had done it, it was over. They had the rest of their lives to just be themselves.

Photographs of their friends, anniversary parties, trips to the seaside. Their skiing trip, Kate on skis and Alice strapped to Ger's back. Jean had taken a lot of the pictures, so she wasn't in many; but it didn't matter. She remembered each one like it was yesterday.

Jean approached the desk warily. She unlocked it and surveyed the neatly docketed papers. Gerard was an obsessive filer of paperwork, believing each and every scrap to be of importance. This might take hours.

She would need wine.

A few hours later, Jean was on her second glass of wine, and had her sleeves rolled up and a smudge of dust on her cheek. She was hot and dirty but cheerful. Why hadn't she done this sooner, she thought, as she ruthlessly tossed yet more papers onto a pile to be shredded. Kate had been right; until she consigned these carefully hoarded slips of paper to the shredder, until she acknowledged that Gerard was never coming back to demand the instructions for the lawn mower or the toaster warranty, she would never truly move on.

And then, with relief coursing through her veins along with the red wine, she saw it. The thing she had been dreading, without knowing what form it would take.

A thick, cream-coloured envelope addressed to Gerard. Unquestionably important. There was no point in delaying now; there was a dull inevitability to it. She reached out for it. The unexpected, the sting in the tail, the crack in the glass. Waiting for her, as she had always known it would be.

Dear Gerard Whyte,

I am the solicitor for the estate of Ms Eve Carstairs, who died on 21st September of this year.

I enclose documents indicating myself and Mr Scott as executor. The purpose of this letter is to inform you that you have been named in Ms Carstairs' will as the beneficiary of the remains of her estate, including most urgently a property in Kilcrenny, Raasay. Copies of the deeds are attached.

There are time constraints involved in taking possession of the property. Please respond in writing or by telephone so that we can speak further and arrange a meeting at our offices in Leith or Oban. Please do not delay; the matter is of some urgency. Identification will be required.

I will await your reply.

Very truly yours, John Moncrieff.

16

'So,' said Ada, crunching the last of her biscuit. 'Maggie's turn today. Are you up to it, Maggie?'

'Aye,' said Maggie. 'Just give me a minute.' She took a deep breath, closed her eyes, then opened them again, smiling radiantly. 'My girlfriend was called Amelia,' she said. 'I was the only one who called her Milly. We lived just a few streets away – she ran a jewellery shop. We were opposites; she loved music and singing, and she was always laughing. I was the serious one.

'Milly had bad asthma her whole life, she was used to it. One day she said she wanted to go to this festival, on the West Coast. I hated festivals, but she persuaded me. It would be chill, she said, there was this band playing that she loved.' Maggie laughed. 'I always thought they were shite.'

'Anyway, we went and saw the band, and Milly was just over the moon. She loved it so much. Talking to everyone and their dog. The next day we went on a hike and we had a big bonfire in the evening. That's what they think the trigger was, the exercise and then all the smoke. She had an attack.' Her face contorted briefly. 'I don't want to talk about that. I'm glad I went along to the godawful festival, though. She wasn't alone at the end.'

She held out her wrist, on which there hung a slim gold bracelet.

'Milly made this for me to celebrate our first anniversary. She was a really talented jeweller, some of you might have been to her shop. I wasn't one for jewellery, but I wore this because of her. I tried to take it off after she died but in the end, I had to put it back on, even though it hurt. I felt wrong without it.'

Kate ran her thumb over her wedding ring. She knew that sensation.

Maggie slipped the bracelet over her wrist and held it out to show them. 'She had an inscription engraved on the inside. Would you believe, I didn't notice it until after she died? She'd call me a dozy cow for that. But the writing is so small.' She lifted it to the light. '*If I'm late, start without me.* That's a Tallulah Bankhead quote, a bit rude. Milly loved Tallulah. It's a joke. Almost like she knew she wouldn't always be there to make me laugh.'

17

KATE

Kate was running late to her first PTA meeting, and she was covered in mud thanks to a lorry splashing her as she sprinted along the high street. She also had the mother of all headaches.

She had stayed up late working on a solution that Marco and his dad would hopefully both find acceptable. Once upon a time, Kate had been able to work magic with the most uninspiring brief. Now, when it mattered most, she felt lost. Sending off the brief that morning, she had the uncomfortable feeling that she hadn't done her best work, but had no idea how to make it better.

She found the PTA convened in one of the classrooms, overlooking the playground. Rain spattered the windows and there was a circle of parents sitting in tense silence. Clearly, the dramatic events of earlier in the term were still fresh.

Veronica was going through a stack of paperwork, looking chic in a crisp white shirt, jeans and stilettos, a look that Kate couldn't have pulled off in a million years.

'Kate! Glad you could make it,' she said, making a neat tick by Kate's name. 'Refreshments are in the corner. Take a seat and fill in a new joiners' form.'

Kate found an empty seat in the circle. She smiled at the other parents but didn't receive so much as a flicker in return – everyone looked too nervous. She began filling out her form. Veronica sat slightly apart with Tamara and Lois on either side. Lois waved at Kate, but Tamara ignored her.

Kate was so tired her head swam and her eyes felt gritty. 'Is there any coffee?' she asked the woman beside her, who jumped. It was Tracy Phelps, class 2A.

'Just green tea,' Tracy whispered. 'Fewer toxins.'

'Right,' said Kate. Grief group 1, PTA 0, she thought. Bad coffee was still coffee. At least here, she hoped, no one would cry.

'Right, is everyone here?' called Veronica, and Kate felt a wave of anxious energy surge through the room, as everyone sat up straighter. Veronica clearly ran a tight ship.

She had to hand it to Veronica, she thought, glancing round the room; she had assembled a crack team. All of what Kate and Adam called the 'power parents' were in the room. Sergio, the conductor of a famous national orchestra sat in the corner, with his husband Euan, who was also resentfully filling in the new joiners' form. Kate recognised the owner of a trendy children's clothing company, a conceptual artist, a journalist for a big national newspaper and the owner of an expensive local bakery and cheese shop.

Dan Sumpter, Lois's husband, was there, with his laptop. He always seemed friendly, waving to Kate in the playground. He wore faded band T-shirts and blue jeans and ran a successful website design company.

All the movers and shakers. What she was doing here, Kate had no idea. It felt like the first day of school. She caught Dan's eye, and he gave her the faintest wink in solidarity. She wondered whether he too had been dragged here against his will.

'Welcome all,' said Veronica. She had a bottle of thick green liquid in front of her. 'This is where the fun kicks off and the hard work kicks in.' She took a sip from her bottle. 'Now, first event of the social calendar is the Christmas party, which Craig and I are old hands at hosting, so *that* should go well, at least. It's the fete I want to focus on. I want to knock last year's total raised into a paper hat.'

Tamara gave a chirpy 'woohoo!' but no one else made a sound.

'Before we get down to it, I'd like to welcome some new members to the group. Dan, who will be responsible for revamping our website and bringing the PTA kicking and screaming into the new decade. Euan, who is a whiz at organisation. And Kate, our local interior design genius, who we all know as one of the most stylish among us.' There was a pause while everyone took in Kate's filthy trainers and leggings. 'Kate will be bringing all of her visual flair to the Christmas fete. Guys, I hope you know what you're in for! Joining the PTA halfway through the Christmas rush is not for the faint of heart.' She glanced at Tamara. 'Now, on to the fete. Over to you, Tamara.'

Tamara nodded. 'We all know parents will pay through the nose if it means they can get their shopping nailed in a morning, so let's make it easy for them to do that. No plastic tat this year, okay?' She narrowed her eyes at Tracy, who shrank back in her chair.

There was a chorus of muted agreement.

'And of course, we have our celebrity guest.' Tamara smoothed her hair and smiled modestly. 'You all know I work in publishing. I've secured Karen Perkiss to come and do a book signing and a reading of her new book, *Tommy Bites Back.*'

There was a murmur of genuine excitement in the group. Even Kate was impressed. Karen Perkiss was a bona fide celebrity author, whose most famous character, Tommy the Tiger, was beloved by parents and children alike. Max would be thrilled.

'She does have certain, ah, requirements,' said Tamara, flicking open her notebook. 'A separate tent, an organised queuing system, a Sharpie, and she'd like her personal musician to accompany the reading.'

'Done, done and done,' said Veronica. 'Tell her it's in the bag. Erika, you're doing cheese and cakes; Sergio, music. The usual decorations and jumpers. The same as last year, pretty much. It all feels a bit *lacklustre*. Kate . . . Is there anything you think we could do to punch things up a bit?'

'Um,' said Kate, thinking frantically. The school fete was usually a dull affair, with a handful of parents trying to sell ugly homemade gifts that half the parents couldn't afford and the other half bought out of guilt. 'We should sell stuff people actually want as opposed to buying because they feel they should, and there should be enough free things to include the kids without pocket money. I'm thinking the parents will buy more if they're warm, well fed and slightly drunk.'

Veronica leaned forward, eyes gleaming. 'I like your thinking. Mulled wine?'

Kate nodded. 'Cider. Hot chocolate for the kids. It's a bit last minute, but maybe there's still time to make it a real event – face painting; guess the weight of the yule log, but a really sumptuous one from the bakery; a choir, parents will love to see their kids singing; pretzels . . . Would a brazier for marshmallows be a health and safety nightmare?'

'Not if it's properly staffed,' said Veronica, scribbling frantically in her notebook. Tamara was looking sour. 'You're so right Kate, we should make it more inclusive, plus imagine the kids hopped up on sugar, it'll be a riot. In a good way. I knew we could rely on you.'

Veronica turned to Dan. 'How's the website going, Dan?'

'Coming along nicely,' said Dan meekly. He turned his laptop screen around to show them all a website page. 'I thought this could work. Simple, good usability, it'll be easy to maintain . . .'

'What do you all think?' Veronica said.

'Gorgeous,' gushed Tamara. 'I love the pink and the green.'

'Kate?' asked Veronica.

'I'm not sure about the colourway, actually,' said Kate. She was growing in confidence now. 'Just because we're eighty per cent women doesn't mean it has to be pastel.'

'Mmm. I agree with Kate; let's have something a bit punchier and cooler,' said Veronica. 'Why don't you send me over some ideas?' Kate nodded and Tamara shot her a look of positive venom.

In the distance, the school bell rang, and everyone reached for their coats. 'Go on,' said Veronica, dismissing them. 'Dan, can you stay behind for five minutes to run through the copy changes?'

The parents pushed their chairs back into place and sped for the exit, forming a loose huddle in the playground. They all looked preoccupied, no doubt calculating how they could squeeze the extensive Christmas fair prep into their already overcrowded schedules.

'How was it today?' asked Kate, when Emmie and Max emerged.

'Good,' said Emmie. There was a worried pucker to her brow. Kate noticed Toxic Lydia, trotting through the playground, holding on to her mum's hand.

'Oh good, Lydia's back,' said Kate, sighing. 'I hope she had a nice holiday. Did you see Olivier? I want to hear how rehearsals are going.'

Emmie shook her head. 'I'm not allowed to talk to Olivier any more,' she whispered. 'Lydia said.'

'Of course you can talk to Olivier,' said Kate. How was she going to tackle this one? Veronica was standing by the gate with Hugo and Sienna, tapping her foot. *How on earth has she got here so fast?* thought Kate. The woman had actual superpowers.

'Kate,' Veronica said. 'I've been waiting for you.'

'That sounds ominous,' said Kate, jokily. 'Am I sacked from the PTA already?'

'Ha,' said Veronica. She tapped her daughter on the shoulder. 'Sienna, I've told you a million times. Stop picking your nose.' She turned back to Kate. 'Not at all, you'll be an asset to the team, just like I knew you would be. But while I was sitting in the meeting, I had the most brilliant idea. I can't think why it hasn't occurred to me sooner! Shall we walk?'

'But I'm hungry,' pouted Sienna.

Veronica swiftly dispensed homemade granola bars and the children set off ahead, with Kate and Veronica walking behind.

'Now, as you know, Kate, I'm very into meditation and yoga; it's why I'm so relaxed. I've been thinking for years about opening up a wellness retreat on one of the islands. Somewhere remote and unspoilt where people can really get away from it all, you know? Simple, organic food, peace and tranquillity, wildlife walks in beautiful surroundings. Finally, I've managed to locate the perfect site. A beautiful little schoolteacher's cottage, on a private beach on the island of Raasay. Utterly isolated. A barn and outbuildings. Everything we need.'

'You bought a house on an island?' Kate said. This seemed ambitious even for Veronica.

'Not quite,' said Veronica, frowning. 'I haven't bought it yet. There are a few technicalities to iron out. But I *will* be. It needs refurbishing, of course. That's where you come in, Kate.'

'Where I come in? I don't know the first thing about yoga or wellness.'

'But you *do* know about interior design. I can commission you to be the designer. Isn't it perfect?' Veronica clapped her hands. 'Unless you're too busy. You've got that little caffe project on the go, don't you?'

Kate bit her lip.

'It sounds amazing,' she said cautiously. 'I'm really grateful you thought of me for it. Maybe you could send me some pictures, so I could get a sense of the place?'

Veronica beamed. 'Of course,' she said. 'You will positively fall in love with it, just like I did.'

'I'm just not sure I have the experience . . .'

Veronica waved her hand. 'Nonsense. I'd like to help you out. No mum left behind and all that. You've chosen such a precarious career. No benefits or security to speak of.'

'Thanks,' muttered Kate.

'You can have a decent budget. Craig doesn't care much what I do with it, he's happy in his basement.'

'What's in his basement?' asked Kate curiously.

'God knows,' said Veronica, running a hand through her silky hair. 'Model railway? Crack den? I couldn't care less. Here, just look at it.' She stopped and held up an image on her phone.

Kate took the phone and peered at it. A white cottage, set low just above a shingle beach. The sun shone down, and the sky was blue and vast.

'It does look lovely,' Kate said honestly.

'I knew it,' crowed Veronica. 'Why don't you come round for a coffee on the weekend and I'll show you the rest of the pictures? Saturday? I'll text you.'

Veronica gave her a brief wave, gathered up her children, and strode off down the street. Kate watched them go.

A wellness centre, of all things. Still, thought Kate with rising optimism, it was another job. Maybe, just maybe, things were coming together at last.

18

JEAN

Jean stared out of the train window, watching the country-side rush past in a daze.

The solicitor's appointment had been a shock, to put it mildly. Extraordinary. She rubbed her forehead. Things like this just didn't happen to people like her.

She wanted to phone her daughters to see what they thought. But how could she explain it to Kate and Ally when she didn't even understand herself? *Yet another secret to keep*, she thought. They were starting to add up.

She wished that Gerard was here to consult. He was always so calm, so shrewd. He would know what to do.

The solicitor, a dry little man called John Moncrieff, hadn't been able to tell her much more beyond the contents of the original letter. Their client was Eve Carstairs, a woman of vast independent wealth who in recent years had ploughed much of it into various charities.

By all accounts she had led a life of glamour and travel, married three times, and then, a few years ago, appeared out of the blue on the isle of Raasay. She had bought a cottage, started a local caffe and, eventually, a bookshop in one of the outbuildings.

'A personal project, it seems,' John Moncrieff had said dryly. 'She left instructions in her will that Gerard Whyte be found and, once identification was complete, take possession of the house, land, outbuildings, and income for upkeep. Of course, when we didn't hear back, we looked into it and discovered his, ah, demise. We attempted to contact his next of kin, but that letter went unanswered too.'

Jean thought guiltily of the weeks she had left post unanswered. 'Are you sure you've got the right Gerard Whyte?' she had asked.

The solicitor had smiled faintly. 'Absolutely sure. Believe me, we have done our homework. We were having to face the possibility that no one would respond. There was quite a lot of interest in the property from prospective buyers, one was *most* persistent. It was a pleasant surprise to hear from you, after so long. My colleague Mr Scott knew the lady personally and he is very concerned that Eve's wishes be carried out.'

'What happens to the cottage?' Jean had asked. 'Now that Gerard's dead, I mean.'

'It passes to his next of kin,' Mr Moncrieff had said. 'It is yours outright, to do as you wish with. There's only one, ah, condition in Ms Carstairs's will. That Gerard, or in the event of his death we can assume *you*, make a journey to the cottage before taking ownership.'

'So, I can't sell it without going there?'

He had nodded. 'That's right. And there are time constraints. Ms Carstairs was rather eccentric. Possession has to be made this year.'

'This year?' Jean had gasped. 'But that's ridiculous. I can't go haring up to the Highlands the week before Christmas.'

'I know it's unorthodox,' Mr Moncrieff had said apologetically. 'If you are unable to travel, I would suggest we send a proxy. Perhaps you have family who might be able to go?'

Jean had nodded. Alice could make the trip, she thought. But for some reason, she didn't want to tell her daughters about it. There were too many questions still.

Who was Eve Carstairs? And why had she left Gerard a house?

Maybe Eve Carstairs was some old family friend of the Whyte's, Jean thought hopefully, someone from before her time. Maybe the answer lay so far in the past that it would never be discovered. But no. The Whytes weren't the sort to have wealthy, glamorous friends with property to will away.

Jean bought a cup of tea from the onboard drinks trolley operator, and wistfully stirred sugar into it. In the end, their wedding had been a quiet affair – just her, Gerard, both their parents and a handful of friends. The baby, of course, the secret guest. Only Gerard and Jean technically knew about the baby, although Jean was sure they all suspected the reason for the rushed engagement.

Her mother wore a maroon coat with a little hat and Gerard's mother a virtually identical outfit in green. Jean wore a white dress with a puffy veil set back on her head. Gerard had been his usual contained self in a blue suit.

Jean remembered one moment clearly. They had cut the cake and eaten it with bowls of ice cream from her parents' shop. Gerard's parents were arguing loudly. Jean's mother looked exhausted and stunned. Her father was eating ice cream fast and glancing at his watch.

Jean had looked at Gerard. *Her husband,* she thought proudly. There had been an expression on his face that she had never seen before. His eyes were darting round the room in what, if Jean hadn't known better, might have been panic. He was holding her hand, so tight that his knuckles were white.

'Hey,' Jean had said, tugging at his hand. 'You don't need to hold on to me so tight. I'm not going anywhere.'

Gerard had blinked and laughed. 'Sorry.' He slipped a warm hand over the slight curve of her belly. 'Thank god that's over,' he said. 'Now it can be just us, can't it, for the rest of our lives.'

If Jean had thought about it, then, she might have wondered. He sounded so *sure*. At odds with the worry in his eyes. Almost as though he was trying to convince himself.

19

KATE

'Alice tells me you're set on hosting Christmas this year,' said Jean, as they hurried up the stairs. They were late for grief group and it was Kate's fault. 'Is that really a good idea?'

'Of course,' said Kate, avoiding Jean's eye. 'Why not? There's tons of room.'

Inside, Ada was ordering other people to set out the chairs in her loud, carrying voice.

'It's just – well, wouldn't you rather wait until you're a bit more sorted before hosting Christmas for six people?' said Jean.

'I'm perfectly sorted,' said Kate, bristling. 'That reminds me, Mum; can you babysit at some point this Saturday? I need to meet a client.'

'I could do the afternoon,' said Jean. 'The morning I'm busy.'

'More golf?' said Kate, selecting a biscuit from the plate Frances was offering.

'Yes. I mean, no,' said Jean, in such an odd voice that Kate looked at her curiously. 'It's a coffee morning.'

'Which is it?' said Kate, narrowing her eyes. 'Golf or a coffee morning?'

'A, um, golf coffee morning,' said Jean, inspecting the plate of biscuits.

'The afternoon is fine,' said Kate, eyeing her suspiciously. 'A mum at the school wants me to consult on some mad-sounding vanity project. A wellness centre on Raasay, for goodness sake.'

'That's nice of her to think of you,' said Jean, beaming. 'Do you think she knows work has been a bit . . . slow?'

'I think she's got more cash than she knows what to do with,' Kate said. 'The cottage looks lovely though,' she added wistfully. 'It made me want to go to the sea. We used to go all the time as kids. Dad was like a different person on the beach, wasn't he? Not a care in the world.'

Ada took a seat and clapped her hands. 'Quiet now everyone. Frances is going to speak today,' she said.

Frances, looking more like a mermaid than ever in a pale green sweater and faded, pale blue jeans, leaned forward and pulled something out of her bag. A small, glass perfume bottle with a golden stopper.

'This belonged to my sister, Georgie,' she said. Her voice was so soft they all unconsciously shifted forward a few inches to hear her better.

'I read that sometimes when people grieve, they remember bad things about the person,' Frances said. 'It's your brain telling you it wasn't all rosy. That hasn't happened for me. All I remember about Georgie are the good things.

'She was the sweetest little sister you could imagine. Always patient, when she had an attack. She couldn't do things that everyone else could do but she never moaned about it. Most teenage girls would, don't you think?

'Anyway, this is what reminds me of her.' Frances held up the bottle. There was an inch of liquid in the bottom. 'It's her perfume. She was given it on her thirteenth birthday. I remember kicking off about it, because Mum hadn't got me a posh perfume until I was sixteen. I was all, *why does Georgie get it younger, it's not fair*. I didn't understand.

'Did you know that scent has the strongest link to memory in the brain? It acts quicker on the brain too. Quicker even than music. When I miss Georgie, this is what I smell. Bluebells. Grass. The smell of damp earth after the rain. That's Georgie.'

20

KATE

Saturday afternoon, Kate dropped the kids round with Jean and then headed to Veronica's house. She had never been inside before, but she knew which house it was – it was famous in the neighbourhood.

It was large, set in a sweeping crescent, with a cream front door and, rather optimistically Kate thought given the climate, an olive tree out front.

Kate rang the doorbell and waited. A few seconds later, Veronica arrived, wearing leggings and an oversized sweater. Her smooth hair was tumbled into a messy bun, with a few artful strands coming loose. She looked glowing, the faintest sheen of sweat on her temples.

'Kate, come in.' She tapped a sign just inside the door that read, SHOES OFF, SMILES ON. 'I was just finishing up a pilates class.'

Kate fumbled with the laces of her muddy boots in the hallway and peeled off her jacket. Against the array of tasteful camel, navy and grey coats on the peg, her anorak stood out starkly.

'Down here,' called Veronica.

Kate followed her voice down the hallway, which was also painted cream. Large black-and-white photographs of Hugo and Sienna marched along the walls, first as babies and then toddlers, then in their school uniforms, culminating in an enormous photo of Veronica, kneeling, pregnant and semi-naked, tastefully covered by a waterfall of dark hair over one shoulder.

Kate stopped to admire a photo of Veronica and Craig on their wedding day. Craig was muscular and beaming in a kilt and Veronica was in a backless wedding gown with an enormous train, veil blowing in the wind. There was a castle in the background.

'This looks like a still from a movie,' Kate said in awe.

Veronica reached out and straightened the frame. 'It was a great day,' she said. 'As you can imagine, I planned it down to a T. Careful with the decorations will you, I've just got this lot up.'

Kate noticed that swathes of ivy were woven through the bannister and golden ribbons adorned each photograph. A candle burning in the hall gave out the scent of pine. It seemed that Christmas had arrived in Veronica's house too.

Veronica led Kate through to the kitchen, a gleaming white space. There was a kitchen island with a few sleek appliances on it. Another sign on the wall, painted on driftwood, read EVERY MISTAKE MAKES ME STRONGER. Kate couldn't imagine Veronica making many mistakes at all.

If Christmas had arrived in the hallway, it had exploded in the kitchen. Bowls of chestnuts and clementines filled the surfaces and in the corner was a vast tree, decorated with sparkling white snowflakes, silver apples and dripping with icicles.

Veronica was throwing frozen fruit into a blender. 'Smoothie with coconut oil,' she said. 'Want some? Very filling, but it does give you cramps.'

'Thanks.' Kate hopped onto a stool and looked around. 'How on earth do you keep this place so clean?'

'We have a cleaner four times a week.' Veronica said, raising her voice over the drone of the Vitamix.

She poured the drink into two glasses, garnished them with a strawberry, and handed one to Kate.

'Here,' she said, pushing a sheaf of papers in a folder over the kitchen island to Kate.

Kate opened the folder. There was the cottage on the beach. In the field behind were the barn and outbuildings. She turned to the next page. A sparse interior, with a wood-burner, sheepskins, cosy armchairs. A wide kitchen table, an old-fashioned stove. And then another, larger room, lined neatly with shelves stacked with books. A few scattered tables and a coffee machine.

'The woman had it going as a sort of local bookshop slash caffe,' said Veronica. 'Hasn't been touched since she died a few years ago. Bit of an oddball by all accounts. Didn't go in for much in the way of modernisation, despite being loaded, so it's pretty rustic.'

'It's gorgeous,' Kate said sincerely. 'And you really think people will go all that way for a retreat?'

'The remoteness is part of the charm,' said Veronica. 'We'll have to gut it, of course. New floors and an extension. Revamp that barn. Rooms for the hot stone massages and plunge pool. Sky's the limit Kate, you can really go for it.'

'The sky's the limit,' murmured Kate. Something in her didn't like the idea of gutting the pretty cottage and adding on an extension, no matter how tasteful. The way it stood, low and proud on the little beach, caught at her heart. 'It would be great to try and work with local materials, so it's sympathetic to the landscape . . .'

'Yup, yup, love it,' said Veronica. 'But it needs to be rustic *luxury*, you know? This lot will like the idea of island life, but they'll want their home comforts.' Her phone rang. She fished it out of the pocket of her leggings and frowned at it.

'You can get that if you want,' said Kate, nodding at the phone. Veronica shook her head and muted the call.

'It can wait,' she said. 'Now, enough about the project. How are *you*? Christmas is such a tough time of year. Only two weeks to go.'

'I'm all right,' said Kate. She hadn't pegged Veronica as wanting a heart to heart. 'Gosh is it that soon? I've somehow invited all the family to ours, and I'm not really prepared. I just want to give the kids the best Christmas I can, you know? They've had two awful ones in a row.'

Veronica pushed a square white package across the table. 'Take this. Candle of serenity. Soy-based, non-toxic. Very relaxing.' Her phone buzzed again and, without looking, Veronica swiftly declined the call.

'What sort of time frame are you thinking for the cottage?' said Kate, trying to steer things away from Christmas.

'Well, there are a few issues to iron out,' said Veronica. 'The lawyers are having a hard time tracking down the owner so they're putting off the sale. But I'll wear them down. Make them an offer they can't refuse. If they haven't heard by the end of the year, then we can start twisting their arm. Ideally I'd start marketing the course next summer.'

Kate lifted up the picture of the cottage again. The idea of stripping away those uneven floorboards and painting it a universal beige made her feel sad.

'Why don't I pull a brief together next week and we can talk?' she said.

'Sounds like a plan,' said Veronica. Her phone was buzzing again, angrily now, like a wasp. 'Oh for goodness' sake. Give me a minute, will you?'

She walked out, leaving Kate alone in the cavernous kitchen. She took advantage of Veronica's absence to pour the smoothie down the sink and rinse the glass out. Then she headed in search of the bathroom.

She eventually found one, all mirrored surfaces, thick cream towels and fresh flowers. She washed her hands and used the expensive French hand lotion and even spritzed on some of the fig-scented perfume that was in the cabinet. Just using Veronica's bathroom made her feel more pulled together.

Kate stepped out into the hall and realised she could hear Veronica on the stairs, talking on the phone. Something about her tone – low and unexpectedly furtive – made her pause. She had never heard Veronica sound anything less than self-assured.

'I told you not to call,' Veronica was saying. She definitely sounded unusually flustered, Kate thought. 'Okay, fine. Just give me a minute to get rid of her.'

Kate slipped out of the bathroom and retreated up the corridor at speed. A few minutes later, Veronica came back into the kitchen. She had changed out of her leggings and was now wearing a silky blouse and tight jeans.

'Kate, I'm afraid I'll have to chuck you out,' said Veronica, slipping into some vertiginous pink heels. Kate noted that she was also wearing a touch of coral lipstick, and her shining dark hair was pulled back into a neat chignon in the nape of her neck. 'Forgot I have the dentist.'

'You're very fancy for the dentist,' Kate said, and she had the satisfaction of watching a faint trace of pink rise in Veronica's cheeks.

Kate allowed herself to be led down the hallway. 'I'll email you the brief Monday.'

'Look forward to it,' said Veronica, opening the front door and looking distractedly down the street. She ushered Kate out. 'I'll see you at the PTA tomorrow.'

Kate turned and looked up and down the street. Empty in both directions. *What*, she thought, *was going on there?*

21

JEAN

Standing in the study, Jean looked at the cork board above Gerard's desk. She had removed all the kid's artwork and had instead pinned the letter from the solicitors onto it.

A cottage in Raasay and a shingle beach. Something stirred in the depths of Jean's memory, but it was too deeply buried. She hesitated for a moment, and then, slowly, she pinned up the polaroid of the Edinburgh Fringe beside the letter.

A group of kids, squinting in the sunshine, battered trainers, scruffy jumpers. Students away from home for the first time. Posh kids playing at being grownups. Totally innocent, she told herself. So why did she feel it might be important?

Jean looked closer at the two girls. One of them was small and dark; the other had yellow hair like a halo, piles of it, and a sharp, pretty face. Tall too, almost up to Ger's shoulder.

She ran her fingers over the dull gold of her wedding ring. That first year of marriage had been strange. Not quite what she had expected. Anticlimactic, in spite of all the shock and upheaval of baby Katy's birth.

Gerard would be out morning to night with work. When he came home, Jean tried to have dinner on the table waiting for him – the food her mother had taught her to make. Soup or stew, mince and potatoes, sugo and meatballs.

She enjoyed the cooking, without her mother breathing down her neck and telling her she was doing it wrong. But she didn't much like the hours when it was just her and the baby.

Her friends were all still working and going out and having fun. The neighbours were few and far between, and all older. Her family were busy with the caffe. There wasn't really anyone around to spend time with.

Jean decided to try and make something out of their little patch of grass out back. One of their neighbours, a gruff, retired sheep farmer, brought her plants and advice. She grew tomatoes, sweet peas, while the baby lay on a blanket and watched the branches of the tree above shifting with the breeze. She would pick mint and crush it between her fingers, then hold them to the baby's tiny nose to sniff.

Sometimes, as she paused from planting seedlings or taking dinner out of the oven, a treacherous thought would snake into her mind that this was not what she wanted. She might be in Edinburgh now, working as a secretary for one of the big law firms. She might be putting by some money of her own.

Then the baby would do some new trick – a smile, a chubby foot in her mouth – and Gerard would come home from work and Jean would put her arms around him, smelling dust and soot and cigarettes and his own unique smell, and she would feel as though it was good, this life of theirs. Not better or worse than what she might have had but, at the very least, all theirs.

22

KATE

'What's that?' asked Emmie suspiciously, as Kate set down two plates.

'Homemade baked beans,' said Kate. It didn't look anything like the picture Veronica had put up on Instagram. Veronica's hadn't been a horrible brown colour. 'Just eat it, will you?'

Kate sat down with her laptop at the kitchen table and a glass of wine and opened up her document for Caffe Firenze. Marco had asked for still more revisions. 'A bit bland,' had been his brutal verdict.

'Why can't we just have beans from a tin like normal?' said Emmie.

'Because the ones from the tin are full of salt and sugar,' Kate parroted, scrolling through images. 'These incorporate three of your five a day.'

Emmie prodded her food with a fork. 'What are these lumps?'

'Grated carrot,' said Kate.

'It looks like the bottom of a witch's cauldron,' said Max. He cackled. 'Or poo. A plate of poo.'

'Max!' Kate snapped the lid of her laptop shut. 'That is unbelievably rude. Can't you see that I'm trying?'

The children scowled and shrugged, and Kate felt guilty.

'Listen, why don't we get our Christmas decorations up this week? I'll get them from the attic tonight,' she said. They were silent. A lump rose in Kate's throat. 'We'll get a tree,' she said, with difficulty. 'We'll get a tree next week, how about that? We can decorate it together. Play Christmas songs like we used to.'

'I don't want Christmas this year,' said Max. He kicked the table leg. 'Bad things happen at Christmas.'

'Me neither,' said Emmie, staring at her plate. A single tear splashed onto her beans. 'We used to get the tree with Daddy.'

Kate scooped both children up and swept them into her lap. 'I know, loves,' she said into their hair. 'I miss him too. But this Christmas is going to be really good. Just like Christmas should be.' She kissed them each on the nose. 'Nothing bad will happen, I promise. Now, who wants cheese on toast?'

Later, when the kids were in bed, Kate approached the trap-door to the attic where the decorations were. She wrestled with the hook to open the door and drew down the ladder, then stared up apprehensively into the darkened space above.

Gingerly, she climbed up the ladder and stuck her head into the gloom.

The attic had always been Adam's territory. Kate hadn't been able to get the decorations down last year. Now, as she stood on the top rung of the ladder, breathing in the musty air, the misery of that day came sweeping back.

Something brushed against her face and she bit back a scream, but it was just the light cord. She tugged it and a dim light above came on.

Kate searched for the boxes of decorations in the gloom, trying not to touch anything. The past felt unnervingly close. There was a box of Adam's schoolbooks and certificates, another of photographs. Their skiing gear, from when they used to do things like ski. The kids' bikes and a scooter with a missing wheel.

Soon Kate was dusty and itchy, and convinced that spiders were in her hair. At last, she found the cluster of boxes with the word XMAS scrawled in Emmie's unsteady felt tip.

Shuffling up and down the wobbly ladder with the various boxes, convinced each time that she would fall and break a limb, Kate cursed the fact that she hadn't done this when the kids were awake. At least then one of them could have held the ladder.

At last, the boxes were piled up in the hallway. Don't look inside, Kate told herself, eyeing them warily. Just don't do it.

She was sobbing over a small wooden angel, when there was a brisk ring at the doorbell. Wiping her face, she went to buzz them in.

It was Jean, holding a plastic Tupperware box. 'Hello love,' she said. 'I made Christmas cookies! I remembered how much the kids love them, and . . .' She took in Kate's tear-stained face and stopped. 'Oh, love,' she said, pulling Kate into a hug. 'Come here. What happened?'

'Nothing. I just got the Christmas decorations down from the attic,' Kate mumbled damply into Jean's shoulder, as Jean led her into the kitchen.

'Sweetheart,' said Jean, gently picking cobwebs out of Kate's hair. 'Come on. Let me make you a cuppa.'

'I don't have any tea,' Kate said, wiping her nose. She sat at the table and picked at skin on her nail. 'I'm a total failure.'

'I'll find something,' said Jean soothingly, rifling through the cupboard. 'Aha,' she said, holding up a dusty teabag.

She sniffed it. 'It's tea of some sort anyway. Now, what's really going on?'

'Everyone else has their decorations up and it all looks perfect,' said Kate. 'They're all spray painting pine cones and making stollen. The kids had such terrible Christmases the last two years and I want this to be special. But it was always Adam who used to get the decorations down. Adam would take them to get a tree and then we'd put music on and drink hot chocolate. This year is going to be rubbish, I know it is. We're all dreading it, and me most of all.'

'Let it all out,' said Jean. She handed Kate the mug of tea and rubbed her back. 'It won't be rubbish. It'll be different, but different doesn't mean bad. Why don't I come along and get the tree with you? We can make it fun?'

'Thanks, Mum,' Kate said, taking a sip of the mystery tea. 'We were going to go tomorrow.'

'Tomorrow,' said Jean, her eyes darting. 'That should be fine. I just need to move something.'

'Don't worry,' said Kate. 'I think maybe the kids and I should do it on our own.' *You always seem so busy these days*, she thought but did not say.

They sat in silence for a while. Her mother was leafing through the sheaf of photos of the cottage in Raasay that Veronica had given her.

'What's this?' Jean asked, holding up one of the cottage.

'It's the place in Raasay I told you about,' said Kate. 'That the mum from school wants done up for a yoga retreat. Nice isn't it? Loads of character. Shame it's going to be gutted.'

Jean was frowning. 'She's buying *this* cottage?' she said, in a stifled voice.

'I think they need to find the owner before the sale can go through. But she thinks she can buy it end of the year.'

Her mother stared at the photo for a long minute, then shook her head and tucked it back in among the others. 'It's lovely,' she said briskly. 'But I bet it's freezing in winter. Listen, I've got to get back, need to feed that cat. Roddy's been in on his own all day.'

'Why? Where have you been?' said Kate suspiciously.

'Food bank,' said Jean smoothly. *A touch* too *smoothly,* Kate thought.

'I thought food bank was on Wednesdays,' she said.

'They asked me to do an extra shift,' said Jean.

She stood and dropped a kiss onto her daughter's head. 'Go to bed will you, love? Things always look brighter in the morning. And don't put too much pressure on yourself when it comes to Christmas. The kids won't care about spray-painted pine cones.'

Kate nodded. She listened to the click as the door shut behind Jean. She rested her chin on her hands and looked again at the little cottage. She imagined walking along the shingle beach, feet slipping over the stones. Taking off her shoes, putting her feet in that cold sea, breathing in the air, and walking home again with salt on her lips to curl up by a roaring fire. She wouldn't do much to the interior, she thought; restore some of the floorboards maybe.

Her phone buzzed with a text and she groped for it, still looking at the picture. It was Matthias and the text was predictably to the point.

'Shall we get the tree tomorrow, midday?'

Kate stared at her phone, her heart beating quickly in her chest. It would be so easy to type a polite excuse and leave it at that. But she didn't want to. Shamefully, she wanted someone to go with her to the market, to help her choose a tree and help her take it home.

'Thanks that would be great,' she typed fast before she could change her mind, then pressed send.

It was just an outing to buy a tree. What harm could it do?

23

KATE

Kate chewed her nail.

She felt over-caffeinated and anxious. She had stayed up late working on the designs for Marco, perfecting what she was hoping was the ideal blend of old meets new, sleek meets kitsch, retro-modern fusion, and had sent them all over to him. Surely, she would have nailed it this time, she thought.

She smoothed her hair in the mirror. She had got changed five times that morning, trying to imagine what Veronica might wear to go and buy a Christmas tree. Skinny jeans, maybe, and a thick cream jumper and a cashmere hat.

In the end, Kate ended up wearing her usual school-run jeans. None of her old clothes fit, either her body or her life. Besides, she thought crossly, why was she making so much effort? Matthias was helping out, that was all. Nevertheless, she had washed her hair.

Emmie and Max shrieked from the window, snapping Kate out of her reverie. 'He's here!' they called.

'Great,' said Kate, leaping nervously to her feet. 'Anyone need a last-minute wee? Snack? Drink of water?'

'No,' said Emmie. 'Why are you talking so fast? And what's that stuff around your eyes?'

'It's nothing, come on,' said Kate, grabbing their coats and ushering them outside.

Fortunately, the only nervous energy seemed to be coming from her – Matthias looked infuriatingly calm and unfazed, as though chauffeuring single mothers around was nothing unusual.

The kids were thrilled to be travelling in a van. Kate and Matthias set about shifting booster seats around and then she scrambled into the front seat next to him. There was plenty of space between them and yet it felt oddly intimate. If anyone saw them, she thought, they would assume they were a family.

Calm down, Kate told herself. He's driving you to buy a tree.

'Where are we going?' she asked. 'IKEA? The garden centre?'

'I think we can do better than that,' Matthias said. 'I took the liberty of booking us tickets for the Victorian Christmas Experience. I thought it would be nicer.'

'It's awesome,' Olivier told her. 'We went a few weeks ago. Santa is there! You get a present!'

'That sounds very Christmassy indeed,' said Kate.

'It is,' said Matthias firmly, starting the van. 'It's time Christmas started in your family.'

Kate couldn't exactly argue with that.

The Christmas Experience was in an old manor house set in the grounds of a park outside the city. The trees were strung with fairy lights and the paths snaked to a front door, from which warm light poured appealingly. Inside the hall was an enormous Christmas tree in front of a log-burning fire, and a sign saying FATHER CHRISTMAS THIS WAY.

For all that Kate was prepared to hate it, she couldn't quite bring herself to. The Father Christmas in his grotto was straight out of central casting, with a ruddy, cheerful face and snowy white beard. He produced Lego sets for both children from his sack and laughed merrily on cue. Staff with trays of mince pies and mulled wine circled the main hall. There was a wreath-making workshop – an idea which Kate decided to steal for the PTA Christmas fair – and a shop selling decorations.

'You can each choose one,' said Matthias.

Emmie chose a llama, Max a Christmas pudding and Olivier a fat, glittery, red apple. Matthias took them off to pay.

'Here,' Matthias said to Kate, handing her a small paper bag. 'You should have something to hang on the tree too.'

'Thanks,' said Kate, feeling herself going pink. 'I'll open it later.'

Outside in the yard, they found their perfect tree, not too big and not too small, almost instantly. Somewhere along the way, Matthias invited them back for lunch and Kate agreed. They lugged the tree back to the van and then, as he started the engine, *All I Want for Christmas (Is You)* came blaring out. Kate burst out laughing.

'This is a Christmas conspiracy,' she said.

'Are you feeling festive yet?' Matthias asked her. 'You must be, by now.'

'A little bit,' she admitted. 'You wore me down.' Their eyes met, just for a second, while the kids chattered in the back. Then Matthias turned and spoke to the children.

'Ready for lunch?' he said.

'If you're sure that's okay,' Kate said to Matthias.

'Very sure,' he said, and they drove back to the city, the children shrieking the lyrics loudly all the way.

★   ★   ★

On the way back, the children had started a raucous, toilet-humour game of I-Spy that continued into the flat and Olivier's room. Kate supervised them for a while but then gave up. They were too excited.

She went to find Matthias in the kitchen.

'It smells amazing in here,' she said. 'What is it?'

'Roast chicken,' he said. 'What can I get you to drink?' he asked.

'Coffee, please,' she said. 'I know, it's nearly three, I'm dicing with danger.'

'How is your sleep?'

'Like a baby,' she lied. Her phone was ringing. Marco, at bloody last. She pounced on it.

'Hi,' said Kate, trying to sound calmer than she felt. 'Marco, how nice to hear from you.'

'Kathy, hi. I've had a look at your proposal. It's dead nice, really stylish . . . but . . .'

'But?' she said, her heart sinking.

'I just don't think it suits,' said Marco. He sounded apologetic, which made things worse. 'A wee bit slick still, you know?'

'We can change it, no problem,' gabbled Kate. 'I'll send over some alternatives. I'll—'

'It's not working,' Marco said, and the quiet kindness in his voice was like a dagger to Kate's heart. 'It's a bit special to us, we want to get it right. Sorry about that, Kath.'

Marco hung up. Kate dropped her head onto the table, too miserable to pretend anything other than utter despair.

'Was that your one client?' Matthias said from the stove.

'Yeah.' She lifted her head. 'And he just sacked me. Well, technically I do have one more client, but I don't know if that'll happen or not.'

'I'm sorry,' Matthias said. 'Why did he sack you?'

'He said I didn't meet the brief,' said Kate. She scowled down at her phone resting on the elegant wooden tabletop. 'It's some scabby caffe. Talk about delusions of grandeur.'

'Did you meet the brief?'

She turned her scowl on Matthias, who was basting the chicken. '*I* think so, obviously,' she said.

'What did he want you to do?'

'Um.' Kate thought back to her meeting with Marco and the notes she'd taken. She realised she couldn't quite remember. 'He wanted to keep his dad and the old-timers happy, but he's got a new chef in, so something a bit fresher. Which I would have done. I think.'

Matthias shrugged. 'He is the client,' he said simply. He leaned forward and poured her coffee. Even though he didn't touch her, Kate could feel the heat of his arm through his shirt.

'I'm cutting you off after one,' he said. 'Let's talk of something else. How was your first PTA meeting?'

Kate was surprised that he'd remembered. 'Not too bad. Veronica runs a tight ship. I'm quite enjoying planning the fair, and there are some amazing people on the team, I think it could be good this year, for a change.' She took a sip of coffee. 'Why does your coffee always taste better than mine?'

He paused, still standing close to her. Her heart beat faster, perhaps not just from the coffee.

'There's a technique to making good coffee,' he said. 'I'll show you.' She took another sip of coffee, trying to hide her pink cheeks. To her relief, he moved away, back to the stove.

'Let me set the table,' she said, jumping up.

He nodded to a drawer. Kate opened it. Neat, shining rows of cutlery. Cloth napkins. Everything in its place. She watched as he added what looked like half a pack of butter to the mashed potatoes.

'You'd get on well with my mother,' she said. 'Only her obsession is olive oil. And salt.'

'She likes to cook?'

'Loves it. All old-school Italian food. So does my sister. They're both so good at it that I never bothered learning.'

He shook his head. 'Food is a way of taking care of yourself. Very young, my mother taught me the basics.'

'Can you make biscuits? The famous speculoos?'

'Exactly. I'll bring you some.' He stuck his head out of the door before she could reply that she could take care of herself very well, thank you. 'Kids, dinner is ready.'

The chicken was perfect, lemony and garlicky, the potatoes buttery, each vegetable cooked to perfection. There was gravy and salad and crusty white bread. Max and Emmie tore into the food and Kate found herself wolfing it down too. It tasted like the most delicious thing she had ever eaten. She hardly paused between mouthfuls. Olivier watched her with an appalled expression.

'You need to chew your food, Kate,' he said. He added, fairly, 'I need to learn to chew my food too. Papa always says so.'

'Do you ever have fish fingers?' asked Max. 'Chips? Beans?'

'I love fish fingers,' said Olivier. 'We hardly ever get them.'

'They're nice,' said Emmie. 'But you go off them when you have them every night.'

Kate shot her a dirty look and changed the subject. 'How's the Christmas play coming along?'

Olivier beamed. 'It's going well,' he said. 'You're all going to love it. We sail to a mysterious island and find the baby Jesus.'

'This sounds like the best Christmas play ever!' said Kate. 'Ms Roger clearly has an eye for raw talent.'

After dinner Emmie lit the third Advent candle and then Matthias put on a film for the kids. It was only then that she felt awkwardness descend. Again, it felt too intimate without the children to distract them. Like she was slipping all too easily into a fantasy of cosy domesticity. Lured in by roast chicken and central heating.

'I'll wash up,' she said, pushing back her chair and standing.

'No, you are my guest,' Matthias said.

'Please, it's the least I can do after that. Best meal I've had in ages.' She took the plates and rinsed them, stacking them into the dishwasher, then put the roasting pan into the sink and filled it with hot water and suds. She had a feeling that Matthias was probably particular about his dishwasher-stacking methods, but it gave her something to do.

'Really, I'll do it,' said Matthias, moving to stand behind her. He took the dishcloth, his arm brushing against hers, and again she felt an electric jolt. 'You're going to break something.'

'Ha, ha,' Kate said. 'Thanks for having us over,' she said suddenly. 'I really appreciate the meal. And just – someone to talk to. I think I've been going a bit mad lately.'

'Any time you want to talk,' he said. He nodded towards the sitting-room doors. 'You go and hang out with the kids. They're watching *The Grinch Who Stole Christmas*. Sounds right up your street.'

When Kate lay in bed that night, she replayed the feeling of his arm brushing hers. Of the warmth of his body.

She needed to get a life, she thought. Fast.

24

KATE

'Stefan was really into his wine,' said Ada. 'I used to tease him all the time, because he wasn't much of a drinker. Too busy training. Hard work being a semi-pro footballer. It was all protein and carb loading, squats and pull ups. But then he had this crazy wine cellar.

'"What are you going to do with all of that wine," I would say, "drink it on your deathbed?" He would say it was a hobby, like cars or sport. Talk to me about vintages and vineyards and all sorts. "I'll leave it all to you in my will, Ma," he'd say. "You can drink the cellar dry then. Enjoy it."

'You don't think of young people getting a stroke. Especially people as healthy as Stefan. He hadn't even had a chance to live yet. All I could think about was that my boy got to do what he loved his whole life and there's not many who can say that, can they?

'I didn't think he'd have made a will, given he was that young. But he had done, I think they make all the players do it. He'd left the flat to me and he said especially the wine cellar. His idea of a joke, I think. I go in there and look at all the wine and imagine him looking down at me. "All yours now, Ma. Enjoy it."'

Ada reached into her bag and pulled out a bottle, which she set on the table. Kate leaned forward to read the label. *Moet & Chandon Grand Vintage 1994.*

'It's his birthday this week,' Ada said. 'He was going to be twenty-six. I thought we could celebrate.'

Ada picked up the bottle, peeled off the foil, and prised the cork out. It gave a loud pop.

She poured the wine into the coffee cups. Kate took hers.

'A toast, then,' said Rory. 'To Stefan. Slange.'

They raised their glasses. 'To Stefan,' they said. 'To Stefan.'

Kate hurried into her flat just after nine. 'I'm sorry I'm late,' she said, calling out from the hallway and unwinding her scarf. 'Couldn't get a bus.'

She hurried into the sitting room and found Alice curled up on the sofa under a blanket, drinking wine and watching the TV. She was in town seeing friends and had offered to babysit during grief group.

'Were the kids okay?'

'They were delightful,' said Alice. 'I just went in to check on them and they're sleeping like angels. Cute, sweaty little angels.' She leaned forward and paused the film.

Kate jumped onto the sofa beside Alice and tucked her feet under her. 'They're only angels with you,' she said. 'Don't stop watching a film on my account. What is it?'

'Just some stupid Christmas rom com,' said Alice, rolling her eyes. 'They'll all get married in the end. Nice tree, by the way.'

'A friend took me to Santa's Grotto,' said Kate.

'Which friend? Nat and Fergus?'

'No, um, some dad from school.'

'I untangled those Christmas lights for you,' Alice said. 'And this box arrived.'

'It's the material for my PTA fete Christmas wreaths,' said Kate, pouncing on the cardboard box and tearing it open. 'Look!' She held up a felt robin. 'How cute is this?'

'It's very cute,' said Alice, looking amused. 'I didn't know you were so into Christmas crafts.'

Kate sat back on her heels. 'I think I'm coming round to them. Remember how magical Christmas was when we were kids?' she asked. 'I was so sure that if I just stayed awake, I would catch Santa, but I never could. And then in the morning, the stockings at the end of the bed . . .'

'A chocolate orange *and* a tangerine,' Alice said. 'We were lucky.'

'Spoilt rotten, more like,' said Kate. 'How many eight-year-olds get riding lessons?'

'Sometimes I fantasise about Mum's Christmas lunch,' said Alice. 'I can never get it as good, no matter how much I try. She could make anything magic, couldn't she?'

Kate nodded. 'I wish I could,' she said. 'All I'm teaching the kids is that Christmas sucks and people die.'

Alice nudged Kate. 'You're doing great. Oh, I nearly forgot. A guy came round. Matthew? Matt? Anyway, he left this for you.' She handed Kate a Tupperware box. 'He was extremely good looking.'

Kate opened the lid. There were crisp, brown biscuits inside.

'Speculoos,' she murmured. 'It's just a dad from school.'

'Is this the same dad who took you to get a tree?' said Alice. 'Is this a *single* dad?'

'Yes. But don't get excited.' Kate said. 'He's just being nice.'

'I've heard that one before.' Alice popped a biscuit in her mouth. 'Men are never "just being nice" when it comes to you. Yummy. See you next week.'

When the door had shut behind Alice, Kate tugged the discarded blanket around her, and poured some more wine into her sister's empty glass. Then she pressed play on the film and reached for the biscuits.

She stayed there, huddled under the blanket, watching the Christmas film – Alice had been right, they did get married in the end – and eating biscuits, until each sweet, buttery mouthful was gone.

25

KATE

On the bus to the PTA meeting, Kate snuck a quick, guilty look at Veronica's Instagram, knowing it would make her feel worse about herself but unable to resist. Hugo and Sienna, wearing fluffy dressing gowns and slippers, hair damp from the bath, were perched on a bed covered in clean white linen, mugs of hot chocolate in hand, grinning toothily into the camera. The image had a bleached, hazy quality, as though it had been taken in a villa in the south of France rather than on a chilly evening in Edinburgh.

The caption read:

> Hot chocolate on a school-night.
> Sometimes it's the simple things.
> Recipe for my spiced cacao sugar-
> free hot chocolate below. Perfect for
> Christmas Eve. Dressing gowns #gifted.
> #sugarfreenotfunfree #smallbusiness #Advent.

Kate sighed. How could anyone's life be so perfect?

She had spent the morning trying to wrestle her ideas for Veronica's wellness centre onto paper, but every time Kate tried to engage with Veronica's vision – blonde wood, cream walls, expensive fixtures and fittings – she would look at the little cottage, with its uneven floorboards and rough-hewn shelves, and her heart would give a little thud of longing. She couldn't afford to mess up again, after she had so royally screwed up with Marco. She had to nail this one.

Kate got off the bus, still scrolling, and realised she was at Veronica's front door. She stuck her phone quickly into her pocket and rang the doorbell. She didn't want to be exposed as Veronica's biggest superfan.

'Kate,' Veronica said, opening the door. 'How's my island retreat coming along?'

'Really well,' lied Kate. 'I should have some ideas to show you soon.'

'Excellent,' said Veronica. 'What I love about you, Kate, is that you're so decisive.' She strode down the corridor, calling out. 'Shame I can't say the same for you, Dan.'

Dan Sumpter was already there, sitting hunched over a cup of tea.

'Coffee, Kate?' Veronica asked.

'I'd love one, thanks. Black with milk on the side if that's okay.'

Veronica swept off and Dan let out a heavy sigh.

'She wants this new website by next Friday,' he whispered to Kate. 'I tried to tell her that it can take *weeks* to finesse. I have a full-time job.'

Kate laughed. 'I don't think she hears the word no very often.'

'Why on earth did you join this walking nightmare?'

'I realised resistance was futile,' said Kate, hopping up onto one of the stools. 'Why did you?'

Dan grinned, a dimple appearing in one cheek. He

was rather sweet-looking, Kate thought, with his baggy anorak and shock of dark hair that stood up every which way. Much less slick than the other parents. He and high-powered lawyer Lois made an odd couple. 'Lois is heavily involved. Veronica said we should keep it in the family.'

'Like the mafia,' said Kate. 'Speaking of websites, I should get some tips from you. Mine is a disaster.'

'I'd be happy to take a look for you,' he said.

'I wasn't angling for a consultation,' said Kate. 'You're already doing pro bono for the PTA.'

'It would be no bother.' He grinned, his dimple peeking out again. 'For someone I'm not actively terrified of.'

Kate grinned back. 'I promise not to shout at you.'

Other members were slowly filing in. Everyone looked apprehensive. Kate wondered whether Veronica inspired them all with the same mixture of fear and admiration that she felt.

Veronica clapped her hands. 'You all know what you're doing. Decoration workshop on the table in the hall, truffle making here on the aga, and Kate will be running a wreath-making workshop in the sitting room.'

'I don't really know what I'm doing,' said Kate, leading a cluster of parents into Veronica's beautiful, elegant sitting room, complete with a grand piano and what looked like Scottish colourist paintings on the walls. 'I just watched a YouTube tutorial.'

'Oh well,' said Sergio, settling down and picking up an armful of twigs. 'Rustic is in this year.'

They worked quietly for a while. 'Psst,' said Euan. He waved a bottle of prosecco. 'We've got some booze.' Kate hesitated. 'Go on,' he said. 'It makes these things go much faster.'

'All right then,' she said, holding out her tea mug. 'Everyone seems a bit scared. Is this because of what happened last term?'

Sergio nodded. 'You mean the exodus. That was scarring. There never used to be this much drama in the PTA. When I first joined it was all community spirit and knitted socks. I think some of the personalities involved have made things a little—'

'Toxic? Terrifying?'

'Take your pick,' he said. 'But say what you like, since Veronica took over, they've raised shitloads of money. It's a double-edged sword.'

Veronica appeared in the doorway. 'Nice work guys!' she said cheerfully. 'I hate to break this up, but the school bell is about to ring. Kate, would you be happy to finish that lot up at home?'

'Absolutely,' said Kate, gathering up the wreaths, which were made to different standards of competence. She could finesse them at home.

As they neared the school gates, Veronica said, 'Kate, why don't we go into town next week? I've got an appointment with Daniel M and I'm sure he could squeeze you in too. He'll do pretty much anything for me.'

'Who's Daniel M?' said Kate, forcing the stiff school gate open.

'Only the best hairdresser in the city! Very exclusive. Anyway, I thought he could sort you out a bit.' She gestured at Kate's hair. 'You always had the most gorgeous hair.'

Kate ran a hand protectively over her hair. 'I don't really like going to the hairdresser,' she lied. 'I get bored sitting there with nothing to do, reading magazines.' The idea sounded like heaven.

Veronica sighed. 'Just a little trim and a root refresh . . .'

'It looks good to me as it is,' said Dan beside them, and Kate shot him a look of gratitude.

The bell rang, and the children began filing out. Kate craned her head, looking for her kids and waved vigorously when she saw them. No matter how infuriating her children were in the morning, by the time pickup came around she was pleased to see them. Dan's little girl, Livvie, threw herself into his arms.

'See you tomorrow,' he said, then whispered, 'stay strong' to Kate. Kate watched as he walked up the steps, tugging his anorak over his head. He was nice. Normal. Kind. A good dad. Livvie and Lois were lucky, she thought wistfully.

'Come on, you two,' she said, trying to sound cheerful. 'Let's go home.'

'Mum,' said Emmie, skipping alongside her. 'I'm starving.'

Kate fumbled in her pocket for a packet of opened crackers. 'Here, have one of these.'

Max bit into one tentatively. 'They've gone all soft,' he said. 'What's for tea? And don't say fish fingers! We had that for lunch.'

'Did you? Damn,' said Kate. 'They're not very adventurous, your school, are they? Maybe Matthias is right about the lunches.'

'That's all we have at home too, though,' said Max.

'All right, don't rub it in,' said Kate. 'But you know what, the joke is on you, because tonight we're getting pizza and . . .' she stretched out the silence like a reality show host, 'we're decorating the tree!'

The children looked apprehensive rather than excited. 'Okay,' said Emmie.

'I know what you're thinking,' said Kate, putting her arm around her daughter and remembering what Jean had said.

'It won't be the same as when Daddy was here. But it can still be really good, in its own way.'

Surprisingly, it was. Kate put music on, old Christmas songs that Adam had loved. They put up the decorations, the ugly beautiful ones the kids made at school and the chic ones Kate and Adam had collected before they'd had children.

Kate tried not to micromanage the arrangements, even when Max loaded the bottom corner of the tree with heavy baubles. Their pizza arrived, thick with gooey plastic cheese. When it came to pinning the angel on the top, a task that Adam had always done, Kate lifted Emmie up high, so that she could reach it.

'Wait! Don't forget the decorations Matthias got us,' said Emmie.

'Of course.' Kate dug around in her handbag and found them. A little llama and a pudding.

'Where's the one you got?' asked Emmie.

Kate lifted out the little paper package Matthias had given her. She peeled back the paper and saw a delicate glass bauble, with a miniature Christmas tree inside. When she shook it, little flakes of snow sprang up and drifted down again. She hung it high up on the tree so the kids couldn't mess with it.

At last, they were done. They stood back to admire their work.

'What do you think, guys?' Kate said.

Emmie let out a deep and happy sigh.

'I think it's perfect, Mummy,' she said.

It wasn't perfect, Kate thought. Perfect would mean that Adam was there with them, on his knees fussing over the tree in its stand, checking it had enough water. But it was still really good, in its own way.

26

JEAN

Jean sat cross-legged, surrounded by piles of papers. She had emptied Ger's desk drawers and then his bookshelves.

Raasay. Eve Carstairs. That little cottage. She knew that name, that place. She had seen it somewhere before, she knew she had.

She lifted up a drawing Ger had kept, of children's hand-prints. So Gerard had been sentimental, a little.

She thought of that summer, when Gerard had come back from the Fringe. It had been bliss to have him home again. To watch him with the baby. Lying back against the bedhead, shirtsleeves rolled up, Kate on his chest. The two of them flushed with summer heat and sleep. He seemed at once more remote than ever – a handsome stranger – and dearly familiar. A father, now.

When Jean had asked him what the Fringe had been like, he had said, 'Not much to write home about. Usual posh students messing about.'

A permanent job came up at the shipyard. His boss had liked him, seen something in him, promoted him quickly. Suddenly Gerard had longer hours and an office. He had a wife and a baby and a job, all three at once. No wonder, Jean thought, that he looked worried sometimes. She felt scared herself. As if she couldn't believe that all of this had happened to them so fast, and that now there was no turning back.

Jean pushed another pile of papers aside. She had seen that cottage before. Somewhere.

27

KATE

Kate's week began well. She almost felt happy, which made her nervous.

Veronica had loved the plans for the island cottage. Buoyed by the thought of potential income, Kate finally set to work on the flat. She might have given up on her grand renovation plans, but she could patch it up enough to sell, she thought. First thing on Monday, she rang the estate agent who had sold them the flat two years earlier and told them it was to go back on the market.

'Of course I remember you!' the estate agent said. 'You and your handsome husband and beautiful wee kiddies. I remember telling someone in the office you looked like the perfect family. I'll be excited to see what you've done with the place.'

Kate snorted. 'Don't get your hopes up,' she said. 'I just want a quick sale.'

Then, Dan texted Kate to tell her he had taken a look at her website. 'I think we can get something up and running even if it's basic,' he had said. They had arranged to meet at a caffe round the corner from the school. And, icing on the cake, she got a text from Erika, a PTA mum whose son was in Max's class, offering to take Max climbing after school.

'Veronica told me about your situation,' her text read. 'I'm happy to help.'

Kate bristled at the idea that Veronica had been calling in sympathy favours on her behalf, but Max was thrilled.

Kate had nearly finished the wreaths and they looked good, though she said so herself. She had more artistic flair than she'd thought. The Christmas fair was coming together beautifully, with donations pouring in and some excellent stalls. A local restaurant with a Michelin star had agreed to donate a meal as the raffle prize.

Kate had googled how to manage Christmas dinner in a small oven with a semi-functioning hob and bought an enormous turkey which she put in the freezer. To top it all, the weather forecast was hinting at snow for Christmas.

For the first time in months, Kate felt a flickering of hope. Perhaps things were turning a corner.

At pickup that Monday, though, Emmie came running out bright-eyed and flushed and Kate's heart sank. She recognised that expression; Emmie was holding back tears.

'What happened, baby?' she asked softly, drawing Emmie close.

'Lydia said . . .' said Emmie, gulping, '. . . she said I had to choose. I can't be friends with her and Olivier. It has to be just her.'

'Is this because you and Olivier are doing the Christmas play together?'

Emmie nodded miserably.

'Lydia said I have to quit the play and not tell Ms Roger why.'

It was one of those times when Kate felt woefully under-prepared as a parent. She wanted to tell Emmie that Lydia could get lost, but instinct told her it would be better to let Emmie decide that on her own.

'Come on,' she said. 'Your brother's got a playdate. Let's go and sit somewhere warm and have a hot drink and some cake. Then we can decide what to do.'

They went to a bakery in the Old Town and sat with hot drinks. After Emmie had devoured several greasy pastries, she looked a little happier.

'What should I do?' she said at last. She was pulling her last bit of bun into strings and eating them. 'I like Olivier, and I want to do the play, but Lydia is my *best friend*.'

'I know, honey. And I remember friends meaning a lot at your age.' Kate dabbed up some crumbs. 'I always think it's good to have a few different friends, though.'

'I'm only allowed one,' Emmie said tearfully.

'I don't have just one best friend, though, do I?' said Kate. 'I have Auntie Alice when I want to have a cosy chat. Nat when I want to have a laugh and a rant about the world. Your Granny Jean when I want a cuddle. Fergus when I need advice.'

'Matthias for when we need a Christmas tree?'

Kate hesitated. 'Matthias for the Christmas tree,' she said.

Emmie wiped her nose with the back of her hand. 'Were you and Daddy best friends?'

'Of course we were, the very best. But I needed my other friends too.'

There was silence, while Emmie licked her fingers thoughtfully.

Kate glanced at her watch. 'Time to go and get your brother. Why don't we sleep on this? I bet you'll wake up tomorrow morning and know exactly what to do.'

'Okay,' said Emmie doubtfully, putting on her coat. 'I hope so. I wanted to be Pirate Queen more than anything.'

★　　★　　★

The next morning, Emmie sulked through breakfast, threw her shoe at Max and then, at the school gates, burst into tears.

'You said I'd wake up and know what to do!' she sobbed.

'I thought you would!' said Kate, feeling wretched. 'It doesn't always work.' She glanced at her watch. 'I have to go and meet Dan now about my website. Please, promise me you won't quit the play just yet. One more sleep and I think we'll have a solution.'

She forced a sobbing Emmie through the gates and sprinted to the caffe. She could see Dan through the glass frontage, two coffees and a laptop in front of him, as well as a pad and pen.

'Dan, hi!' Kate said, sitting down. She started unwinding her scarf and peeling off her coat. 'Thank you so much for doing this.'

'It's no bother,' he said, sitting up a little straighter. 'It just took me a few hours.' He grinned. 'It can be daunting, when you don't know what you're doing.'

'Which, let me guess, most creative types don't?'

'Let's say it's not always their strength.' He nudged one of the coffees towards her. 'Black, hot milk on the side, right?'

'Thanks,' she said, taking a grateful sip.

'It's what you always order, my nerd brain remembered.' He turned the laptop towards her. 'This is what I was thinking for your home page. Really simple navigation. It's not very whizzy but usability is key here. Tell me anything you don't like, I can sort it.'

'This looks fantastic,' Kate said, her eyes widening as he clicked through. 'Did you really just spend a few hours on this?'

'If you know your stuff it doesn't take long,' he said. He let out a huge yawn. 'Sorry. Lois had a big deadline and Livvie had earache, so I spent the whole night sleeping on her bedroom floor. I found a Barbie under my back this morning.'

'I should have been the one buying you coffee,' said Kate sympathetically. *Dan was so lovely*, she thought. A good husband and father. Adam, for all his strengths, had never spent the night with the kids when they were sick. His job had always come first. It had always been her mopping foreheads and holding sick bowls.

'You can get me one after the first big client hit via your shiny new website. Deal?'

'Deal,' she said, scanning the page. 'Honestly, this looks amazing. I can't thank you enough.'

Dan cleared his throat. 'I'd be happy to meet again to talk through your copy if you'd like. I think we could optimise your SEO.'

There was a soft knocking on the glass window and Kate looked up to see Alice, looking like a doll in a camel coat and woolly hat, her cheeks pink with cold. Mark was at her side, dour-faced and hugely out of place in his flat cap, Barbour and cords.

'Come in!' mouthed Kate, beckoning, and Alice hurried through the door. Mark followed, his expression resigned. He probably thought caffes were a city-dwelling waste of time.

'What are you doing in town?' asked Kate, standing and hugging her sister. As usual she smelt of roses.

'We came through to do some shopping,' said Alice. 'Mark's not happy about it,' she added dimpling at him. 'He'd rather be at home with the chickens.'

'Poor Mark,' Kate said lightly. 'Why don't you have a cake stop?'

'Oooh yes!' said Alice.

'If that's what you want, Alice,' said Mark stoically, as though they had just suggested he rip his fingernails off for fun.

'I should get going,' said Dan, standing.

'Sorry,' Kate said, 'Dan, this is my sister Alice and her boyfriend, Mark. Guys, this is Dan, from the kids' school. He's a digital whizz and he's done the most amazing job salvaging my terrible website. He's my hero.'

Dan stood and shook hands with Alice and Mark. 'It's really not as big a favour as you think,' he said modestly. 'Kate, I'll see you at the next PTA gathering.'

Alice sat down in Dan's seat and pulled off her gloves. 'I'll have a hot chocolate, please, Mark, and one of those cinnamon rolls.'

'Oat milk flat white, please,' said Kate, thinking of her microbiome.

'Oat milk,' said Mark, his shoulders slumping. He went off to join the queue.

'Poor Mark,' Alice said, watching him. 'He's like a fish out of water in town.' She smoothed down her hair. 'That's nice of – Dan, was it? – to help you out with your website. Another dad helping out?'

Kate rolled her eyes. 'This one is happily married. You need to stop matchmaking me with every man you see within a mile radius.'

'I know what you're like,' said Alice, standing to help Mark with the tray. 'Or rather what men are like around you. Fergus doing pickup, Matthias and his biscuits, Dan working his magic on your website. It's like school all over again.'

'I think you're giving me way too much credit,' said Kate, taking her coffee gratefully. 'Anyway, like I said, Dan is just helping out.'

'Okay,' said Alice. 'Whatever you say.'

28

JEAN

It came to her in the night, and she sat bolt upright.

Raasay. A postcard on the doormat, over five years ago now. Sailboats bobbing on a calm sea, a shingle beach, a little white house. The writing on the back, in a bold, slanting hand:

Remember this? E

Gerard had been out doing the shopping and Jean had picked it up. She had turned it over, frowning. None of their friends were by the sea and the girls weren't on holiday.

She was going to carry it through to the kitchen table like they always did with the mail, but something, some impulse, made her put it back on the doormat, so that it would be the first thing Gerard saw when he walked in. She wanted to see whether he would mention it, and it didn't surprise her at all that he never did.

Where had it gone, she wondered. She would like to see it again, just to be sure.

29

KATE

It was the night of the PTA Christmas party, the most glamorous occasion of the year, and Kate didn't know what to wear.

She sighed and surveyed her wardrobe. Once, way back, so long ago that she could barely remember, she had been able to dress up a second-hand blouse so that everyone would ask where it was from.

Jean would be here any minute to babysit and she wasn't even dressed. Kate pushed past the blouses and skirts shoved on hangers to the back of her wardrobe, where her dresses were. Most of them were too small for her now. They represented a different time, when her and Adam had gone to parties together. They would be running late, always, and, as the doorbell rang for the babysitter, Kate would quickly put on some eyeliner and red lipstick, and then pull on one of these dresses.

She would step out of the bedroom and Adam would say, 'Look at Mum. Isn't she lovely, kids?' and the children would say that she looked like a beautiful mummy, and then she and Adam would disappear into the night, giggling at the unexpected freedom, Adam's hand resting in the small of her back.

Knowing that if the party was boring or full of strangers, they had each other. Telegraphing across the room with just the flicker of an eyebrow if they needed rescuing from a conversation.

Now, Kate's hand stopped on a wrap dress. Black crepe with red roses. Adam had loved this one, she remembered. On impulse, Kate pulled it on. It did up, just about. Eyeliner, smudged a little bit, mascara. No lipstick.

She took a step back and looked at herself in the mirror. *Not bad*, she thought, grinning suddenly. It felt like a bit much, but why not? It was nearly Christmas, after all.

By the time Kate arrived, the party was in full swing. The hallway was crammed with parents; some Kate recognised and some she could have sworn she had never seen before. Maybe everyone just looked different in their finery, as opposed to bedraggled in the playground.

Veronica appeared out of the crowd, elegant in a chic navy dress that revealed one toned shoulder.

'Kate, lovely to see you,' she said, putting a cool cheek to Kate's flushed one. 'I do love your vintage chic. Not everyone could wear such a strong print.' She tapped the sign by the door. 'If you don't mind . . .'

'Shoes off, smiles on.' Kate obediently kicked off her heels. She felt suddenly overdressed and overheated in contrast with Veronica's low-key simplicity.

'Let me get you a drink,' Veronica said. She glanced around, and as if on cue Craig appeared at her elbow with a tray of fizzing champagne. Kate took one.

'Amazing party, you two. As usual,' Kate said, looking around. She was pretty sure the flat had been professionally decorated. Candles flickered on every surface and there were wreaths of holly pinned to the walls. 'You guys do these things so well.'

'Nothing to do with me. All down to Veronica,' Craig

said, looking fondly at his wife and slipping a hefty arm around her waist. 'I just have to show up and look good.'

Kate laughed dutifully.

'Kate, Veronica mentioned you were interested in one of my PT sessions? I can add you to the waiting list.' He looked her up and down professionally. 'I cover all ages, all abilities.'

'Maybe one for January, Craig,' said Kate. 'When I've got more in the way of willpower and disposable income.'

'Yes, let her get through Christmas first,' said Veronica. 'It's not easy for everyone to remain disciplined at this time of year. I know that I've been letting myself go a bit. Speaking of which, how is Christmas planning going, Kate?'

'Good, thanks. We got a tree and everything.'

'We're doing a sustainable Christmas this year,' explained Veronica. 'Everything sourced from local businesses or second hand.'

'Better than buying some last-minute crap from Amazon,' said Craig, and Kate laughed uneasily, rethinking the kids' Christmas list. 'Dan, hi mate.'

He shook hands with Dan, who had just arrived with Lois, wearing a shirt over his usual band T-shirt and jeans. Next to Craig, Dan seemed smaller and scruffier than ever. Lois was wearing her suit and looked like she'd just rushed over from work.

'Thanks for having us, Craig,' said Dan. 'And Veronica. It's quite the event.' He turned to Kate and smiled shyly. 'Hi Kate. Any hits on that website yet?'

She grinned back. 'Any day now, I'm sure. Dan designed me a new website,' she explained to Veronica and Craig.

'That was kind of him,' said Veronica. 'Why don't you guys go inside?'

Kate saw Nat in the corner, chatting to Matthias, excused herself and went over.

'Hello,' said Nat, hugging Kate. She was buzzing with excitement. 'I can't believe we're out! Isn't this a great party! Look at all this booze! And canapés. Actual waiters! Poor Fergus drew the short straw babysitting tonight. I had a feeling this would be a good party.'

'Everyone is so glamorous,' said Kate. 'Veronica looks like she's heading to the Oscars after-party. I feel like a troll.'

'You look gorgeous,' said Nat stoutly. 'I love that dress. Doesn't she look great, Matthias?'

'It is a very nice dress,' said Matthias.

'Thanks,' said Kate. 'But I'm not taking fashion advice from the man who wears a corduroy blazer.' Instead of his blazer, though, tonight he was wearing a nice shirt, Kate noticed. Soft navy, with flecks of grey. Maybe his ex had bought it for him.

'Hey. Leave him alone,' said Nat protectively. Clearly, Matthias had made it into her inner circle of trust. She took a gulp of champagne. 'Isn't it great to be out without children? Do you know what I was thinking the other day, Kate? How we were going to cycle through France one year, just the two of us. We still should. Remember, you used to cycle everywhere.'

'I did love it,' said Kate, ruefully. 'The bike is probably in a state though. It's been in the shed all year, rusting nicely. I can't remember the last time I rode it.'

In truth, Kate knew exactly when she had last ridden her bike, down to the minute. December 1st of last year. Cycling across the Meadows, the winter sunshine in her eyes, wind in her hair and light rain on her face. She had been flying. She had felt . . . free.

And then, at 10.07, her phone had rung. The Call that would change everything.

'Who's watching Olivier?' Kate asked Matthias. 'Or is he home alone, rustling up some waffles as we speak?'

Matthias took a sip of his drink. 'His mother is in town,' he said. 'Lily arrived this morning.'

'Oh,' said Kate, disconcerted. 'She's – she's staying with you? In your flat?'

Only a few days ago, *she* had been in Matthias's flat. Now Lily the ex was there. As she had a perfect right to be, Kate told herself. Get a grip.

'She wants to see Olivier as much as possible,' Matthias was saying. 'In fact, now she's here I'll have some free time. Why don't I come and have a look at your bike? I fixed up Olivier's bike from scrap.'

'Good with your hands,' said Nat, and winked at Kate, who rolled her eyes. Like Jean, Nat could manage about two drinks before becoming tipsy.

'I could come over on the weekend,' continued Matthias. 'Saturday at ten?'

'Okay, great,' Kate said. 'If you're sure. I'll throw in a poorly made coffee.'

'Deal,' he said.

Kate pushed her fringe off her forehead. The room was hot. Biscuits, Christmas tree excursions, and now Matthias was fixing her bike. It was all a bit unsettling. Either that, or she should have eaten before she came out. The champagne sat uneasily on her empty stomach.

'I'm going to the toilet,' she said. 'Save me a canapé, will you?'

Upstairs, in Veronica's palace of a bathroom, Kate peed and washed her hands. She lifted out one particularly tempting glass bottle, labeled *Orchid Essence Rejuvenating Oil*, unscrewed it, and inhaled deeply. She rubbed some onto the backs of her hands.

Kate opened the door to find Dan outside. 'Oh, hi,' she said, holding the door open. 'All yours.'

He didn't move. 'I was actually waiting for *you*, Kate.'

'Waiting for me?' she asked. The queasy feeling in her stomach intensified. 'Do you want to talk about the website?'

'The website?' He gave an odd laugh. 'No, I—'

The next thing Kate knew, Dan had backed her into the bathroom, shut the door and pressed his lips to hers. Horrified, she jerked away, and he ended up wetly kissing her ear. Kate put her palms square on his bony chest and shoved, and he staggered backwards into the door.

'What the hell are you doing?' Kate hissed. 'It's the PTA Christmas drinks! Your wife is downstairs!'

Dan stared at her, his hair rumpled, breathing hard. 'I've been thinking about you for weeks. We really click, Kate.'

'This isn't appropriate!' Kate snapped. 'Do I need to spell out why?'

He scowled. 'You've been flirting with me too.'

Have I been flirting with you? Kate thought wildly. Surely she would have noticed.

'Let's just forget this happened,' she said. She wiped her mouth and straightened the front of her dress. 'I think everyone's had a bit too much to drink. But I've never flirted with you. I lost my husband last year, in case you've forgotten.'

'Got us all under your thumb, don't you?' Dan said nastily.

Kate took a deep breath, willing herself not to lose her temper. 'I agreed to you helping me with the website. I *didn't* agree to an assignation in Veronica and Craig's toilet.'

He scowled. 'Jesus. It's nothing.'

Kate's temper kicked in. 'If it's *nothing*, then why don't I tell your wife what just happened and see what she thinks?'

The colour drained from his face and she laughed. 'Don't worry, I won't. But only because I don't want to hurt anyone. Get out of my way, Dan.'

She opened the bathroom door a furtive crack, checked the coast was clear and slipped out. Just as she reached the stairs, though, he caught up with her.

'Look, this is just a misunderstanding, okay?' he said anxiously. 'I'm happily married. I think we should just forget this ever happened . . .'

'Nothing I'd like more,' snapped Kate. But she saw that he was looking past her, a look of dawning horror on his face. Kate spun around to see Tamara, halfway up the stairs, face alight with glee.

'Oh I *am* sorry,' she said. 'Am I interrupting something?'

Back downstairs, Kate returned to the throng of neighbours in the front room holding drinks and canapés. To her immense relief, she saw that Nat and Matthias were still in their spot, now with replenished glasses. Nat was flushed and giggling, and even Matthias looked less serious than usual.

'Believe me, I know it for a fact,' Nat was saying. 'Look at her. No wrinkles whatsoever. But apparently if you have too much of it, eventually the muscles in your face die and you turn grey.'

'That would be off-putting,' said Matthias. He held out a napkin to Kate. 'I saved you a canapé,' he said.

'Thanks,' said Kate, taking it automatically. Then, flushing, she handed it back. 'Actually, no thanks. I don't need you to do me any favours.'

Nat and Matthias both stared at her, their mouths slightly open.

'You,' said Matthias slowly, 'are being strange. Even for you.'

'Are you okay, Kate?' asked Nat, squinting at her drunkenly. 'He's not wrong, you seem a bit upset.'

Kate watched as, behind them, Dan came into the room, followed by Tamara. He looked intensely shifty and Kate's heart sank.

'I'm going to go,' Kate said. Her voice was a bit high pitched, she thought, but otherwise normal. 'Mum's babysitting and I don't want to be too late back.'

'I'm coming with you,' said Nat suddenly. 'You're definitely being weird.'

'Please don't,' said Kate. 'I'm fine. Just a bit too much wine on an empty stomach.'

She wound her way through the crowd towards the exit. She couldn't face trying to find her coat or asking someone to get it for her. She'd rather abandon it than run into either Dan or Tamara again. She found her shoes in the pile and pulled them on. As she neared the front door and freedom, she felt a firm hand on her arm. Still jittery, she yelped and spun around.

'Kate.' It was Veronica, still immaculate. 'Tamara said you were leaving.'

'Yes, I've got to get back for the babysitter. Thanks for the party,' gabbled Kate, backing away.

'What a shame,' said Veronica. She tilted her head to one side, watching Kate with unblinking dark eyes. Tamara and Lois appeared behind her, like sinister bodyguards. 'You won't forget the PTA meeting tomorrow afternoon, will you? We're all so much looking forward to it.'

'Of course not,' Kate murmured, groping blindly for the latch. She jerked the door open. And then she was outside, in the chill night air, walking fast.

30

KATE

The morning after the party, Kate woke groggy. It had taken her hours to fall asleep, because she couldn't stop reliving the nightmarish encounter – first with Dan in the bathroom and then with Tamara on the stairs. She managed to get the kids dressed and out of the front door and at the last minute remembered the Christmas wreaths she was meant to be bringing to the PTA meeting.

The PTA meeting. *I can't cancel*, she thought as she struggled under the weight of the cardboard box. It would look bad. But she was dreading it. At least, she thought, she was seeing her mother and Alice for Christmas shopping later. What was she so worried about? They could hardly stone her. Could they?

'Come on, Mummy,' said Emmie, tugging at her coat. 'Why are you walking so slowly?'

'No reason,' said Kate.

In the playground, she saw the circle of Primary 1 and 2 parents gathered by the school gates, waiting for the bell. She edged over to them and was sure a silence fell. She looked around for Fergus but his kids went to breakfast club.

'Hi,' she said to Tracy, who was always friendly.

'Um, hi,' said Tracy, staring straight ahead.

Cautiously, Kate looked behind her and saw Tamara, Veronica and Lois watching her. Lois's eyes were hard and ringed with red. Tamara gave her a slow, chilling smile. Kate shivered and turned away.

The PTA meeting was at 9.30 so she had half an hour to kill after drop-off. Kate went to the corner shop for milk and bread and then hovered outside Veronica's house. Part of her wanted to turn tail and run for home. But why should she? After all, she had done nothing wrong. If Dan had the gall to show his face today, there was no reason she couldn't.

Thanks to her dithering, she was now late. Taking a deep breath, she rang the doorbell.

Veronica answered, looking reassuringly immaculate.

'Kate, you're the last one, chop-chop.'

It didn't sound like they were organising a stoning, Kate thought.

She followed Veronica into the sitting room clutching her box of wreaths. Euan gave her the smallest wave, before Sergio elbowed him in the ribs. Tracy looked frozen with dread. Tamara gave the smallest, disbelieving shake of her head.

'I can't believe she turned up,' she said, in an audible whisper. 'What a nerve.'

Kate took a seat in the circle, box on her lap, and tried to take deep, calming breaths. Her phone buzzed in her pocket. She took it out and checked her text.

It was Alice. 'Still on for later?'

'Absolutely!'

Alice texted back. 'Good. Mulled wine, shopping and cake, can't wait. And I have NEWS.'

Kate smiled. *Mark had done it*, she thought. *He had popped the question.*

'Can we tempt you away from your phone, Kate?' said Tamara. 'Because this meeting was meant to start eleven minutes ago.'

'Of course,' said Kate, sticking her phone quickly in her pocket. 'Sorry.'

She looked round the circle again. Dan was examining his nails, a look of pious injury on his face. Lois was looking at her with barely disguised contempt. She was wearing a black suit and had a briefcase. She must be off to court later, but it gave her an unnervingly legalistic air. Tamara was smirking into her coffee. Tracy's eyes were round and Sergio looked agog with excitement. Euan gave her a sympathetic smile.

The frostiness in the playground had just been a taster, Kate realised; this was going to be about as uncomfortable as she had expected.

Only Veronica seemed her usual self.

'Coffee, Kate?' asked Veronica, her hand poised over a cafetiere.

'Yes please,' said Kate. Her head was hammering. *If I can survive this*, she thought, *I can survive anything*.

'I don't have sugar, I'm afraid,' said Veronica, handing Kate the cup. 'Just agave syrup. Now. Let's run through the checklist for Saturday. Kate, did you bring the wreaths?'

'Right here,' said Kate meekly. She opened the box and held up one of the wreaths. 'Are these okay? I thought a bit of gold might be nice.'

'Bit tacky,' said Lois. 'Bit obvious. But I suppose that makes sense, coming from you.'

Everyone else stared at their laps. Silently, Kate put the wreath back in the box.

'The Karen Perkiss signing,' Veronica continued determinedly. 'Tamara?'

Tamara cleared her throat importantly. 'The warehouse have agreed to fast-track us the advance copies, so we'll be stealing a march on the local bookshops. The tent and musician are sorted. We just need someone to meet and greet the talent.' Tamara peered at her notes. 'Although she's short one character. Shame it's not a snake,' she said, smirking. 'Because I know someone who would do a great job. But it's Tommy Tiger himself, so if anyone under five foot feels like taking one for the team and dressing up, Karen would appreciate it. The costume is provided.'

'I'll do that,' said Sergio. 'Are you kidding, Tommy Tiger? Pablo will be thrilled.'

'Whatever makes you happy,' said Veronica. 'Would anyone like some brunch? I've made a beetroot tarte tatin.'

'Not for me, thanks,' said Kate, putting down her cup. 'In fact, I've got to head. I've got to meet my mum and sister.'

'I guess you're used to quick exits,' said Tamara. 'Must be an occupational hazard when you go around kissing people's husbands.'

The silence that fell was sub-zero. Kate glared at Tamara, then at Lois, who was examining her nails.

'I see you've all made your mind up about what happened,' Kate said, as coolly as she could manage. 'If you'll excuse me.'

She stood on shaking legs, clutching her box, and picked her way through the chairs. She went into the hallway and pulled on her boots, put on her warm coat and opened the front door. It was starting to snow.

She was halfway down the front steps when she heard the door open again behind her.

'Kate.' She turned to see Veronica holding out Kate's jacket. 'You left this behind last night.' Snow began to fall, glittering like diamonds in her dark hair.

'Thanks,' said Kate. She wedged the box on her hip and reached out for the jacket. 'Sorry about all that. Bit of a misunderstanding I think.'

Veronica took a step closer. 'Listen, Kate. I try to keep team morale high,' she said. 'I've spoken to Tamara and we think until you and Lois resolve whatever issue you're having, you should consider your membership of the PTA suspended.'

Unexpected tears pricked Kate's eyes.

'You're chucking me out of the PTA?' she said. 'Shouldn't there be some sort of due process? What happened to innocent until proven guilty?'

'We're not chucking you out, goodness. It's just a temporary suspension,' said Veronica. 'Till things calm down. You can still have a stall at the fete . . .'

'How generous of you,' said Kate. 'You didn't even listen to my side of the story. I guess it's easier for you lot to believe I'm a desperate single mum than that your precious super-dad Dan is a sleazeball creep.' She did up her coat angrily. 'So yes, I'm still coming to the fete by the way. I'll see you on Saturday.'

She walked off with her head held high and a lump of hurt rage in her throat. At the end of the street, she glanced back and saw that Veronica was still standing on the doorstep, looking after her, snow mantling her hair and shoulders.

Kate thought she had beaten her ever-punctual sister by arriving in Stockbridge three minutes early, but Alice was already waiting for her on a bench, next to a crowd of shoppers and a trio of pipers.

A school choir was singing and there was an enormous tree twinkling with lights. Shops had their doors open and staff dressed in Santa hats out front, holding out trays of cardamom buns and hot chocolate.

'I was trying to be early,' said Kate, kissing her sister and dropping onto the bench beside her. 'And you *still* beat me. God have I had a bad morning. I was at a PTA meeting from hell.'

'Don't worry about it,' said Alice. 'You're not even late, I just wanted to get into town early and soak up the atmosphere. Here, I got you a mulled wine.'

'Thanks,' said Kate. 'Where's Mum?'

'Running late,' said Alice.

'She's late a lot these days,' said Kate. 'Something is up with her, I know it.'

Alice rolled her eyes. 'You're just being paranoid. Look, there she is.'

Jean hurried towards them, wearing what Kate recognised as her smart coat, which Jean only took out for special occasions such as trips to the theatre or Christmas shopping.

'How are my girls?' beamed Jean. She kissed them both. 'I hope you're going to let me spoil you today.'

They began to stroll through the streets.

'Didn't you say you had news, Ally?' said Kate, giving her mother a sly look. 'Don't keep us in suspense.'

'I sure do,' said Alice, beaming. 'Well, it's Mark's news too, really. Guess what?'

'What?' asked Kate, nudging Jean.

'We're getting bees! Me and Mark. Bees!'

Kate stared. 'Bees?' she said blankly.

'Yes!' Alice clapped her hands. 'I wanted to do the responsible thing and not commit till we were ready. We've spoken to some of the neighbours and they're happy to help, and then we can all share the honey. The hives are arriving next week. Bees are very self-sufficient, actually. You can have some honey too!'

'That's your big news,' said Kate. 'Bees?'

'It's big news to me,' Alice said, a little more quietly. 'I've been wanting hives for years now. You know that.'

'I think it's great,' said Jean firmly. 'And I for one will be queuing up for some of the honey. How's the Christmas fete going, Kate?'

'Well, it's going really well. But I think I'm going to leave the PTA.'

'Why?' said Alice. 'I thought you were enjoying it.'

'I was, but . . . there was a misunderstanding. One of the dads came on to me at the Christmas party, and now they all hate me and they want to suspend me. Can you believe it?'

'Don't tell me. The IT guy in the caffe?' said Alice, smiling. She looked amused, like this was all one big joke. 'Sounds about right, for you. It'll blow over.'

Kate stopped in the street and glared at Alice, oblivious to the fact she was blocking the traffic. 'What do you mean, *sounds about right for me*?' she said.

'Nothing,' said Alice quickly. 'It's just – drama follows you around, doesn't it? Especially man drama. Remember school!'

Kate hadn't felt angry with her sister, not properly angry, for a long time. Now, she could feel rage begin to stir. Goodie two shoes Alice with her safe life and her organic vegetables and her bees.

'Let's go and sit down,' said Jean nervously. 'We can have a drink and cool off a bit.'

'You think I gave that guy the wrong idea?' Kate said dangerously.

'I could have told you that day in the caffe that there would be trouble,' said Alice. 'He had that puppy-dog look. You're oblivious and you get yourself into these situations.'

Kate snapped. 'At least I don't play it so safe I never *do* anything.'

'Excuse me?' A faint flush was stealing up Alice's cheeks. 'You, of all people, are going to lecture *me* about playing it safe? Not all of us were lucky to walk into the perfect marriage with the perfect man straight out of university, Kate.'

'You think I'm lucky?' snapped Kate. 'You have no idea. As always. You're in your boring little Stepford bubble and you're too self-absorbed to notice anyone but yourself.'

The sisters glared at each other. Then Alice turned and stormed off.

Jean and Kate stood in silence for a moment. 'I'm sorry, Mum,' Kate said at last. Her anger had faded as quickly as it had erupted, and she felt guilty and embarrassed. 'I ruined your special day out.'

Jean visibly gathered herself. 'Oh, you didn't ruin anything,' she said. 'Come on. Let me buy you that cake.'

They sat in the nearest caffe and Jean ordered tea. 'She was being smug and self-righteous,' Kate said miserably. 'Implying it was all my fault.'

'I think Alice feels like things came easy for you,' said Jean. 'Not recently, of course. But meeting Adam so young, and him being a financial wizard, and the pair of you always seeming so happy.'

'Well, she's wrong,' said Kate. Before she could stop herself, the words came spilling out. 'Adam and I weren't happy. Actually, we were going to get a divorce.'

Jean stared at Kate open-mouthed.

'That's right,' said Kate, ploughing on. 'The day he died, Adam was on his way back from the lawyers to start proceedings. And as for him being a financial wizard, let's just say he fooled all of us, but I'm the one suffering for it.'

There was a silence, and then Jean said softly, 'Oh love. I'm so sorry. Why didn't you tell me?'

Kate shrugged. 'I didn't want to worry you. I was embarrassed. You get told you're a golden couple enough times, you start to believe your own hype.' She laughed shakily. 'I wish someone had told me there's no such thing as a perfect marriage.'

Jean swallowed. 'Of course there isn't,' she said. 'Every marriage has its flaws.'

'Not you and Dad, though,' said Kate, pouring milk into her tea. 'Which gives me hope, frankly, that true love is out there still.'

31

KATE

The next morning started badly and went downhill fast from there.

They all slept late. Max was snotty and had a barking cough. He refused to eat his cereal, then complained that it had gone soggy. Emmie had a tantrum, first because her tights were too itchy and then because she couldn't find her pencil case.

'Come on, shoes on,' called Kate from the hallway. She stuffed their snacks into their rucksacks. Silence. 'Shoes on,' she shrieked, so loudly she was sure she would give herself an embolism. 'Shoes on!'

'I can't find my jumper,' wailed Emmie. There was silence from Max.

'It's on your floor; come on, come on,' yelled Kate, tugging on her own boots. 'Please, we'll be late. Max, where *are* you?'

Silence. She stormed down the hallway, shedding mud from her boots as she went, and found Max hunched over a sheet of paper, his tongue poking through his teeth with concentration.

'Put that down and get in the hallway,' Kate said.

'I need to write this letter to Santa,' said Max, his back to her. 'How do you spell axolotl?'

'You *need* to put your shoes on,' said Kate, dangerously.

'I'm nearly finished . . .'

Kate reached over his shoulder and tore the paper in two.

'There,' she said. 'You're finished.'

There was a moment of silence while Max stared at the paper on the floor, and then he let out an ear-splitting wail. Emmie was watching from the doorway with wide eyes, holding her school jumper.

'Hallway. Shoes. Now,' Kate snarled.

The children edged past her into the hallway and put their shoes on. Max was still crying and Emmie was eyeing Kate warily. The guilt just made her more angry.

They walked to school in a frosty silence, the children trotting to keep up with Kate's long strides.

The group of parents at the gates fell silent as they approached. Kate walked right past them with her head high, not bothering to check whether the kids were following.

'Have a good day,' she said coldly, handing them their rucksacks. 'See you later.'

'Okay, Mummy,' said Max, his lip wobbling.

Feeling terrible but unable to back down now, Kate turned and stalked past the other parents.

'Oh Kate,' Tamara called after her. 'I've got you down for one ticket at the play this week, is that right?'

'Yeah,' said Kate, turning. 'I haven't suddenly found a plus one I'm afraid.'

Tamara smirked. 'Never know, with you,' she said.

Like ice in spring, something seemed to melt inside Kate. The PTA, Christmas wreaths, turkeys, advent, probiotics and smoothies. Holes in the wall and dust in their clothes and invoices and bills unpaid. Grief group and Adam and her father and Hamish the hamster, tucked away under the ground.

It was all too much.

Back at home, Kate changed into her pyjamas and took a tray of brownies out of the freezer that some well-meaning person had brought round in the aftermath of Adam's death. She pulled a sheet off her bed and got onto the sofa underneath it. Her phone rang – Veronica – and she stuffed it under a pillow, then flicked on the TV.

Nat rang around ten. 'Weren't we having coffee this morning?'

'Sorry,' Kate said. 'I'm really sick.' She forked some more frozen brownie into her mouth. 'I think it's this stomach flu that's been going around. Had to leg it home to the toilet. Barely made it, to be honest, it was disgusting.'

'Jeez,' said Nat. 'I hope we can dodge that. No worries, feel better.'

Kate took a deep breath. 'Do you ever properly lose it with James?' she asked.

'All the time,' said Nat. 'Fergus is the calm one. Why do you ask?'

'I lost it this morning,' said Kate. She dug a chunk of chocolate out with her finger. 'I behaved worse than the kids.'

'You're under a lot of stress,' said Nat gently. 'And you're not well. I hope you'll be all right for the school play. James has been talking about nothing else. Apparently, Olivier has been drilling them on their lines. He's a sweet boy, isn't he?'

'Yeah, he is. I'll be there,' Kate said. 'I've got to go, Nat. Feeling really rough.'

After she had hung up, she watched a cooking programme, then a detective series about rival antique dealers, then a soap. She ignored a call from Jean and one from Alice. She went on a gossip website and read about an actor struggling with sex addiction. She stayed in bed until she was almost late for pickup, then got off the sofa, put a coat on over her pyjamas, pulled on her boots and walked out of the door with nothing more than her keys.

I'm cracking up, she thought. So this is what it's like. It felt oddly relaxing.

32

KATE

The doorbell summoned Kate from what felt like the deepest sleep of her life. She groaned and tugged the pillow over her head.

It rang again, longer this time. Kate swung her legs onto the floor.

She stumbled down the stairs and fumbled with the latch. Matthias stood outside, sleet on the shoulders of his coat. She stared at him blankly.

'What are you doing here?' she asked. Her voice was hoarse, as though she had smoked a packet of cigarettes. Now that she thought of it, something smelled of cigarettes. It was her.

'I have come to look at the bike,' he said. He frowned. 'We said Saturday, didn't we?'

'Oh.' She pushed a hand through her tangled hair. She was aware suddenly of the height of him, of his broad shoulders, dark hair black with the rain. His body filled the doorway. Only his glasses gave him the look of a mild-mannered academic.

'Yeah, I forgot. Sorry, come in.' Her head was throbbing with something unfamiliar, something she hadn't felt for a long time – the nauseous, creeping approach of a full-blown hangover.

Matthias brought a rush of cold air into the flat with him. It made Kate realise how stale the flat smelt. Kate led him into the sitting room and stopped.

They stood there in the doorway, surveying the scene. Kate's shoes were dropped in the middle of the sitting-room floor and her coat lay crumpled beside them. Her handbag was open, and scattered across the floor were her keys, wallet and lipstick.

There was an empty wine bottle on the table, a mug half full of wine. There was also, she saw with horror, a bottle of cooking brandy. A carton of ice cream, a soupy inch in the bottom, and a smeared spoon sat beside it. A half-eaten piece of toast. There was a saucer full of cigarette butts.

It came back to her. She had dropped the kids off at Nat's, pleading her stomach bug, bought a packet of cigarettes and some ice cream, and then proceeded to drink everything in the flat.

How much of a loser was she?

'You had friends over last night?' Matthias said, looking around at the room. 'A party?'

'Nope,' she said grimly. 'Just me.'

He still didn't react, but he did take his jacket off and lay it carefully on the sofa. 'I shall make coffee.'

'You don't have to make the coffee,' she muttered. 'You don't have to be nice.'

'I'm not,' he said. 'You should take a shower.'

'You don't have to go too far the other way,' she said. She hesitated, irritation warring with exhaustion and the desire to stand under a hot shower and feel clean again. 'I warn you, you'll hate the kitchen. Nothing is where it should be.'

She went to the bathroom. The mirror was grimy and spotted with toothpaste. There was an impression of her pillow on her face and eyeliner was smudged down her cheek. What on earth had she been thinking, getting drunk alone? It was irresponsible. What if one of the kids had got sick and Fergus or Nat had been trying to ring her? What if Jean had fallen in the street, or been mugged? She shuddered and flipped on the spray.

It felt strange to be showering when Matthias was next door, rustling up coffee. She sped through the shower, scrubbing cigarette smoke out of her hair, and hurried back into the bedroom, where she dressed quickly in jeans and a jumper. Then she plugged in her phone, which had run out of battery. There was a new text from Nat:

'Tried to call you. I hope you're feeling a bit better today. The kids are having breakfast, then we might take them all to see that film about the robot dog? Looks grim. Give us a shout when you want to pick up.'

Tears prickled Kate's eyes. She didn't deserve Nat.

'That would be amazing,' she texted back. 'I love you.'

She went back into the kitchen, where Matthias stood with his back to her, busy over the stove. He was wearing another nice shirt. Forest green, this time. Maybe Lily had taken him shopping.

Without turning around, he said, 'You know, there is almost nothing in your fridge. Not even milk.'

'I know, I know.' She pushed back her wet hair.

'You do have eggs and some bread. I'll bring it through, if you want to sit down on the couch.'

A wave of exhaustion hit her. Obediently, she went next door and sat down. The sounds of Matthias moving about in the kitchen, pans clanging, the coffee bubbling, were comforting. She shut her eyes.

When she opened them, she was horizontal on the sofa and there was a plate on the table in front of her. Scrambled eggs, butter-yellow, and a slice of bread and butter. There was a cup of coffee, a glass of water and two paracetamol. Matthias was sitting in the armchair, engrossed in an interior design magazine.

'This looks great,' she said, sitting up and wiping what she suspected might be drool from her cheek. She didn't want to think what interesting shapes her damp hair had dried into. 'Thank you.'

'No problem,' he said.

'I didn't use to be this much of a fuck-up, you know,' she said. She picked up her fork. 'I used to have my shit together. I had a business. A husband. A life. I wasn't always a mess.'

He lifted his eyes from the magazine and looked at her for a moment. 'I don't think you're a fuck-up,' he said quietly.

'Not that I care what you think,' she said. 'Not that I care what any of them think. Screw the PTA.'

Maybe she was still drunk. She took a bite of the eggs. They were delicious and she was suddenly ravenous. It had been so long since she had eaten breakfast at a time when normal people did. It felt like an extraordinary act of what Veronica might call *self-care*.

'These eggs are really good,' she said, fighting the urge to stuff them in her mouth. 'You bake. You cook. Is there anything you don't do?'

He smiled faintly and turned a page.

'My head is still killing me.'

'You should go for a walk,' he said, setting down the magazine. 'It's not raining in this city for once, we should make the most of it.'

She slumped back on the sofa. 'Can't I just lie very still until I feel human again?'

He stood and held out a hand. She put hers into it; it looked small in his large palm.

'Come on,' he said. 'You can show me around my neighbourhood.'

They walked down the canal in the winter sunshine. Couples walked past and people with dogs. It felt fresh and clean. Kate saw a family staggering under the weight of a Christmas tree.

'How did you end up in Edinburgh?' Kate asked.

'I went to London for work,' he said. 'Then it got expensive. I liked the sound of Scotland.'

'Do you still like it?' she asked.

He nodded. 'Not the weather, so much. The coffee could be better.'

Kate shook her head. 'Scotland has one of the largest Italian populations outside Italy – there's *fantastic* coffee here. You just have to know the right places to go. One of them is right down here.'

They sat in the Italian deli, Matthias hunched on a tiny stool.

'Take my word for it,' said Kate. 'My mum's family are Italian and they've been coming here for cannoli for years.'

The waitress brought little cups of hot, bitter espresso.

'See?' said Kate. 'Right up your street.'

He took a sip. 'It's good,' he admitted. 'Why did you rush off so quickly at the party the other night?'

'You don't beat about the bush, do you?' He looked puzzled, and she explained, 'It's a saying. It means you're very direct.'

'I have been told that,' he said.

'I left because – oh it's stupid. One of the dads tried to kiss me and everyone got the wrong idea and now I have to leave the PTA.' Kate fiddled with a packet of sugar. 'They think I'm out to break up marriages.'

'You've been busy, then,' he said.

'I think,' she said, 'that I might be losing it. I did pickup in my pyjamas yesterday. I feel broken.'

He smiled at her. 'You're not broken. Just . . .'

'A bit battered?'

'Exactly. Aren't we all?'

She laughed. They turned and watched the sunshine on the canal and listened to the carol singers until it was time for Kate to go and get the kids and, as she walked back along the canal, the wind in her face, she realised that Matthias was right. She *did* feel better.

33

KATE

Kate forced herself to attend grief group. If she'd missed it, Jean would have been suspicious.

'Welcome, everyone,' the group leader, Ada, said. 'Ooft it's hot in here tonight, isn't it? I need to tell them to turn down the heating.'

They all nodded. It *was* hot. Instead of making Kate feel sleepy, the heat was making her tense, on edge. Something was bothering her, like a splinter under the skin. There was something here she was missing, an undercurrent, but she was too slow to see it. She looked round at them all – Rory, quiet and watchful; Maggie, flushed in a sweater; Frances, plaiting one of her braids which had come loose; Jean, upright in her chair as always, expression alert.

'I want to take this moment to thank you all for your bravery in these meetings,' said Ada.

She leaned forward and took a biscuit.

'It's hard to confront loss, because it means we have to look at the whole story. Not just the good bits, not just the bad bits, but all of the bits in between. Being honest is the hardest thing.' She lifted her cup of tea. 'I salute you. Now, I think today is Kate's turn to talk, isn't it?'

All the faces turned to look at Kate. She ran her fingers over Adam's watch, which she had brought with her. Adam loved that watch. It had been his grandfather's and then his dad's. He would take it off and put it somewhere safe whenever he went swimming. They'd gone swimming together every Saturday at the baths, the same time every week . . .

Before Kate knew what she was doing, she was on her feet. 'Sorry, everyone,' she said. 'I have to go now.'

Kate made it out of the building before the tears came. She hadn't cried at her dad's funeral. She hadn't cried at her husband's. Why now, in an overheated room above a community centre?

She found herself outside the caffe she and Emmie usually came to and went inside. It was quiet, closing up, but no one seemed to mind. She found a table in the corner, laid her head on the table and cried noisily for several minutes. It was like she had an endless supply of tears and couldn't staunch the flow. Then, through the crook of her arm, she saw a familiar pair of shoes. Tailored trousers, cropped at the ankle and smart loafers.

'You left your coat behind. Oh, Kate.' Jean crouched beside her, stroking her hair. 'Darling girl.'

Kate sat up, wiping her eyes. 'I'm sorry,' she said. 'I didn't mean to embarrass you in front of your group. They must think I'm an idiot.'

'You could never embarrass me,' Jean said. She slipped into the seat opposite. 'I was being selfish, making you come to group. Especially given everything you and Adam were going through . . . it was much too soon.'

Kate shook her head. 'It's not that,' she said. 'I feel like a fraud. Everyone is grieving so *well* in there.'

'Grief is complicated.'

'You and Dad adored each other,' sighed Kate. 'At least that part was straightforward.'

There was a pause and then Jean said, 'Why don't we go home, and I'll make you Katie's pasta?'

Kate laughed. 'Like I'm five and off school?'

Jean squeezed her hand. 'Like you're five.'

Back at her mother's flat, Kate washed her face and brushed her hair in her mother's bedroom. She noticed that her father's bedside table had been cleared and when she opened the wardrobe, she saw that his things were gone. As much as she had wanted this, her chest tightened.

She wandered down the hall and looked into the study. There was a cork board on the wall and Jean had pinned a polaroid to it – a group of kids squinting into the sunshine. It looked like it had been taken in the eighties. Kate looked closer. She recognised one of the men as her father – unbelievably young, face bleached by the sun. A girl next to him with a mass of golden hair. Her mother must have found it while she was clearing out his things.

There was a letter pinned to the board too, stiff cream paper – something from a solicitor's office addressed to her father.

Back in the hall, Kate could hear her mother humming along to the radio in the kitchen, and smell frying garlic and onions. The sounds and smells of her mother cooking were as familiar as the worn carpet in the hallway and the stain on the wall where she had thrown a cup of coffee as a teenager, and the faded green velvet sofa. There were cardboard boxes in the corridor, neatly labelled for charity. Her mum had certainly upheld her part of the bargain.

Photos lined the hallway. Her parents, looking so young. Gerard, straight backed, long-limbed, handsome, his arm slung proudly around Jean on their wedding day. Jean, looking enchanting in a silk dress, hair pinned back with flowers. The smallest swelling in her belly that was Kate.

Her grandparents, outside their ice-cream parlour in Portobello, with Jean as a little girl standing between them, her cheeks round, a look of intense mischief on her face.

Running into the surf and then salty chips afterwards. Ice cream on the steps, crunchy sand in the sweetness. Her mother tucking their skirts into their knickers and chasing them into the sea. Her father waiting with big towels to dry them off, their legs blue with cold. Sunburnt and sleepy on the way home. Tumbling into bed, salt still on their lips, falling asleep to the sound of the sea and her parents talking downstairs. Her mum's laugh and her dad's low chuckle.

What an extraordinary childhood. Golden. She had taken happiness for granted. She had no idea how cruel and surprising life would turn out to be.

As a teenager, when her parents had become slightly more interesting to her, Kate had wondered what both sets of grandparents had made of each other – her mother's noisy, Italian-Scottish family, all big meals and arguments, and the quieter Whytes.

Kate had asked her parents about it once. They had been in the kitchen, much like now – her mother listening to the radio and drinking wine, stirring something on the stove, the smell of garlic, steam on the windows, Alice doing homework, her father home from work, washing his hands at the sink.

'Did your parents like each other?' Kate had asked. 'They're pretty different.'

'Oh, they got on with it in the end, didn't they, love?' Jean had said to Gerard. Her back was to them, stirring onions.

'They did,' he said. 'Although they didn't like it much at first.' He had slipped a hand around Jean's waist, kissed the nape of her neck. 'More fool them.'

Kate smiled at the memory. She had cringed at the time. As a teenager, the idea of her parents kissing or touching had been the *worst*. Now, the story of the immigrant's daughter and the boy from the wrong side of the tracks seemed more romantic than anything.

The last photographs on the wall were framed copies of Kate's magazine covers and clippings.

> Ones to watch: Scotland's Youngest,
> Hottest Designers.
> Whyte Hot talent: Shaking it up in the
> world of interiors.

'Wine, love?' called Jean from the kitchen. 'I've got a bottle of red open.'

'Go on then,' said Kate, coming in. Jean handed her a glass.

'I remember one time you were away visiting Granny and I got sick,' Kate said. 'I asked Dad to make Katie's pasta. He didn't have a clue what to do.'

Jean laughed. 'Your father's forte was toast, toast and maybe at a pinch some more toast,' she said with a smile.

Kate wandered into the sitting room. It felt lighter, somehow, and Kate realised that a few of her father's things were gone – there were no pipes or ashtrays, no fishing magazines. There was a map spread out on the floor and she crouched down and looked at it. A map of the Hebrides. Kate squinted closer. Someone had marked a neat little cross somewhere called Kilchattan.

'What's this, Ma?' she called through. 'Planning a holiday?'

There was a pause before Jean answered. 'Aye, one day,' she said at last. 'Never been up there, can you believe it? Your father went as a boy, I think.'

Kate sank into the battered sofa, as she had so many times it probably held the muscle memory of her body – crying over exams or a boy, or eating crisps after school and watching *Neighbours*.

Jean brought through a bowl of hot, buttery pasta covered in cheese and pepper. Kate took a spoonful, and just like that she was five again. Their door had always been open and their table always full, and there had always been something delicious on the stove. How had she failed so spectacularly to duplicate that comfort in her own home?

There was a stack of photographs on the low table, and she picked them up. 'What are these, Ma?' she asked, through a mouthful of pasta.

'I found them when I was clearing out and thought you might like to have a look,' Jean said. 'Pictures of my parents' place. Dad and I would go for a drink after school, just to wind my parents up. I didn't think much of it then, but that caffe was a stunner.'

Kate turned the pictures over. There was Capaldis, with its white Formica-topped tables, the pistachio-green bar, linoleum and wood panelling.

'Oh, look at you!' she cried. Her mother and father, sitting in a booth, bottles of Coke in front of them, grinning conspiratorially. Her mother looked so pretty, beautiful really, with her mop of curly hair and wide mouth curved in its lovely, contagious smile. And her father so dashing and handsome. No wonder they had both fallen for each other that young. The surprising thing was how that love had endured into something deeper, had withstood children and house moves and sickness, and now death. The perfect marriage.

'We were just kids,' Jean said. 'Eighteen, Jeezo. Can't believe my parents let me go through with it, baby or no baby.'

Jean had dragged a stool over to the bookcase and was standing on it, scanning the shelves. 'What are you looking for, Mum?' Kate asked.

'I wanted to find something for grief group,' Jean said, running her fingers across the spines. 'That book of poems your father loved so much . . .'

'Poetry?' said Kate. 'Thought he was more of an Ian Rankin man.'

'Mostly,' Jean said absently. 'But he loved this one book – ah-ha!'

She stretched up and tugged down a slim volume. 'Here,' she said. 'He carted this around whenever we moved. I can finally open the hallowed pages. Rupert Brooke.'

'I can't imagine Dad reading poetry.' She glanced at her watch. 'I should get back for the kids, Mum. Do you mind if I take these photos for a few days?'

Jean hopped neatly down. 'Of course not. And mind you come to the next group, okay? You mustn't be embarrassed. People are always running out crying, it's standard.'

'Even you?' Kate asked.

Jean laughed. 'There's still time,' she said. 'Come on, I'll drop you home.'

34

JEAN

That night, Jean Whyte lay in bed and remembered.

One morning in the summer of 1980 he was gone.

Jean had woken up and the bed was cold beside her. Not so unusual; he left for work early and she was often so exhausted after a night with the baby that she rarely woke when he slipped out.

Now, sunshine dappled bars of light across the quilt. It must be late; she and Katie had both slept longer than usual. The baby was whimpering sleepily. Jean picked Kate up, fed her, changed her and then went downstairs, cuddling her into the crook of her neck. Kissed that soft head with its wisps of dark blonde hair.

Their little kitchen was full of sunshine and the tiles were warm under her bare feet. Jean glanced at the clock and saw that it was gone nine. She hadn't slept like that in months.

She laid the baby down on the fluffy rug near the stove, and then put a pot of coffee on and sliced some bread. She ate bread and butter and drank her coffee, cooing at the baby, who was kicking her legs in the air.

It was only then she had seen it. A piece of their thick writing paper, folded sharply down the middle, resting against a jam jar of daffodils she had picked only yesterday.

Her own name in Gerard's neat, cramped handwriting. He had left her a note. She smiled and reached for it.

Dear Jean,
    I've gone away for a while.
    There's plenty of money in the bank and you can draw out anything you need. I won't be in work. I can't explain now but I need a bit of time.
    Anything I say will be trite. I'm writing because I don't want you to worry, but of course you will. I promise I will always look after you and Katie and I love the both of you so much.
    G

Forcing herself to move carefully, Jean had picked Kate up and gone upstairs, put her in her cot. The baby started crying almost immediately.

She opened the wardrobe. A few things were gone, she could tell at one frantic glance – Gerard's old canvas knapsack, a few jumpers, his jeans. His wedding suit was hanging neatly. She dug her hands into the pockets of his jackets – nothing, not even a receipt. His office shoes, polished to a high shine, were still there. Shirts hanging, ironed and pressed by her. Ties rolled up in this drawer. Cufflinks, glinting in the morning light.

Heart beating, she went down into the hall and picked up the phone. The number for Gerard's work was pinned to the noticeboard, but she knew it by heart. She had rung it countless times this last year to ask what he would like for dinner, to get him to bring home milk or nappies. She began dialling but her fingers were too numb. She had to stop, hang up, and start again.

Scott Ferguson picked up, Scott who had got drunk at

the Christmas party and told Jean she had nice legs and that he wouldn't apologise for saying so.

'Fergusons' Shipyard,' he said briskly.

'Hiya Scott, it's Jean Whyte,' she said, surprised at how calm she sounded.

'Jean! How's our man doing?'

'He's . . .' She hesitated, choosing her words carefully. 'He's not in work,' she said at last.

There was a silence, and then Scott said, sounding slightly confused, 'Aye, he rang first thing. Terrible flu, he said he'd be off the rest of the week.'

'Yes,' she said. 'He's asleep now. I was just checking you knew.'

She hung up the receiver gently. The baby was crying more loudly now. Jean went upstairs again to the cot and scooped her out. Held her to her chest. Kate stopped crying immediately. People always asked Jean if Kate was a good baby, and really, what did that mean? All babies were good.

'Where's Daddy gone, hmm?' Jean said. She walked to the window, looked out at the sun-dappled garden below. Her baby felt feather-light in her arms. 'Where's Daddy gone, eh?'

35

KATE

That evening, Kate was getting a second chance at grief group. It was their last one before they stopped for the holidays. Their 'party'. A bowl of crisps and some bottles of warm wine sat in the centre and Ada had handed out paper hats.

The circle of people seemed to press closer that evening. All these people who had loved purely and uncomplicatedly and were grieving the same way.

And her, sticking out like a sore thumb.

Kate took a deep breath.

'My husband Adam and I met at university,' she said. 'He was studying business and I was doing art. He was a real charmer. Funny, loads of mates. Mr Popular. We had an end of year prom and we were crowned king and queen. Gross, I know.

'We were like ... oil and water. He was responsible. I couldn't keep so much as a plant alive. Together we made a good team. I thought we did, anyway.'

She rubbed the dull gold of the watch with her thumb. 'This was Adam's watch. It belonged to his grandfather and then his father and I guess it will go to Max one day, if he wants it. Adam was careful about everything, but he was *really* careful about this watch. He'd always take it off if he went in the shower or went swimming or ...'

Kate stopped. *Not again*, she thought.

She could feel a trickle of cold sweat make its way slowly from her neck, gathering in the small of her back.

Like a film unfolding in her mind, she saw Adam laying the watch down carefully on the shelf in the swimming baths. Saw him helping Max into his swimming trunks, supporting each chubby leg in his hands. It was so real that Kate could smell the chlorine. Her ears were ringing.

She pushed back her chair and stood. 'Sorry about this,' she said. 'Again.'

Outside, she turned left out of the building and then, not knowing what to do or where to go, she began to run. It was dark now. She sprinted over the bridge. Her chest burned and she had to slow briefly to a brisk walk but as soon as she could breathe, she began running again.

She reached the big hill near the school. Her phone rang and she ignored it. Jean. Then it buzzed with a text. Kate pulled out her phone and read it, leaning against the wall, chest heaving.

'Katie, are you all right?'

She texted, 'I'm fine, I'm sorry I embarrassed you AGAIN. What a disaster. I've gone home to bed.'

'You could never embarrass me. Get some sleep and we'll speak tomorrow.'

Kate shoved her phone into her pocket. She began running again, feet skidding on the slippery cobbles. A stitch burned in her side. She didn't want to go home. The children would be asleep. Nat would chat to her for a bit and leave and then it would just be Kate and the holes in the wall.

She ran on, lungs bursting. It was only when she looked up that she realised she was on Matthias's street and virtually outside his door. *Any time you want to talk*. She skidded to a halt and glanced at her phone to check the time. It was only nine. Olivier would probably be in bed. It wasn't too late to ring, was it?

Before she could change her mind, Kate stumbled to his door, jammed her finger on the doorbell, then dropped down to catch her breath, legs trembling with the unexpected activity. There was a pause before the intercom crackled.

'Who is it?'

She staggered upright. 'It's Kate,' she gasped into the intercom.

A pause. 'Who?'

She could slip away now, she thought; if Matthias mentioned it in the morning, she would strenuously deny the whole thing.

'Kate Whyte. You know. Emmie's mum?' Silence. 'Um. Class 4c.'

There was a longer pause. She imagined Matthias staring at the intercom in horror. Then she saw a tall figure approaching, distorted by the glass, and the door opened.

He was wearing a soft-looking, faded T-shirt and pyjama bottoms and his feet were bare. His hair was rumpled, as though he'd been sleeping.

'I couldn't hear anything through the intercom,' he explained. He was frowning, but he seemed more puzzled than annoyed. 'I thought it was you.'

She spread out her hands and waved them jazzily. 'It's me,' she said. 'Surprise! You said I could come by if I ever wanted to talk so here I am. Although you're probably busy.' His pyjama bottoms were comically short on him, stopping almost mid-calf and he had huge feet with bony ankles. 'You were in bed. I shouldn't have disturbed you. Wait, is Lily here?'

He held the door open. 'I was watching TV,' he said. 'Lily is at a friend's. Come in.'

She followed him inside, conscious suddenly that her face was damp, either with sweat or tears, she wasn't sure. She wiped it surreptitiously with her sleeve.

Inside the flat, everything was as tidy and serene as usual. She could smell something. *Woodsmoke,* she thought. Like a campfire on a winter evening. She felt delirious.

'How do you make it so nice here?' she asked, wandering into the sitting room uninvited. She traced a finger along the shelf. 'No dust. Not even the normal, socially acceptable amount. I love it.'

'Is that why you came round?' he asked, sounding amused. He watched her from the doorway. 'To be somewhere clean?'

'Yes,' she said. She took off her coat and held it close to her chest, still breathing hard. 'Plus, I remembered that you have a whole drawer full of fancy tea.'

'I do,' he said. He prised her coat out of her hands and laid it on a chair. 'Why don't I make some? You can have a good look round,' he added. 'I know you're dying to.'

'Is it that obvious?' He went next door and put the kettle on. She walked around the sitting room, scanning for any revealing detail. Shelves of neatly stacked books, mostly with French spines. A guitar was propped against the wall.

'You play the guitar?' she called.

'I play the cello, remember,' he said. 'For the Scottish Symphony Orchestra. The guitar is just for fun.'

There was a series of framed photos on the mantlepiece, including Olivier with what must be various grandparents, and one of Lily, with Olivier in a fuzzy snowsuit on her lap. Kate studied her – she was predictably lovely, all loose tousled hair and sharp cheekbones. Spitefully, Kate pushed the photo crooked. It looked so jarring in the orderly room that she straightened it again, feeling guilty.

She pulled a photo album off the shelf and flipped through it. Olivier as a baby, swaddled in a blanket. Olivier with chocolate cake all over his face. Olivier in a school play, dressed as a fox. Olivier in a swing, shouting with laughter.

'I have green tea, fresh mint, raspberry, lemon and ginger or verbena,' Matthias said.

'Which do you recommend?' she asked.

'The verbena, for sleep. You have circles under your eyes.'

'Thanks for pointing them out.' Kate slid the album back into place on the shelf.

'I thought you slept fine.'

'All right, Sherlock. You've got me.' She wandered back through to the kitchen. 'Can I look through your fridge?' she asked. 'I want to see if you've got half a rotting carrot lurking in there, like the rest of us.'

'Sure,' he said. He poured hot water into cups. 'Knock yourself out.'

The fridge was well stocked, like an advert for nutrition. Milk, in glass bottles. Expensive-looking cheese, wrapped in wax paper. The salad drawer was stuffed with fresh vegetables – peppers, lettuce, cucumber, leeks – all of which probably featured in Matthias's delicious, home-cooked meals. A glass jar of pickles with a homemade label on the front. Next to the fridge, butter in a glass dish and a wire basket of eggs.

'This kitchen makes me want to cry,' Kate said. 'I'm so jealous.'

Matthias handed her the mug of tea and she breathed in the fragrant steam.

'Why do you not finish the building work on your flat, Kate?' he asked.

She laughed. 'Again, so direct.' He was silent. All the usual lies formed on the tip of her tongue. *We're waiting for the contractors. The right architect. A bit of free time.*

'I can't,' she said. 'Partly because I don't have any money but also the creative spark is gone. I don't think I'll be able to sell it. The kids won't ever have a real home.'

'They have a home,' he said gently. 'With you.'

She took a scalding hot swallow of tea to burn away the lump in her throat. 'You must think I'm totally crazy, coming over like this and going through your fridge.'

'No.' The mug looked tiny cradled in his large hands. 'Actually, yes, you are a bit crazy. But I don't mind.'

'My mum is making me go to this grief group with her,' said Kate. 'You sit around in a circle and talk about the people you've lost. Tonight, it was my turn to talk about Adam. I couldn't do it. I ran away. Again.'

'And you came here?'

'And I came here.'

Their eyes locked. The tidy kitchen felt static suddenly, like the air before a storm. Kate drank the rest of her tea in one swallow and put down the cup carefully, with hands that shook slightly.

'I'll leave you alone,' she said. 'I'll probably be embarrassed in the playground tomorrow. Thank you for letting me in and making me tea instead of telling me to get lost.'

He stood up. 'Wait. It is your turn to light the Advent candle.'

She laughed. 'Really?'

'Of course.'

He handed her a lighter and she bent over the candles. All were lit but one. Flicking the lighter, she held the flame over the last.

'There,' she said, as it caught. 'Christmas is officially here.'

He smiled. 'Would you like to come for dinner with me one night, Kate?'

She stared at him. 'Dinner, with me?'

'Yes,' he said. 'The two of us, no children. In a restaurant.'

'All right,' she said. 'I mean, yes I would like that, thank you very much.' She took a deep breath. 'See you next week,' she said.

'Absolutely.' He held the door open for her. 'I'll text you. Goodnight, Kate.'

Outside, she began to walk quickly towards her flat, her quick breath creating a cloud in the frosty air.

She had realised something in Matthias's kitchen. That right now there was no one else she would rather tell her secrets to. She wanted to pour them all out by the light of the advent candles. Which, she thought, was very unsettling indeed.

36

KATE

Kate joined the tail end of the queue of parents filing into the gym. Tamara and Tracy were sitting behind a folding table, huddled in thick jumpers, collecting money and dispensing tickets.

Tamara stared at Kate as she approached the front of the queue. 'Were you wearing pyjamas to pickup the other day?'

'Hi,' said Kate, holding out her £3. 'Just one please, as discussed.'

'I suppose you do love a bit of drama, don't you Kate?' said Tamara. 'Well, enjoy.'

Kate went through into the gym and found an empty seat at the end of the row. Everywhere people were sitting in twos, laughing and chatting and pointing when a little face peeked behind the curtain. It felt like she was surrounded by a sea of couples. She caught sight of Carrie Hooper, another single mum, sitting alone, and gave her a little wave of solidarity. Lois and Dan sat in the front row, backs straight, looking ahead, not touching.

She could see Matthias near the front too, chatting to Euan, and to her horror she saw Lily on the other side of him. Kate could only make out a mane of gorgeously tousled hair. As Kate watched, Lily leaned forward to whisper something to Matthias, who nodded. Kate sunk lower in her seat, wishing she had washed her hair and changed out of her ratty leggings. At least she wasn't wearing her pyjamas; that was something.

Then the lights went down, the head came out to welcome them, and THE SEASICK PIRATE'S CHRISTMAS began.

'That was amazing,' said Kate, sweeping the children into a hug. 'You guys were awesome!' She hugged them so tightly that Max yelped. She buried her face in their warm little bodies. 'I'm sorry Mummy's been so grumpy lately,' she whispered. 'I've been super stressed about work.'

Emmie frowned. 'But you don't do any work to be stressed about, Mummy,' she said.

'Well, that's true,' Kate said, standing. She saw Olivier and held out her hand for a high five. 'The man of the hour. What an amazing play. I can't believe that all came out of your big brain. The pirate ship delivering presents at the end – that was inspired.'

'Thanks,' said Olivier modestly. 'I was worried after the dress rehearsal this morning, but I think it came together all right.'

'It was better than all right!' said Kate. 'I laughed. I cried. Sometimes both together.'

That wasn't a lie; she had spent the best part of the play with silent tears streaming down her cheeks. The sight of her children in their costumes, faces shining in the stage lights, had broken her.

Matthias came over. 'Feeling better today?' he said to Kate.

'Yes, thanks,' she said, her cheeks starting to burn despite herself.

'Olivier's mum is here. I thought you might like to say hi,' he said. He nodded to where Kate could see Lily, who still had her back to her, chatting to Euan and Sergio.

'I would love that more than anything,' said Kate insincerely. 'But I left a casserole in the oven and I don't want it to dry out.'

Matthias narrowed his eyes. 'There is a lot in that statement that I have a problem believing.'

She ignored him. 'Right, you two, let's go. It's late and you need to wind down after such an amazing performance. Congratulations again, Olivier.'

On their way out, Kate was so busy trying to avoid Lily that she ran into Veronica instead, standing by the door and counting money.

'Kate,' she said. 'I thought that was you. Are you still coming to the fete on Saturday?'

'I certainly am,' said Kate. 'I'm done caring what anyone thinks.' She winked at Veronica. 'You should try it some time.'

37

KATE

Thursday and Kate was early for grief group, for once. As she approached, she saw Jean leaning against the wall, waiting for her, looking in the opposite direction. From this distance she might have been a girl, with her slight figure and curls blowing in the wind.

Kate was about to call out to her when she noticed another figure walking towards Jean. Rory. For some reason, Kate hung back. She watched as Rory's dark, rather serious face broke into a smile under the gleam of a street lamp. Jean lifted her hand in greeting and they spoke briefly, and then Rory went inside.

It was nothing at all, but for some reason, Kate felt uneasy. Mum was so vulnerable right now. Maybe it had been a mistake to persuade her to clear out Dad's stuff.

Kate reached her mother and gave her a hug. 'How are you, Mum?' she asked.

'Grand,' Jean said. Her face was pale under the streetlights. 'A bit tired.'

Her mother didn't seem tired, though, Kate thought. She seemed alert, excited almost. They walked up the steps together.

Kate gave her a sidelong glance. 'Is it your turn to speak today? You don't have to if you don't want to.'

'It's nice to remember.' Jean patted her handbag. 'I've got Dad's book with me to talk about.'

'Mum, you'd tell me if anything was ... I don't know, *wrong*, wouldn't you?'

'Kate, don't be so dramatic,' said Jean, laughing. 'Everything is absolutely fine.'

She walked ahead up the steps and into the building, and as she held the door open for Kate, she smiled. A warm, open smile, as though she hadn't a care in the world. Kate knew then, as surely as she knew the feel of Jean's hand on her forehead or the smell of her perfume, that her mother was lying.

'You all know I first met my husband, Gerard, at school,' said Jean. Her lovely voice, with its gentle lilt, filled the room. She seemed calmer now than she had done outside, cradling a mug of coffee in her hands.

She held up the book. 'Gerard was a big reader, always,' she said. 'Mostly thrillers or crime, a bit of historical stuff. But I remembered he loved this book. Poetry of all things. People can always surprise you, even after they've gone.'

She opened the book and paused, looking down at the page with a puzzled expression on her face. Kate craned her neck and saw an inscription there, in a slanting hand, and a postcard resting in the pages. There was a silence that bloomed and expanded in the room.

'Are you okay, Mum?' Kate whispered.

Jean nodded once, slowly. 'Of course,' she murmured softly. Then she looked up and smiled at them all, cleared her throat, and began to read.

These I have loved:
White plates and cups, clean-gleaming,
Ringed with blue lines; and feathery, faery dust;

This Year, Maybe

Wet roofs, beneath the lamp-light; the strong crust
Of friendly bread; and many-tasting food;
Rainbows; and the blue bitter smoke of wood;
Radiant raindrops couching in cool flowers.

38

JEAN

Gerard had been gone for six days. On the seventh day, Jean got home from the shops with Katie in the pram, and he was there.

Sitting at the kitchen table, hands resting on his knees, tense as though he had been watching the door for hours. He looked tired and a bit sunburnt.

'Katie needs a nap,' Jean said, without looking at him. She went upstairs with Kate and put her down in the cot. She took her time singing songs and drawing the curtains, waiting until the baby was drowsy.

Then she stood for a moment on the landing, trying to catch her breath. Her anger was a wild animal that she had to catch by the tail. When she was in a rage, she might do anything – set fire to the house. Tear it all down.

Did she want to do that? Part of her did.

She took a deep breath and walked downstairs. Gerard was sitting in the same position. He looked wretched, and that annoyed her even more.

'So, you've come back,' she said. She sat down opposite him. 'I didn't tell your folks or mine, by the way. Didn't want them to all despise you like I have, in case you came back.'

He reached for her and she jerked her hand away. 'Do me

a favour, Ger,' she said coldly. 'Running out on your wife and baby. What sort of man does that?'

'I am sorry,' he said humbly. 'I'll tell you everything, right now.'

Something shifted within her, then. The hot anger subsided and for the first time a little voice, calm and practical, told her to hold fire. To think of little Katie upstairs. This cottage, their home. Gerard, dark circles under his eyes, a flush on his cheekbones from the sun, hair dishevelled. The boy she had wanted at fourteen and still wanted now. Their life together, which seemed suddenly so ineffably precious.

'I don't want to hear it,' she said.

His eyes were anguished. 'But Jeanie . . .'

'Do you want to come back?' she asked. She held his gaze.

'Aye, of course I do,' he said miserably. 'Jeanie, this is the only place I've ever wanted to be. I went mad for a while, that's all. If you let me—'

'If you want to come back, then you can't tell me about it,' she said. 'We don't speak of it again. Whatever it was, it never happened.'

That, she thought, would be the price Gerard would pay. Whatever had happened that week in September, he would have to live with it his whole life. That could be his punishment.

It hadn't occurred to Jean that she might be punishing herself instead.

39

KATE

That week, Matthias had sent Kate a text suggesting a date and time for dinner, Saturday night at a new bistro in town that had been getting great reviews. Nat was babysitting. Kate was a mixture of nerves and excitement. As she threw a pair of jeans to the floor in a rage, her phone rang. Jean, at last – she'd been trying to call her mother all day. She pounced on it.

'Mum, finally,' she said. 'Have you been ignoring my calls?'

Jean laughed. 'You're being dramatic again, love. I had a bad head. I thought I might pop round now though, if you fancied it? I've got some deli bits. We could have a drink and a chat.'

Kate hesitated. The casual note in her mother's voice didn't fool her for a second. Jean was up to something, and this could be her chance to find out what.

On the other hand, Matthias would have left for the restaurant by now. It would be rude to cancel. Besides, if she was honest, she didn't *want* to cancel.

'I'm meeting someone for dinner.' She took a deep breath. 'It's not a date or anything. I can cancel, if it's important.'

'Oh, darling,' Jean said. Her voice was bubbling with laughter. 'Don't be silly. Go on your not-a-date. Live a little. We can catch up another time.'

'Promise?' said Kate warily.

'Of course, have fun.'

Jean rang off. Kate stared at the phone. She had a bad feeling – like she had missed something important.

The doorbell rang. Nat. 'Coming,' she yelled. She opened the front door wearing her pants and bra. 'When did I forget how to get dressed?'

'Just go like that,' said Nat. 'Make his day.'

Nat kicked off her boots and unzipped her jacket. 'I think someone is nervous about their big date.'

'It's not a date. He's European,' said Kate. 'Probably has dinner with women at the drop of a hat.'

'And yet, you washed your hair.'

'That's just polite,' muttered Kate. She crouched down, sifting through the pile of clothes. 'None of this stuff fits.'

Nat knelt beside her. 'Hmm. What do people wear for non-dates? I think this,' she said eventually, holding out a soft green jumper, 'and the jeans you're wearing now, and boots. And your red lipstick. It used to be your thing and you haven't worn it in ages.'

A year, thought Kate. Pretty much exactly.

'What are you scared of, Kate?'

'I'm not scared,' said Kate unconvincingly. 'Okay, I'm terrified. What if we have nothing to say to each other? He's not exactly a big talker, is he? What if it's two hours of silence?'

Nat tossed her the jumper. 'Put some clothes on, will you?'

Kate tugged the jumper over her head. She hadn't worn it for years – it was too delicate to wear around the children. She stood back. It brought out the green in her eyes and the colour in her cheeks. Her hair, freshly washed for once, tumbled around her shoulders.

'Lovely,' said Nat. 'Now, lipstick. Go on.'

'Fine,' said Kate, digging in her makeup bag for her trusted red lipstick, worn down to a stump. She put it on, the feel of it waxy and strange on her mouth.

'Gorgeous,' said Nat, slipping an arm round her and looking at her reflection. 'That's my girl. I knew she was in there somewhere.'

Kate looked back at her reflection. She looked almost familiar. Only the old Kate could never have imagined the last year.

'You know what?' said Nat, meeting Kate's eyes in the mirror. 'I don't think Matthias *does* have dinner with women at the drop of a hat. I think he's a bit shy. I like him anyway, and you know I hate practically everybody.' Nat gave her a little shove. 'Go on. Have fun.'

'Thanks for babysitting,' Kate said, tugging on her coat and giving Nat a kiss on the cheek. 'I'll see you about ten. No later.'

'You'd better,' said Nat, winking. 'It's not a date, after all.'

Kate walked through the restaurant, aware of a sense of general calm and hush, wood veneer, black and white tiles, soft lights. She felt oddly nervous. Matthias was sitting at a banquette, and he stood when she got to the table.

'Hello,' he said.

'Hi.' It all felt excruciatingly polite. 'Sorry I'm late.' She looked around. 'This is really nice.'

'Yes,' he said, sitting back down. 'I thought it would be nice for you to get out.'

She frowned. 'Hang on. Did you ask me out because you felt sorry for me?'

His heavy brows came down. 'No.'

'Because if that's the case, you can take your sympathy and stuff it.'

'Kate.' He spoke very slowly and clearly. 'I asked you for a drink because I've been wanting to ever since I met you.'

'Oh,' said Kate. She could feel herself flushing up to the roots of her hair. 'Really?'

He nodded. The waiter came with menus.

'I don't know how to do this,' Kate whispered. 'I don't know how to go on a date.'

'Me neither.' He was looking at the drinks menu. 'But we both know how to eat in a restaurant, don't we?'

'Sort of,' she said. 'It's been a while. I heard you order drinks and food.'

'You're funny,' he said, his eyes crinkling.

'I used to be,' she said. 'You're not meant to crack jokes as a grieving widow. Why did you and Olivier's mother break up?' He looked up, startled, and she laughed. 'You're not the only one who can be direct.'

'We had already broken up,' he said. 'The pregnancy was a surprise. We decided we both wanted to be parents. She was travelling a lot so we thought it best I should have Olivier most of the time.' He shrugged. 'We are friends.'

'I can't believe anyone is that functional,' she said. 'There must have been at least one screaming row?'

'No, not really. What colour would you say your eyes are? I keep trying to figure it out. Green, grey, blue?'

She flushed again. 'They change all the time,' she managed. 'Depending on the light.'

He looked at her for a long moment. He reached out across the table for her hand, and her heart leapt. His big hand was warm on her wrist. She was sure he must feel her pulse racing beneath his fingers. 'Right now, they are green,' he said.

'Oh. Well, that must be the candlelight,' she said.

He smiled. 'Must be.'

After dinner, they walked through the city back to Marchmont.

He stopped under the streetlight. 'Goodnight,' he said.

'Goodnight,' she said, trying to keep her voice light and relaxed. 'Thanks for everything, you were right. It was really nice to, um, get out of the house.'

He put a hand on her arm. She could feel her heart drumming in her chest. She was shaking, and to hide it she cupped her hands around her elbows. What if he asked if he could kiss her? What would she say? Did she want him to? She risked a quick look at him and saw that he was smiling, almost as if he knew what she was thinking.

'I'll see you tomorrow,' he said. 'It's the fete, isn't it? I'll get to see all of your hard work paying off.'

She grinned, feeling at once disappointed and relieved. 'I don't know about that,' she said. 'You might see me tarred and feathered, more like.'

He shook his head. 'Ignore them. Good night.'

She walked up the road and when she looked back, he was still there, standing under the lamplight and watching her go.

Kate shut her front door and leaned against it, a huge smile spreading over her face. She stayed there for just a moment, relishing it. The warmth of the restaurant, the delicious food and wine, feeling like herself again, sharp, clever.

'Through here,' called Nat from the sitting room. 'I want to hear everything.'

Kate made her expression casual and walked down the corridor. 'Hiya,' she said. 'Kids okay?'

'I assume so,' said Nat. She was sitting cross-legged with a tin of Quality Street in her lap, looking even smaller than usual under a mass of blankets. She muted the TV. 'Haven't heard a peep, so I didn't check I'm afraid. I'm watching a Christmas film about a baker who meets a medieval knight. Did you make these, by the way?' she said, nodding to the heap of Christmas wreaths stacked up by the sofa.

Kate dropped down on the sofa next to Nat. 'I did. They'll be on sale tomorrow.'

'They look incredible, I'll buy one. Well, don't leave me hanging! How was it?'

'Confusing. Weird. Strange to be out with someone who wasn't Adam. Lovely restaurant, lovely food.' She picked at a nail. 'What on earth does he see in me?'

Nat rolled her eyes. 'When I first met you, I took an instant dislike. You were too beautiful. How's that for a feminist contradiction? Speaking of which,' she said, 'there's a rumour going round the playground that you kissed Dan Sumpter at the Christmas party.'

'What!' said Kate weakly. 'Who said that?'

Nat rolled her eyes. 'One of those PTA clones. She didn't know I was standing there. I told her it was bollocks of course, nice and loudly.' She paused. 'Unless it wasn't?'

Kate stared at her lap. 'I lied to you about something. Well, I lied by omission. Dan *did* try it on with me at the PTA Christmas party. I didn't tell you because I was scared you'd think I had it coming.'

'You were scared that I, a lecturer in feminism, would think you *had it coming*?' said Nat.

Kate laughed shakily. 'I worried I was getting a reputation. Veronica was always making these little digs about men doing things for me. My sister said I attract trouble. I was worried you'd think I was a massive flirt, trying to snare Fergus.'

Nat squeezed her hand. 'Dan clearly had sinister motives. But Fergus helps out because you're a mate and he cares about you and the kids. Just like I do. Simple as that. I would never think anything else.'

Kate swallowed. 'You don't think I use people?' she said.

Nat laughed. 'I didn't say *that*. Gorgeous people are used to getting what they want in life. But I don't believe for a second that you lured Dan Sumpter,' she shuddered, 'into a snog at the PTA Christmas party.' She glanced at her watch. 'I've got to go, but don't let this ruin your evening, okay? Matthias is a good one, I can feel it. You deserve some good luck.'

Kate shut the door behind Nat. She felt a sudden dullness in her chest, as though she had come thudding back to reality. What had she been thinking? She had two small children. Her husband had died a year ago. She couldn't date anyone, let alone another parent at the school.

Tonight, she had jumped at the chance to be someone else. Tomorrow she would be chiselling Weetabix off the floor and fretting about the mortgage. It was time she started being sensible – and that meant breaking things off with Matthias before they went any further.

40

KATE

On Saturday Kate got to the fete early to set up the brazier and marshmallow stand. Nat texted her first thing. 'I'll be there for the moral support but later. Feel ropey, think it's some bug.'

The food stall was groaning under baskets of plump mince pies, assorted pies and cheese. Another stall was selling felt Christmas tree decorations and Arran stockings. There was a 'guess the weight of the yule log', with the prize the hefty log itself, decorated with flaked chocolate. Fairy lights were woven among the stalls, and trees donated by the Christmas tree farm filled the air with their clean, spicy scent, mingling with the smell of sugar and cinnamon and charcoal.

If she was leaving the PTA, Kate thought, surveying the scene with grim satisfaction, at least she was going out in style. This was going to be a Christmas fair the like of which Lyndoch Primary had not seen.

Euan was setting out the stall next to hers. He gave her his usual friendly wave.

'Hey, neighbour,' Kate said. 'Did they draw straws over who had to work next to me? You'd better hope being a social pariah isn't contagious.'

Euan grinned. 'It will all blow over. It always does.'

'Will it?' She began to thread marshmallows onto skewers. 'I can't help thinking it would be easier to move to a different country. Start a new life in witness protection.'

A child approached. 'Is that real chocolate or vegan chocolate?' he asked.

'Which do you want it to be?' asked Kate. She dropped her voice conspiratorially. 'Because I've got both.'

The day passed quickly. Kate felt protected behind her stall; she didn't know the majority of parents and children who bought marshmallows and warmed themselves by the brazier which reminded her that the vast majority of the parents didn't have a clue about the machinations of the PTA. The fair was going with a positive swing. There was a buzz in the air, peals of tipsy laughter rang out and children ran around squealing, wearing reindeer antlers and Santa hats.

At about two in the afternoon, Kate saw Matthias. He was watching Olivier trying to throw a hoop over a wooden post. Max was standing next to him, cheering him on.

'Watch the brazier, will you?' she said to Euan. 'Don't let any children fall in or I really will have to leave the country.'

She walked over. 'Hi,' she said, tapping Matthias on the shoulder.

He turned and smiled at her, a warm smile that lit up his eyes.

'I wanted to say thank you for a wonderful evening last night,' she said, trying to focus.

'No problem,' he said. 'We should do it again.'

She took a deep breath. She had been rehearsing what to say all morning.

'As you've probably gathered, things are complicated for me right now,' she said. 'My husband died a year ago and

I'm a bit of a mess. Dinner was lovely but I think we should probably leave it there.' She took a deep breath. 'Sorry.'

He blinked. 'That is okay,' he said.

She hesitated. She hadn't expected it to be quite so brief. Olivier managed to snag one of the pegs and Max whooped and gave him a high five. 'Maybe you should avoid the marshmallow area,' she said. 'I feel a bit awkward now.'

'Okay,' he said again.

There was a pause. Then Kate turned and went back to the stall. She kept her head down and sold marshmallows till her hands were sticky. What had she expected? That he would come running after her and beg her to reconsider?

As the fair was winding down and dusk was settling, Nat appeared, looking pale and fragile, huddled into a thick duvet coat.

'How are you feeling?' asked Kate. She held out a stick. 'Marshmallow? Or is that the last thing you feel like.'

Nat shuddered and handed her a fiver. 'Consider that my donation. But I'm not eating that. I've spent all night throwing up. Must have been what you had the other day.' Kate had forgotten about her fictitious stomach flu. 'Fergus is down with it now. Moaning and groaning, obviously has it much worse than I did.' She rolled her eyes and looked around the playground. 'What a weird atmosphere. People seem *happy*.'

Just then, the buoyant holiday mood was shattered.

A howl of rage, almost primal, sent them turning around in confusion. It was coming from Lois, who was marching with speed towards them, coat flapping with the g-force. Terror seized Kate but Lois marched straight past her. Up to Veronica.

'How could you?' she said. She was shaking, bright spots of red in each cheek. Veronica took an involuntary step back, her eyes wide with fear. 'I thought you were my friend. How could you *sleep with my husband*?'

A terrible hush descended on the playground. Tracy, who had been in the middle of ladling hot apple juice into a cup, poured it onto her foot. Euan clutched Sergio's arm, horror and excitement warring on his face. Nat gasped.

All eyes swivelled to Veronica. The colour had drained from her face. In the light of the twinkling fairy lights she looked ghastly. She moistened her lips with the tip of her tongue.

'I don't know what you mean,' she said. Her voice was pitifully unconvincing.

'You know *exactly* what I mean,' roared Lois. 'I've seen the texts. He confessed everything. *Everything!*'

Kate knew she should look away, but she couldn't. It was like watching a car crash.

'You always had to be so superior didn't you, Veronica,' sneered Lois. 'With your chia seeds and hot yoga. Bossing us all around. And all along you were stabbing me in the back. Did you think I would keep this quiet? Well, I won't. I want everyone – all of them' – she swept her arm around the watching circle of parents – 'to know the truth about you and Dan.'

A hand tugged on Kate's arm. She looked down and saw Max and Emmie, eyes wide, clutching pretzels in mittened hands.

'What's going on?' said Emmie.

'Hush,' said Kate, urgently. She knew she should take them away from the awful scene, but she couldn't seem to make her feet move. She glanced around at the rest of the PTA who looked either thrilled or shocked. Tamara looked as though Christmas had come early. So much for the sisterhood, Kate thought.

'You're pathetic, Veronica,' said Lois. She curled her lip. 'You and Dan are welcome to each other.'

With that, she turned on her heel and stormed off. The crowd parted to let her pass. For a moment there was silence, stretching out so that Kate thought she might scream just to break the tension. Then Veronica dropped the handful of notes she had been counting and sped off after Lois.

Noise broke out, a high-pitched excited buzz.

'Did that just happen?' asked Nat, turning to Kate. 'Or am I still delirious with stomach flu?'

'I think it happened,' said Kate. She felt as stunned as Nat looked.

'Come on,' said Nat. 'This Christmas fair is clearly over. Razed to the ground, one might say. Can I come back to yours for a post-mortem?'

'Of course,' said Kate. She glanced around at the chaos. Tamara was issuing orders in a loud, carrying voice. 'What about the marshmallow stand?'

Nat shrugged. 'You don't owe the PTA anything. Ditch it.'

'You're right,' said Kate. 'Euan, you're in charge of the brazier again. Come on, kids. Let's go.'

'Why was Livvie's mummy shouting at Hugo and Sienna's mummy?' said Emmie as Kate dragged her out of the playground.

'That's between them,' Kate said, walking fast. 'We don't know the full story and . . . oh look at that Christmas tree through the window there. They've got an owl on the top instead of an angel.'

'Hugo's mummy slept with Livvie's daddy? What does that mean?'

'Nothing. It's complicated and grown up. You could help me out here,' she added to Nat.

'You're doing a beautiful job on your own,' Nat said, giggling.

As soon as they got to Kate's, the kids sprinted upstairs to play – or more likely, dissect the events of the fair – and Kate and Nat went into the kitchen.

'Tea or wine?' asked Kate. 'I'm hoping you'll say wine, but you might feel too rough.'

'Are you kidding, after that?' asked Nat. 'Wine, definitely, for medicinal purposes. My god. Veronica, of all people. Queen bee of the PTA. Mum of the Year. How the mighty fall.'

Kate took a bottle of white from the fridge and rinsed two dusty glasses. 'I feel sorry for her though,' she said slowly. 'That was pretty rough.'

'An affair with Dan Sumpter of all people,' said Nat. 'Ugh. He's such a mole. And Veronica's a goddess. I can't believe she didn't stick up for you either, when everyone was being horrible.'

Kate smiled weakly. 'Too right. I felt like I had a scarlet letter tattooed on my forehead.'

'Hey, at least Veronica's taken the heat off you there,' said Nat.

'Yeah,' said Kate. 'I suppose she has.'

They drank their wine in silence. Upstairs, Kate could hear the children shrieking.

'Tamara looked so pleased with herself, didn't she?' said Nat. 'It's all gone a bit *Mean Girls*.'

'I know,' Kate said. 'While Dan presumably gets off scot-free. It's so unfair.'

Nat looked at her over the rim of her wine glass. 'You know what the sisterly thing to do would be.'

'What?' said Kate. Then, seeing the mischief in her friend's eyes, 'Oh no.'

'Yes,' said Nat triumphantly. 'We should take the kids round to ours so they can watch telly with Fergus. And then we should go and befriend Veronica.'

'Veronica,' Kate yelled through the letterbox. 'Come on, open the door. I know you're in there, I can smell the candle of serenity.'

There was a shuffling of feet, and then the door was opened just an inch. A pair of dark, wary eyes looked at them through the crack.

'We come in peace,' said Kate, holding up the bottle of wine. 'We know that Dan is a shit.'

A pause, and then Veronica opened the door more widely. She looked tired but still poised. Her hair was pulled into a messy bun and she wore pyjamas and a thick cardigan. Kate was sure she wouldn't look half so composed in the middle of a personal crisis.

'What are you doing here?' she said.

'Let us in, will you?' begged Nat. 'It's freezing out here.'

Veronica hesitated, but Kate pushed past her. It was time to take charge of the situation, Veronica-style.

'Let's talk,' she said. 'Come on.'

She led the way to the kitchen, Nat and Veronica following. She found wine glasses – enormous, fragile goblets – in a cabinet. Their cheap corner-shop wine looked out of place in this kitchen but it would do.

'Where are the kids?' Nat asked.

'They're at my mum's,' said Veronica. She sat on a stool, her shoulders slumped. 'Craig's gone to a mate's. He won't speak to me. I've let them all down.' She glanced at Kate, who was pouring the wine. 'I'm sorry, Kate. I should have stuck up for you when all those rumours started about you. I was so confused. Dan told me you'd made a move on him when you were pissed and Tamara said she'd overheard it. I didn't know what was going on. But I should have guessed.'

'You mean when the PTA were shunning me? I'll cope,' said Kate. She sat down at the marble island. 'Come on. Tell us about it.'

Veronica stared at her wine. 'Red wine is really calorific,' she said mechanically, and then took a swig. 'Fuck it.'

'How long was it going on for?' asked Nat.

'Since last term,' said Veronica. 'Do you remember the Halloween disco?'

'I certainly do,' said Kate. The shrill, sugar-fuelled shrieks of fifty children up past their bedtime was a sound burned for ever on her brain. 'Wait. You and Dan were helping out that night, weren't you?'

'Yeah,' said Veronica dully. 'He smuggled some booze in.'

'You were looking after our kids *drunk*?' said Nat, sounding scandalised.

Kate shushed her.

'Not drunk,' said Veronica. 'We just had a beer. He kept finding little ways to touch me. I thought they were accidental at first, but then I went to the toilet and when I came out he was waiting for me.' *Clearly, Dan has a* modus operandi, Kate thought as Veronica sighed. 'We kissed in the cleaning closet.'

'With everyone outside?' squeaked Nat. 'That was risky.'

'I know,' said Veronica dully. 'That was the thrill, I think.' She picked at an invisible thread on her cardigan. 'Why are you here, Kate?'

'I don't know,' said Kate honestly. 'Why did you make me join the PTA? Why did you hire me to renovate your house? Why did you keep giving me probiotics and candles?'

'Because I felt sorry for you,' said Veronica. 'You'd lost your husband and you were clearly lying about having any semblance of a career and you looked awful. No one was looking out for you.' She shrugged. 'I thought I could help. I am nice, you know. No one ever thinks that about me, but I am.'

Kate grinned. Her mother was right; people never stopped surprising you.

'But why *Dan*?' asked Nat, clearly incredulous.

'He was just there,' said Veronica. 'Maybe I was bored. Bored of exercise and pickup and PTA meetings and improving books and vegan meals. He could have been anybody. It was validation, pure and simple.' She sunk her head into her hands. 'I feel like such a fool. I've lost my husband and my best friend. I've ruined everything.'

'People come back from worse,' said Kate encouragingly. 'I lost my husband and look at me now.'

Veronica shot her a pitying look. 'No offence, Kate,' she said. 'But you are a woman on the edge.'

Clearly even a life crisis hadn't dented Veronica's capacity for brutal honesty. 'Hey. I'm hanging in there,' Kate said weakly.

'If you say so,' said Veronica. 'I'm the head of the PTA,' she wailed. 'I run a parenting Instagram account. Now everyone will know I'm a fraud!'

'You can still do all those things! Just with humility,' said Kate. 'Not,' she added hastily, 'that you weren't humble before. But now people will know you aren't perfect, they'll relate to you even more. Being perfect is hard.'

Veronica sighed again. 'I know,' she said. 'Craig and I – we had all these *things*. House, cars, holidays. A new kitchen. Not enough, is it?'

They were silent for a moment. On the one hand, Kate thought, those things sounded pretty good from where she was sitting. But she understood what Veronica meant.

'You were unlucky,' Nat said at last. 'You were vulnerable, and Dan came slithering along. If you hadn't been caught, it would have just fizzled out.'

'Maybe I wanted to get caught, though,' said Veronica. 'Something has to change now, right?' She shook her head. 'At least there's that.'

'You can think about all that tomorrow,' said Kate, bracingly. 'What can we do tonight to cheer you up?'

Veronica gave her a thoughtful look. 'There is one thing.'

'What?' asked Kate suspiciously.

'Would you let me cut your hair?' Veronica said. 'I know I've had a glass of wine, maybe two, but I used to cut hair professionally before I met Craig and I'm really good, honestly. You have such lovely hair, proper Brigitte Bardot. I could just cut the fringe back in and trim the ends a bit. Go on,' she said persuasively. 'It would make me feel much better.'

Kate looked at Nat, who shrugged. 'You know what,' she said, refilling her glass. 'If it makes you feel better, then go for it.'

'Do you think they'll recover, her and Craig?' said Nat, on the way home. 'Your hair looks great by the way. It doesn't surprise me that Veronica is good at cutting hair. She's very precise, even after half a bottle of wine.'

'Thanks,' said Kate. She glanced at Nat. 'Have *you* ever been tempted to have an affair?'

'No way,' said Nat vehemently. 'Think of the effort. Talking to someone new? Worrying about how you look? Dating? I'd rather die alone.'

'Thanks,' grinned Kate. 'You're really inspiring me to hit the dating scene.'

'Oh, you'll be all right,' said Nat. 'Besides, Matthias is besotted.'

'I told him I couldn't see him again,' said Kate.

'Kate!' Nat wailed. 'Why?'

'Because it's far too soon. I don't know what I was think-ing agreeing to dinner. Can you imagine how confusing it would be for the kids?' Kate shook her head. 'Like they haven't been through enough.' They walked for a while in silence. 'I hated Adam, sometimes,' Kate said at last. 'I didn't have an affair, but that was probably down to luck. Right place, right time, right sleazeball – who knows. I can't blame Veronica too much.'

'Hatred is pretty close to love,' said Nat. 'Same sort of general area. Obsessive. Can't eat, can't sleep. You know?'

'Yeah,' said Kate. 'I know.'

Back at the flat, Fergus called weakly out to them from down the hall.

'Down here,' he said. 'You'll be glad to know I'm feeling a bit better. I've graduated to dry toast.'

Nat snorted. 'Coming,' she said. 'Listen, Kate. I get it, about Matthias. This isn't something to jump into. But for the record, he seems like someone who would get it, too. If you just talked to him . . .'

Kate shook her head. 'It's too soon,' she said stubbornly. 'It probably always will be.'

Once Kate had put her sleepy children to bed, she poured a glass of water to dilute the wine. She rang Jean, and the phone went straight to voicemail.

She wandered over to where she had laid out the photo-graphs of Capaldi's on the sitting-room table. Her mother and father before they were any such thing. The eighties, but it might have been a scene from an earlier era – the beautiful pistachio-coloured booths, the Formica. Capaldi's had been the real deal. The last Kate had heard, it had been taken over by a chain restaurant, which depressed her too much to think about.

She went to her shelves and took out her copy of *Classic Italian Cafés*, which had once obsessed her as a young designer, and turned the pages. Even in black-and-white you got that hit of another world. Immigrants from Italy, asserting their identity in a new country, in these Scottish cities and towns with chip shops and ice-cream parlours. Double nougats, little metal dishes, wafers covered in chocolate, soda fountains. Now, so many of them were gone.

On her phone, she began to scroll through the photos she had taken of Caffe Firenze. You could see the past, she thought, in the lovely lines of the bar and those battered booths. Suddenly she realised how incongruous and wrong her proposal to Marco had been. If only she could have another chance to do it right . . .

Kate tried Jean again, and again she got voicemail. She could text Alice to check whether she'd heard from her, but that meant swallowing her pride and apologising. Or she could go round there now, it would only take a few minutes. But the wind was howling outside, and the children were tucked up in bed. Jean was probably fine.

I'll check on Mum tomorrow, Kate thought. Waiting till then couldn't hurt.

41

JEAN

As the train pulled out of the station, Jean closed her eyes, mentally reviewing all her plans. She had everything she needed for the next few days. The flat was tidy. She had filled up Roddy's bowl and left instructions for the girls. Locked up carefully.

She would wait until tomorrow to text Kate. Calling would be too difficult. There would be questions she couldn't answer.

Kate's revelation that she and Adam had been on the brink of divorce had been a shock. Adam had always seemed so charming, as well as being handsome, good-looking and rich. A doting husband and father. Everything you could want in a son-in-law. But then, Jean had never really trusted charming people.

'All right there, hen,' said a burly guard. 'Tickets?'

'Thank you,' she said, holding it out. 'I'm stopping at Oban. Are we running on time?'

'Aye, for now. Depends on this snow.'

'I'm going on to Raasay after.'

He shook his head. 'You won't make it all the way up there, I can tell you that now,' he said. 'Even if the trains are running the ferry won't be.'

Jean lifted her chin. 'I'll make it,' she said.

She had to take possession of the cottage and she had to do it alone. Because whatever answers lay on the island, she had waited a very long time to find them.

42

KATE

Kate had been up all night, working. She read her email to Marco through one more time. She had decided on brutal honesty.

> *Dear Marco,*
>   *I know you won't be expecting to hear from me. Your feedback on my work was absolutely fair enough. I wasn't listening to what you and your dad wanted. But I'm listening now. It might be too late, but I wanted to show you my idea for Caffe Firenze, just in case.*
>   *You were right. It is a bit special. It just took me a while to see it.*
>   *Very best, Kate Whyte*

She attached the document she'd been working on and sent it off, before she could think better of it.

Then she rang Jean. It went straight to voicemail again. That decided things, thought Kate, throwing on a pair of jeans. She was going round.

She was about to rouse the children when her phone buzzed with a text from Jean.

'Finally,' Kate muttered. She opened the message and her stomach lurched.

'I've had to go away unexpectedly. Would you mind going by the flat and feeding Roddy? For a day or two I'm afraid. Explain later, but all fine, PLEASE DON'T WORRY. Lots of love, Mxx'

Kate stared at her phone and read the message again. The next few *days*?

She rang her mother's number, but it went straight to voicemail. Jean had turned it off.

She threw on a jumper and pulled on her trainers. As she headed down the hall though, the doorbell rang.

It was Lois. She was dressed smartly but wearing trainers and carrying her cycle helmet, as if she was on her way to work. The sky outside was iron grey with the promise of snow.

'Kate,' she said. 'Can I come in for a minute?'

She didn't sound furious, Kate thought nervously. 'Sure,' she said, opening the door. 'Come on in. Excuse the mess. I promise none of these wires are actually live.'

'Wow,' said Lois, following her down the corridor, eyeing the disarray. 'This isn't quite what I imagined.'

'Do you want some tea?' asked Kate. It felt very British to offer tea when you were confronted by the other woman. Not that she *was* the other woman, she reminded herself.

'No thanks.'

Kate decided to take the bull by the horns, now that it was sitting in her kitchen.

'Look, Lois,' she said, pulling out a chair and sitting down. 'I don't know what Dan told you about the night of the Christmas party, but I have a feeling it's not the complete truth.'

'Oh, I know that now,' Lois rubbed her forehead tiredly. 'He told me you'd been flirting with him and leading him on for weeks. Cosy coffees together. Texting him. Playing the sad widow. Throwing yourself at him at the Christmas party. I almost bought it. But then I checked his phone.'

'That's when you found out about Veronica?'

Lois nodded. 'My best friend and my husband,' she said softly. 'What a cliché. It's so embarrassing.' She shivered. 'It's freezing in here, Kate.'

'The boiler's gone. You shouldn't feel embarrassed,' said Kate. 'He's the one who messed up.'

Lois shrugged. 'He's a good dad, you know. Just a shitty husband. I guess I've had enough of getting the raw end of the deal.' She stood. 'Anyway I only came to tell you I'm sorry I was so horrible to you. Turns out you can be very smart and very stupid, both at once. I'll see myself out.' She stopped in the doorway. 'You should keep coming to the PTA, by the way,' she said. 'Don't let Tamara win.'

Kate listened to Lois's footsteps go down the corridor and the door click shut. Something was niggling at the edge of her brain. *Very smart and very stupid, both at once.*

She picked up her phone and read Jean's text message again. 'I've had to go away unexpectedly.' She sank into the chair and tried to think.

Like leaves drifting through the wind, images tumbled into her mind. A polaroid tacked to a cork board, her father and beside him a girl with a mass of golden hair. A map, spread out on the sitting-room floor. A whitewashed cottage in Raasay, on a shingle beach. A book of poetry, with something scrawled on the first page and a postcard hidden in the pages. Jean, distracted, busy . . . The pieces were falling into place, but she didn't know what the final picture would be.

One thing she did know. She needed reinforcements.

43

Jean woke to find the conductor standing over her. The rest
of the carriage was empty.

'We're stopping here in Crianlarich. Sorry, hen,' said the
conductor. 'I didn't think we'd get this far, to be honest,
what with that snow.'

Jean yawned and rubbed her eyes. Then she took her
suitcase, clambered down from the train and stood on the
platform, shielding her eyes against the glare. The sun was
bright and, while she had been asleep, the world had turned
white. She turned up her collar and shivered.

'We're running a coach as far as Oban,' the conductor
said. 'It's out front, you go and hop on. They'll put you up
in a hotel there for the night.'

Jean shook her head. 'I have to get to Raasay,' she said.
'It's important.'

'Not today,' he said sympathetically. He held out a hand
for her suitcase. 'Come on, hen, it's just one night. The train
company will reimburse.'

Jean hesitated, then surrendered her bag. She was the
only passenger on the coach. She huddled into her coat and
watched the white landscape whirling past the window.

Gerard had made this same journey, she thought. And
she didn't think he had made it alone.

Ferry or no ferry, she was getting to that island.

44

KATE

The moment Kate stepped through the front door of her mother's flat, she knew that something was wrong. Roddy was mewing and circling her legs. The hallway was cold and dark.

She scooped up the cat and hurried down the chilly hallway, looking in all the rooms as she went. Her heart was beating horribly fast. There's nothing to be scared of, she told herself. Jean was fine, she had to be.

The flat was tidy as always. Every cushion in place – Jean couldn't bear to leave things in a mess. Another trait Kate hadn't inherited.

Kate reached the kitchen. The kitchen was neat, every surface wiped clean. That was when she saw the note on the table, folded and addressed to her and Alice.

My darling girls,
I'm sorry to rush off like this. Something came up to do with your father, which is very confusing. I need some answers.
I'm sorry to be so mysterious. Please don't worry about me, I'll be back soon and then I can explain everything.
Lots of love, gorgeous girls. Thanks for feeding Roddy. And if Rory comes round, tell him I'm sorry.
Mx

Kate read the note through three times, her bewilderment rising. Something had come up to do with her father? What answers did Jean want? And what did Rory have to do with anything?

Just then, there was a knock at the door. Still in a daze, Kate walked down the hall. There was a tall silhouette at the mottled-glass window. She opened the door and found a man standing there, a lean figure with a dark, serious face.

At first she was too upset to recognise him. And then she saw that it was Rory, from grief group.

'Speak of the devil,' she murmured. 'My mother said you might be round.'

He was looking equally startled. 'Kate, hi,' he said. 'Ah. Is Jean in?'

'No,' Kate said. 'She isn't. What are you doing here, Rory?'

'Jean was to meet me last night and she never showed up.' He was looking more worried by the second. 'She didn't call or anything. It's not like her.'

'No,' said Kate grimly. 'It's not. You'd better come on through.'

In the kitchen she sat at the battered wooden table, reading and re-reading the note.

'I'll make some tea, will I?' said Rory. Kate didn't have the energy to do more than nod. He put the kettle on, moving with ease around the kitchen.

'You've been here before,' Kate said.

'Aye,' he said apologetically. 'Not very often. Jean was worried you might pop in.'

'Right,' said Kate. 'Well, we can discuss that in a minute. First, I want to ask you something. Do you have any idea what this note means?' She pushed it across the table to him.

He read it and shook his head. 'No idea,' he said. 'But at least we know she's all right.'

'But where has she gone and why?' wailed Kate. 'I'm worried.'

Rory poured hot water into the mugs. 'This might be my fault.'

Kate narrowed her eyes. 'Why would it be your fault, Rory?' she asked.

He thought for a moment before answering. He was a considered man, Kate thought. There was nothing nervous or careless about him. Even the way he made the tea was careful and precise. And he had kind eyes.

'Your mother and I,' he said, 'have been seeing each other for the last six months. She wanted to wait to tell you girls. Said you'd all had a hard few years, and the timing had to be right. She was especially worried about you.'

There was silence, while Kate grappled with the realisation that her mother had a *boyfriend*. She remembered Jean's insistence that she come along to grief group. That she meet everybody and get to know them. How shy and flustered she'd been that first day.

'She wanted us to meet,' said Kate slowly. 'That's why she kept pestering me to come to group. But there's more, isn't there?' Rory was quiet. 'Why would she take off *now*?'

Rory took a sip of tea. 'I asked her to marry me, and she said yes.' He glanced up and winced at Kate's expression.

The kitchen seemed to swim in front of Kate's eyes. 'You and my mum are *engaged*?' she said faintly. 'When's – when's the wedding?'

'We hadn't discussed that yet,' he said. He smiled. 'The question is, where is the bride?'

Kate pulled herself together and reached for her phone. 'I'm going to call my sister,' she said. 'I think she needs to hear this.'

Alice picked up, still sounding cross.

'What do you mean, Mum's AWOL?' she said. 'That's a bit dramatic, Kate, even for you.'

'She's left a note and everything,' said Kate. 'Said she's gone to find answers, whatever that means. It's something to do with Dad. I *knew* something was up with her. Come round and I'll explain properly.'

Alice sighed. 'Fine,' she said, sounding exasperated. Luckily for you, I'm in the city. 'I'll come over now.'

Kate hung up and stood. 'Wait here a minute will you, Rory?' she said. 'I just want to see what she's taken with her.'

Kate ran upstairs and took an inventory of Jean's bedroom. The smaller of Jean's two suitcases was gone, along with her winter coat, thick boots and winter gloves and scarf. Her comb and toiletries were gone.

She went into the study and walked over to the cork board. There were a few items pinned to it now, like a genteel CSI investigation.

The solicitor's letter on stiff paper, dated September a year ago. Kate hadn't so much as glanced at it before, but now she read it carefully.

Dear Gerard Whyte,

I am the solicitor for the estate of Ms Eve Carstairs, who died on 21st September of this year.

I enclose documents indicating myself and Mr Scott as executor. The purpose of this letter is to inform you that you have been named in Ms Carstairs' will as the beneficiary of the remains of her estate, including most urgently

a property in Crianlarich. Copies of the deeds are
attached.

   There are time constraints involved in taking posses-
sion of the property. Please respond in writing or by tele-
phone so that we can speak further and arrange a meet-
ing at our offices in Leith or Oban. Please do not delay;
the matter is of some urgency. Identification will be
required.

   I will await your reply.
   Very truly yours, John Moncrieff.

Kate rubbed her forehead. Her father had been left a house
– and he had never known about it.

She moved on to the next item. A postcard. Kate pulled
it down. A little white cottage on a beach. She knew that
cottage – she had spent the last few weeks planning to tear
it down. Postmarked Crianlarich, Raasay. And the words, in
bold handwriting, as though someone had pressed down
hard with the pen:

Remember this? E

Next item, that polaroid. Her father squinting at the sun. A
woman with a halo of gold hair.

And on the desk, the book of poetry that Jean had brought
to grief group. Kate flipped it open. There, on the front
page: '*Yours, E.*' The same decisive handwriting . . . E. *Eve*
Carstairs.

What had the little white cottage meant to her father?
And what had Eve Carstairs meant to him? Enough that he
had kept her photograph, a book of poems, a postcard.
Which, thanks to Kate's meddling, Jean had stumbled
across. And now Jean was gone.

The doorbell rang and Kate went to answer it.

'Don't think I've forgiven you,' said Alice, when Kate opened the door. 'I'm still angry, I'm just worried about Mum.' Rory appeared behind Kate in the hall. 'Who's this?' she asked.

Kate said, 'Rory, this is my sister, Alice. Alice, Rory is Mum's . . . fiancé.' She watched with satisfaction as the colour drained from her sister's face.

Rory made another pot of tea and they all sat around the kitchen table.

Alice was staring at Rory as though he had sprouted horns. 'Where did you and Mum meet?' she asked suspiciously. '*When* did you meet? Help me understand this.'

'We met at a grief counselling group,' he said, pouring tea. 'I've known her for about six months.'

'I didn't realise that grief group was such a hot dating scene,' muttered Alice.

'I get that it's a shock,' he said. He gave them an apologetic smile. 'We can all talk about it later. I think the important thing now is to find your mum.'

Kate had brought through the items she'd discovered in Jean's bedroom and laid them out on the kitchen table. She didn't like the idea of exposing Jean's secrets to Rory, but then again Jean hadn't left them much choice.

'Mum had these all pinned up in the study,' she said. 'A photo, a letter to Dad and this postcard. Which makes me think either they're connected, or at least that Mum thought they were.'

Alice read the letter carefully. 'This is so weird,' she said. 'Who the hell was Eve Carstairs? And why did she leave Dad a *house*?'

Kate pushed the polaroid across the table. 'She's one of these people, I think.'

Alice looked at the picture. 'I'd take bets she's this one,' she said, pointing to the elegant blonde.

'Mum had a little CSI investigation going on. Look at the postcard. *Remember this? E.* I think at some point Dad went off and met Eve Carstairs at this cottage.'

'So, E left him the cottage in her will?' said Alice incredulously. 'That's a bit messed up isn't it?' She groaned. 'You're saying that Dad had an affair? I can't believe it.'

'At the very least, Mum thinks he did,' she said. 'I think she's gone off to find this cottage on this island here.'

'You're assuming she'll get there,' said Rory quietly. They had both forgotten he was there. 'Heavy snow is forecast. One of the worst storms in years.'

'Great,' said Alice. 'She's gone to the Highlands in a complete state, in a snowstorm.' She glared at Kate. 'This is your fault. If you hadn't nagged Mum into sorting through Dad's stuff, she wouldn't have found this letter and none of this would have happened.'

Kate pushed back the chair and stood. 'I will deal with it,' she promised. 'I'm going to collect the kids and then we'll make a plan, okay? I promise, we'll get her back.'

45

JEAN

Jean Whyte stood on the harbour, watching the expanse of water.

'There's no ferries running, hen,' called a voice. She turned to see a fisherman washing his hands at an outside tap, a man in his sixties with a white beard. 'There's a storm coming.'

'I need to get across,' Jean said. 'It's very important.'

He laughed. 'Well, I'd offer to take you across myself,' he said. Her eyes widened and he shook his head. 'That was a joke, love. There's a hotel round the way, you can wait out the storm there. Maybe in a few days, they'll be running again.'

Jean held out her hand. 'I'm Jean Whyte,' she said.

'Callum Roberts,' he said, taking it.

'Callum, I can't explain why but it's urgent that I get to that island tonight,' she said. She smiled up at him. 'I'll pay you double the ferry fare. And something extra. It's nearly Christmas. Go on, do us a favour will you, Callum? I'm sure you can get there and back before this storm starts.'

He frowned at her. 'It's just a wee fishing boat,' he said. 'It'll be rocky.'

'I'm an extremely experienced sailor,' she lied.

After a moment, he laughed. 'All right,' he said. 'Seeing as you're so determined. I hope it's worth all this trouble.'

'It will be,' Jean said. 'I'm going to do something I should have done a long time ago.'

46

KATE

Kate rang on the door to Matthias's flat. There was no answer. He must be out. She wasn't sure whether she was disappointed or relieved. Then, the window above opened, and woman stuck her head out.

'The buzzer's broken,' she yelled, in a French accent. 'I'll come down.'

Kate's heart sank. Even at this angle she recognised the lovely face above her. She had forgotten all about Lily, Matthias's ex.

'Don't worry,' she called, but the window had already slammed shut. She groaned. Of all the people she didn't want to encounter right now, it was Matthias's gorgeous ex.

A few seconds later, the woman appeared at the door. She was wearing worn blue jeans and a soft grey T-shirt. Her thick fringe was falling into her eyes and her face was puffy, as though she had just woken up. Her brown feet were dusty and bare. She looked like she should be starring in a French music video.

'Can I help you?' Lily asked. Her voice was hoarse and sleepy.

'I had a message for Matthias,' Kate said. 'Nothing important, just school stuff, the kids are in the same class.

You could just tell him that Kate stopped by, if that's okay.' She started backing away.

'He'll be back soon,' said Lily. She yawned hugely. 'Sorry, I was having a nap. Matt is taking Olivier to buy some shoes.'

'Oh yeah, Olivier loves his shoes, doesn't he?' said Kate, finding herself babbling. 'I wonder if they've gone to that new shop in Stockbridge, that opened the other week. Anyway, like I said it's not important.'

'Is everything okay?' asked Lily.

Kate sighed. Her head ached and her throat felt sore. Her stomach was churning. Her sleepless night was catching up with her, or maybe she was getting Nat's bug. 'I'm having sort of a family emergency.'

'I'm sorry to hear that,' Lily said. 'Why don't you come up for tea and wait for Matt?'

Curiosity and exhaustion warred with embarrassment, and won. 'Okay, then.' Kate followed Lily up the stairs.

Inside Matthias's kitchen, there was a record playing. 'Come on through,' said Lily. She grinned. 'Into his freakishly tidy kitchen.'

'How long are you staying?' asked Kate, taking a seat, and immediately regretting it. It sounded like she wanted Lily on the next plane out of Edinburgh.

'Another week,' said Lily, rifling through the tea drawer. 'I don't often get a few weeks off, so when I do I like to spend it here with my boys. Are you in a lavender and valerian sort of mood or a lemon and ginger one? Or a homemade mint?' She squinted at the label on a jar. 'Who needs this much tea?'

'Um, maybe lemon and ginger,' said Kate, sitting at the table. 'It must be nice for you to see Olivier,' she said. She groaned inwardly. Now it sounded like she was implying that Lily didn't see enough of her own son.

'It is. Olivier says he wants to come on tour next time, though. You might have noticed that he has a flair for the dramatic. I keep trying to stamp it out, because I do not want him in this industry, but you know . . .' She shrugged her elegant shoulders. 'If you are drawn to something, what can you do?'

'I guess,' said Kate. 'That's nice you and Matthias are friends, still.'

'We weren't together very long,' Lily said. 'Olivier was a bit of a surprise. A happy one, of course. Are you married?'

'Yeah. I mean, no. I was, but he died.'

'Ah,' said Lily. 'Sorry to hear that.' She held out a biscuit tin.

'Matthias made macaroons. He's a great cook. I don't know why he's still single. Well, I have a theory.' Lily put the macaroons onto a plate, handed Kate her tea and then dropped into a chair, sprawling gracefully. 'I think he likes someone, but her situation is complicated.'

'Is it?' croaked Kate. She put a macaroon in her mouth so that she would have something to do. 'In what way?'

Lily stirred her tea. 'The woman he likes had a big loss. Matthias doesn't want to push things. He wants to be a friend to her. But also, he likes her very much.' She took a sip of her tea. 'What do you think he should do, Kate?'

Kate swallowed her biscuit. 'He should probably steer well clear. That woman sounds like a mess.'

Lily smiled. 'You know, that's funny, I said the same. I said, Matt, this woman sounds like a lot of drama and you should avoid. Find someone without all that baggage.'

'Oh,' said Kate. 'Right. So, you told him to, um, leave this woman alone?'

'Yes, I did.' Lily looked at Kate steadily over her mug. 'But now, I think I might have changed my mind.'

'Have you?' said Kate. 'Why?'

'I don't know exactly,' said Lily. 'I'm a good judge of character.'

There was a silence, in which they both drank their tea.

'It's a tricky one,' said Kate at last. 'This – this woman might be scared.'

'I am sure,' said Lily. 'No one said love was easy.' There was the sound of footsteps on the stairs and a key turning in a lock. 'But sometimes love is worth it, no?'

'I guess,' muttered Kate. 'If you want to be all optimistic about it.'

'Through here,' called Lily. 'We're in the kitchen.'

Matthias came in, with snow on his shoulders. He was so handsome, Kate thought, despite that horrible jacket.

'I have met Kate,' said Lily. 'She was outside the flat.'

'Yes,' said Matthias. His expression was unreadable. 'She comes over sometimes. When she gets cold. Olivier would like to show you his new shoes.'

Lily stood. 'I'll go and admire them then,' she said. She winked at Kate and went out.

Matthias took her seat opposite Kate. There was an awkward silence. 'I like your hair,' he said at last.

'Thanks,' said Kate. She fiddled with a teaspoon. 'I'm sorry,' she said at last. 'If I was going to tell you we shouldn't go for dinner again, I shouldn't have told you at the Lyndoch Primary Christmas fete.'

'Don't worry about it. Did you come here to tell me that?'

'I'm worried about Mum,' Kate said. 'She's been acting oddly for ages and then this morning she sent me a text asking me to feed Roddy. I went round to hers and she's not there. I think she's gone to find a cottage on an island. Dad and this woman went there years ago, and they had an affair. Can you believe that? I can't.'

There was a pause. 'Is that all?' Matthias asked.

Kate shook her head. 'No. It turns out Mum's engaged to a man from her grief group and she didn't tell us. So, there's that. I want to find her and bring her home.' She watched Matthias apprehensively. 'Are you thinking I'm even more of a mess than before?'

'I am thinking,' he said slowly, 'that you will need some help.'

'So this is your bedroom,' Matthias said. 'It's how I expected.'

Kate's bedroom was as chaotic and cluttered as usual. Books and magazines all over the bed, clothes spilling out of drawers, jam jars of dead flowers, half-drunk cups of coffee, photos and postcards tacked to the mirror.

'That means you think it's a tip,' Kate said.

'I think it's very you,' Matthias said. 'Are you sure you want to go running off after your mother? She left you a note, told you she was fine and not to worry. Perhaps you should take her at her word.'

'Absolutely not. She needs help.' Kate stuffed a heap of Emmie and Max's clothes into the bag and began rummaging through the laundry for some clean T-shirts.

Matthias sat on the bed, took out the kids' clothes Kate had stuffed into the bag, and began neatly folding them again. 'You think she is in trouble?' he said.

'Maybe, yes.' Kate paused, a pair of socks in her hand. 'I was so busy worrying about my own situation that I missed what was going on right under my nose. I need to put that right.'

'The trains are all cancelled,' Matthias said.

'We'll go in Alice's car,' said Kate. 'I can't let Mum run about the country in this weather the way she must be feeling.'

'If that's the Renault parked outside, I don't think it'll get you very far in a snowstorm.'

Kate sighed. 'Then what do you suggest?'

'You can borrow the van,' Matthias said. 'I'll go home now and make sure there are spare blankets, maps, hot water. You can leave first thing tomorrow.'

'I'm sure it will be the best-provisioned van in all of Scotland,' said Kate gratefully. She struggled with the zip of her bag. 'Thanks for this. I wouldn't do this if I wasn't worried.'

'You should trust your mother,' said Matthias. He took the bag off her and zipped it up. 'She seems like a sensible lady.'

'No one is sensible when they're in love or angry,' said Kate. 'I think Mum might be both.'

47

The sun came out as Jean approached the cottage. It made the sand sparkle.

The storm was toying with them – the iron-grey sky had gone as swiftly as it had come on. Jean set out across the beach towards the whitewashed cottage. She passed a family, wrapped up warm against the wind. The little boy was complaining that he was tired. The father scooped him up and put him on his back.

How many beaches had she and Gerard walked on, just like this? Children wrapped first against their chests in slings, then on their backs, then a hand in theirs, little legs trotting to keep up with their stride. Sandy shells and smooth sea glass proudly offered, pushed into their hands. Jean's pockets would be full of shells by the end of the walk, and she would surreptitiously shed some on the way home, the broken ones, with sharp edges. The ones that were whole and smooth and perfect, she kept. Kate and Alice would line them up when they got home. *Come and look at my treasure*, they would say.

48

KATE

'Where are we going, Mummy?' asked Emmie.

'A road trip,' said Kate, tying her boots. 'A fun adventure with me and Auntie Alice. Fergus is going to come and feed Roddy.'

'But why?' asked Emmie. 'Why are we going *anywhere*?'

'We're going to find Granny,' said Alice. She wrapped up in a parka. 'She's taken a little trip, um, by mistake and we're going to bring her home again.'

'Will we be home in time for Christmas?' asked Max anxiously. 'It's in two days.'

'Of course,' said Kate. 'This is just a little trip.' *With a snowstorm on the horizon.* She pushed down that thought.

'Look,' she said. 'There's Matthias.'

Matthias parked the van and got out. He was wearing a heavy coat, boots and gloves.

'Alice, hello,' he said, holding out his hand. Alice grinned at him.

'Of course! The biscuit guy,' she said. 'I knew it.' She opened the back of the van and chucked her suitcase in the back.

Then she reappeared. 'Wait. Why is there a child in the back? Why does he have luggage?'

Kate looked through the window to see Olivier engrossed in a book.

'I thought we should come with you,' said Matthias. He stuck his hands in his pockets. 'If that's okay. You could use an extra pair of hands. It looks like snow and you've never driven the van before. I've got snacks.'

'You don't want to get involved in this,' Kate said. 'What about Christmas?'

Matthias shrugged. 'I'd rather you got there safely,' he said gruffly.

'Let him come,' said Alice, taking Kate's rucksack. 'I don't trust either of us to drive this thing.'

They had just buckled themselves in when there was a knock at the van window. Kate rolled it down. It was Rory, wearing a wax jacket, with a backpack under his arm, looking sheepish.

'What are you doing here, Rory?' Kate asked.

'I thought you'd be setting off about now. I wondered if you'd like an extra pair of hands.' He shuffled his feet. 'I'd like to know Jean's all right.'

Kate glanced at Matthias, who was looking amused. 'We've got lots of room,' he said.

Alice rolled her eyes, but she was smiling. 'Fine,' she said. 'Let's go with your random bloke *and* Mum's random bloke.'

Kate leaned forward and opened the door. 'You can come,' she said to Rory. 'So long as you can cope with eight hours of I Spy and the soundtrack to *Moana* on repeat.'

49

By the time Jean reached the cottage, the blue sky had once again turned grey and the air was bitter.

The solicitor was waiting for her by the cottage, a round man with ruddy cheeks called Kenneth Scott, who lived on Raasay. He seemed too ruddy and cheerful to be a solicitor.

'Remarkable story,' he kept saying happily. 'We had almost given up finding the owner. And we had a persistent prospective buyer. *Very* persistent. Wants to turn the place into some sort of yoga retreat. Never thought for a moment we would keep it in the family.' He glanced at Jean. 'So to speak. Anyway, I never thought you would make it up here before the end of the year, and in this weather too. That's persistence for you.'

'I was very curious to see the place,' Jean said. 'I thought if I didn't get here today I never would.'

Jean's cheeks burned with the cold. She peered through the porch glass. There was a CLOSED sign on the door and the lights were off.

The solicitor fumbled with the keys and ushered her in. The door jangled. Even inside, their breath billowed on the cold air.

'Och, it's frightful now, isn't it,' Kenneth said. 'They weren't lying about the weather turning. I'll put one of the heaters on.'

Jean moved further into the cottage. A photo was hung by the door of an old woman, surrounded by piles of books. Thick grey hair in a long plait that swung over one shoulder. Blue eyes, dark lashes, high cheekbones. A navy fisherman's sweater and jeans and leather boots.

The room was lined with books. At the back were a few tables and chairs, a little caffe area. Jean remembered that this had been the island's bookshop and caffe.

'Come through,' Kenneth called. 'Tea?'

Jean stepped through the arch into the kitchen area, and there it was, leaning against a caddy of biscuits. A white envelope and, in that familiar, slanting black ink, the name *Gerard Whyte*.

50

KATE

Rory and Matthias sat up front in the van, Kate and Alice in the middle row and the kids in the back.

The city bled into the countryside. Occasionally, Kate caught Matthias's eye in the mirror and looked away quickly. She busied herself checking ferry times, while Rory organised a game of I Spy. Alice was crunching polo mints for her carsickness.

'I need a wee,' announced Olivier, after two hours.

'And me,' said Max.

'Okay,' said Matthias. He turned off the motorway into a service station.

'We'll have to be quick,' said Kate, chewing her nail. She unclipped her seatbelt. 'Come on, kids. I'll take you.'

'It's okay, I'll take them,' said Matthias. 'We can get you a coffee.'

'You're taking all three kids?' asked Kate doubtfully. 'Can you handle it?'

'I'll come in and help you,' said Rory. 'What can I get you girls?'

Kate tried to ignore the faintly parental tone in his voice.

'She'll have a cheese sandwich and a lemonade,' said Alice. 'I'll have the same. And salt and vinegar Squares, please.'

Kate caught Alice's eye, and smiled reluctantly. Their childhood service-station meal.

The children scrambled out of the van and the door slammed behind them as they vanished into the service station.

'What's a cheese sandwich without salt and vinegar crisps,' said Kate. There was a pause. 'I'm sorry I said you were scared of living. I got it all wrong.'

'I don't want a wedding or babies. I love yours, but believe me I'm happy to hand them back. You just decided I should want those things because it's what you did.' Alice met Kate's gaze, her brown eyes hurt. 'Give me some credit, Kate. I know what I want in life.'

Kate nodded. 'I get it, Ally. For what it's worth, my life wasn't as sorted as you think.'

There was silence, and then Alice said, 'I was really excited about getting those bees.'

Kate fumbled in Matthias's snack bag and found an orange. She dug her nail under its skin. 'There's something I need to tell you.' She took a deep breath. 'Adam and I were going to get a divorce. He was on his way back from the lawyers when he was killed.'

Alice gasped. 'That is so typical!' she said.

'Thanks for the sympathy,' said Kate, dryly.

'You think you can do everything without help and it drives people mad,' said Alice. 'I can't believe you were going through all this on your own. You had me fooled – I thought you guys were rock solid. What went wrong?'

'I don't even know,' said Kate, peeling the orange. 'He was always away with work and I was stuck at home trying to do the renovation, two kids in a dust trap. I didn't know how much strain he was under.' She took a deep breath. Since she was being honest, she might as well go all the way.

'Adam had been speculating financially. It was how we bought the flat and the car and had all those skiing holidays.'

'He lost money?'

'He lost everything,' said Kate. 'I only found out after he died. There was just enough to cover the funeral and the last few months.' She rubbed her forehead. Her headache was back and she felt hot. 'He always thought he was smarter than other people. It was my fault too,' she added fairly. 'I got used to leaving money stuff to him. More fool me.'

'Why didn't you tell me?' said Alice. 'We could have helped. Me and Mark and Mum—'

'Because you're rolling in it?' said Kate. She shook her head. 'If we could have just been honest with each other. If we could have turned to each other and said – I know it's hard for you, I get it . . . Well, then maybe we could have got through. I won't ever know.'

'We'll help in any way we can,' said Alice.

'Thanks.' Kate grinned. 'Rory was a bit of a surprise, wasn't he?'

Alice giggled. 'He seems nice though.'

'I'm reserving judgement,' said Kate. She tore the orange in two and handed half to Alice.

They sat there in silence, looking out of the fogged windows and eating the orange.

'I'm sorry I said all those stupid things,' said Kate. 'Happiness looks different to everyone, like Mum always says. My way isn't the only way. I've certainly proved that. I think it was easier to focus on you getting hitched than admit the shitshow of my own life.'

'I'm sorry I said you were an outrageous flirt,' said Alice. 'It's hard having a sister like you. Golden child. Golden life.'

'Till it all came crashing down,' Kate said bitterly.

'Hey,' said Alice. She stretched out a hand, sticky with juice, and squeezed Kate's. 'It's just a new beginning. A better one, maybe.'

Kate rolled down the window and breathed in the fresh, sweet, cold air. The children were on their way back, heads bowed against the wind, Matthias and Rory following, clutching white paper bags and steaming Styrofoam cups. She could hear their shouts and cries. Max was laughing.

A new beginning. A better one, maybe. She would take that, she thought.

51

JEAN

Jean sat on the low wall, eating an apple. The letter was in the pocket of her coat. She just had to take it out and read it.

All those years ago, Gerard had wanted to tell her everything. She hadn't let him. That was to have been his punishment. She had kept her side of the bargain and he had kept his. It was as though those seven days had never happened.

What made things so different now? It would still hurt. But she had to know. Jean stood and threw her apple core into the sea. Then she drew out the envelope and peeled back the flap.

No more secrets.

52

Five hours later, they had listened to *Moana* so many times
Kate was sure she could recite it. The children had become
restless and irritable, until even Olivier was kicking the back
of the seat and whingeing. The air in the car was stale,
everything smelt of banana and the children were covered
in a layer of orange dust from the crisps Rory had bought
them.

Every shriek went through Kate's head like a dagger. Her
throat was hurting more with each passing mile. Her stomach churned.

Several miles outside Oban, her phone rang. She pounced
on it, hoping it would be Jean.

'Mum?'

'Hello, is that Kath?'

'Yeah,' she said, trying to block out the children's yelling.
'Marco?'

'I got your email.' She could hear the grin in his voice.
'Love the designs. My dad does too. You've nailed it, Kath.
That woman was right about you.'

Kate let her head fall back and her eyes close in triumph.
Relief washed over her. 'What woman?' she asked.

'Madeleine something. We got in touch to offer her the
gig and she said to give you another shot. Said she knew

you, and that you were the real deal. That's when I got your email.'

Kate laughed. She felt giddy. 'You're really going to sign this off?'

'Aye, this chef wants to start in the spring. Jim Argylle, his name is.'

'Wait. Jim Argylle as in, Jim Argylle the *Topchef* finalist?' said Kate. 'Jim Argylle with the TV show, whose London restaurant is booked up for months in advance?'

'I guess that's the one,' said Marco. 'Says he's coming home. Expecting a big wait list and all. Oh, and some reporter wants to speak to you about it, from the *Herald*. Said they could give you a call, okay?'

'Okay,' said Kate, beaming. 'Thanks for this, Marco. I won't let you down, I promise.'

'That's all right, Kath. Sorry it took so long. Let's speak after Christmas, hey? Have a good one.'

Kate rang off, beaming. She hadn't lost it, after all, she thought. She'd just needed a bit of a nudge in the right direction.

They arrived at the ferry terminal to find the operator shutting up shop. The snow was so thick up here Kate could hardly see.

'Will it be open in the morning?' Kate asked the operator.

'Can't tell at this rate,' they said sympathetically. 'Depends on whether the snow stops. Sorry, hen.'

Kate got back into the van, rubbing her hands and shivering.

'Don't worry,' said Matthias. 'Another night won't hurt. We'll get over in the morning.'

They found a B&B in Oban, near the harbour. The

owner, Mrs Skelly, said she could do them some supper, which turned out to be stew and potatoes.

The others ate hungrily, but Kate pushed it around her plate. The few bits of cheese sandwich from the service station were sitting uneasily on her stomach.

They put the children together in their own room at their insistence; Kate couldn't tell whether it was an inspired or foolhardy move. She and Alice took one room and Rory and Matthias the other.

Alice was watching the TV and painting her toenails. Kate paced up and down the cell-like room like a caged tiger. The smell from the polish was making her feel worse.

'Sit down,' Alice said. 'Watch some TV.'

Kate stopped pacing. 'I can't believe Dad had an affair. Doesn't that bother you?'

Alice sighed. 'Of course it bothers me,' she said, carefully screwing the lid back on the nail polish. 'But marriage is private. We know they were happy.'

'Were they?' said Kate. The room, with its red walls and carpet and hideous fuchsia coverlet was making her feel even more nauseous. 'I don't even know any more. I feel like my whole childhood has gone up in flames. I thought they were perfect.'

'You don't look that well,' said Alice. 'Look it's stopped snowing. Why don't you go for a walk along the harbour? Cool off, in every sense.'

Kate hesitated. 'The kids . . .'

'I'll keep an ear out,' said Alice. 'Go on, walk off some of that stress. If you see a shop open, bring back some chocolate.'

Kate walked down to the harbour pier, trudging through the settling snow. Her head throbbed. A few elderly folk were walking their dogs. The sky was about to turn dark.

She reached the end of the pier and before she knew it, she was crying. She hadn't realised how much crying one person could do in such a short space of time.

'What is wrong with me?' she wailed to the sea.

'That is a good question.'

She knew before she turned around that it was Matthias. She was too exhausted and miserable to pull herself together. She fumbled in her pocket for a tissue, and he handed her a clean one. She blew her nose, but the tears kept coming.

'I don't normally cry,' she told him. 'Actually, that's not true. I seem to cry all the time these days. I can't believe my dad had an affair.'

He put a cool hand over her forehead and she leaned into it, resting her cheek briefly against his broad shoulder. He put his hand on her waist, holding her upright.

'I think maybe you have a fever. Come back to the B&B and you can take some paracetamol.'

She groaned, but let him lead her back down the pier.

Back at the B&B, Kate's bedroom was empty. She checked her phone to see a text from Alice that read, 'Max woke up. Don't bother coming in, they're all asleep and I'm on the floor. Just get some sleep, feel better and for gods' sake, stop worrying.'

She texted back. 'Thanks. I feel gross.'

'Here,' said Matthias. He was holding out a glass of water and two paracetamol. 'Take these.'

She swallowed them obediently. 'I feel sick,' she said. 'Everything hurts. I think you got me a dodgy sandwich.'

His mouth twitched in his half smile that she realised she loved. 'I'm going to speak to Mrs Skelly and see if she has some crackers. Why don't you put on your pyjamas?'

When he had gone, Kate looked at her reflection. Her eyes were glittering and her face was chalk white except for two red circles in her cheeks. Her forehead was sheened with sweat. She looked terrible. Thank goodness she was too ill to care.

Shivering uncontrollably, she got into her pyjamas and slumped on the bed, closing her eyes to stop the room spinning. When she opened them again, Matthias was setting down a tray of crackers and water.

'She wanted to send up her grandmother's cure-all of whisky and lemon. I said we'd give the painkillers a chance.'

'Thanks,' said Kate, her teeth chattering. She retched suddenly.

'Are you going to be sick?' Matthias said.

'No,' she said. 'Yes. Maybe.' She leapt up and staggered to the bathroom.

She threw up and then washed her face and her mouth out, scrubbing her teeth with toothpaste. When she went back into the bedroom, Matthias was lying back on top of the sheets, watching the television. James Stewart running through the streets of Bedford Falls, eyes wide and hair dishevelled.

'I'm sorry you had to hear that,' she croaked.

'I have an eight-year-old, I'm used to it. Come on,' he said. He patted the bed next to him. 'And drink this.' He held out a glass of water. 'Just a sip.'

She took a swallow of the water, then crawled under the sheets, tugged the duvet up to her neck and lay there shivering. Her pyjamas were already damp with sweat. Matthias's hand lay open-palmed on the duvet and she reached for it, her fingers curling through his. 'I can't get sick,' she muttered. 'I need to get to Mum. I need to make Christmas perfect.'

'Watch the movie,' he said softly. 'This is a good bit.'

'You like *It's a Wonderful Life*?' she asked. 'It's so optimistic and cheerful.'

265

He turned to her. Close to, she could see every detail of his face. Dark eyes, strong jaw.

'It's actually very sad,' he said. 'But that makes the ending even better.'

The shivering receded slightly and Kate started to feel warm. The last thing she remembered before she slept was James Stewart hugging his family to him as the Christmas bells rang and an angel got its wings.

CHRISTMAS EVE

53

KATE

When Kate woke the next morning, Matthias was gone.

She sat up cautiously. Her head didn't hurt and the prickling sensation in her arms and legs had gone. She glanced at her watch. 8 a.m. She had slept for thirteen hours.

She checked next door. Alice and the kids were gone, presumably down to breakfast. She could smell bacon and coffee, and it didn't make her stomach heave.

Kate peered out of the window. Snow was thick on the ground, but it wasn't falling any more. She jumped in the shower and washed, brushed her teeth, then pulled on her jeans and sweater. She stood back and looked at herself. She looked pale and tired, but better. And different, somehow.

Nothing had changed since yesterday. Kate was still an insolvent mess. Her mother was somewhere on the islands, and the snow was deep outside.

And yet, as she ran down the faded stairs to the breakfast room, where she could hear childish chatter and the clink of crockery, she couldn't help feeling oddly, unexpectedly cheerful.

'Thanks for getting the kids dressed, Ally,' she said, slipping into her seat. She avoided meeting Matthias's eye. What was the etiquette when you had thrown up in front of someone and then passed out next to them, holding their hand?

'It was no bother. Matt helped me,' said Alice. 'Are you feeling better?'

'Much.' Kate risked a quick glance at Matthias, who looked entirely calm.

'What can I get you, hen?' asked Mrs Skelly, bustling in. 'I hear you weren't well.'

'Just a twenty-four-hour thing,' said Kate. 'All better. I'm actually starving.'

'I'll bring you some tea and toast,' said Mrs Skelly.

'And some coffee, please,' called Kate. 'I'd kill for a coffee.'

'Must be feeling better,' said Matthias. His eyes met hers and Kate felt her insides going all soft and warm again.

Alice cleared her throat. 'Mrs Skelly seemed to think the ferry wouldn't be running,' she said.

'I do have an alternative,' Mrs Skelly said, setting down toast and marmalade, which Kate pounced on. 'My Robert runs the freight ferry. He'll take you over if you can leave in half an hour. Says he'll risk it, the snow shouldn't pick up again till later.'

'Would he?' said Kate, sitting upright, her toast half-buttered. 'That would be amazing.'

Mrs Skelly patted her hand. 'Aye, he likes an adventure,' she said. 'And three kids at sea in a snowstorm should be that.'

54

JEAN

Dear Gerard,

If you've made it this far, then the lawyers must have
found you. The first thing to say, is that I'm sorry for
everything.

I should have left you well enough alone that summer.
All of us thinking we were so important, working on our
first play. That dreadful pub where we first met, all of us
showing off, playing at being grownups. Except you.

I didn't impress you much, another rich student. I
wanted you to notice me.

All those weeks, getting close to you. You'd a wife and a
baby on the way and I didn't even care. The first-night party.
I saw you over the street, standing under the streetlamp, and I
knew if I went over, you'd kiss me. That horrible little room,
with the gas heater and the tiny bed.

You told me it enough times and I knew that you
meant it. You loved your wife and you would go back
home to her. When I woke up that next morning and you
were gone, I thought that was it.

I didn't expect you to show up at my parents' house, that's
for certain. All those months later. The sight of you, so out of
place. Thank goodness they weren't there.

Your wife had the baby, you said. A little girl. We should

go, before my parents come back, I said. And we did. A week in Raasay in the prettiest cottage, with the owner making a sour face because I didn't have a ring.

When I told you to go home that week, I wasn't being noble – I wanted you as much then as I ever did. I just knew it was the right thing, I knew it in my bones. You wanted your family. Plus, my life was just beginning. That summer was my first taste of freedom, and I wanted more.

I don't regret anything that's happened to me in my whole life, except what happened between us. I was such a selfish little thing. I want to make amends for that.

I think I moved to Scotland because you were here. The first thing I saw in the paper was the cottage for sale. It felt like fate. I had nothing better to do, and I had been so happy there, and god knows I had enough money, so I bought it. I wanted to make something good out of it, and I think I did. People from all over the island come here, they pass the time and talk. It's good for the soul. I sent you a postcard, which I shouldn't have done – but I wanted you to remember it too.

When I got sick, I knew I wanted to leave it to you and your family, the cottage and the land. I didn't have any children or family left.

Anyway, it's yours to do with as you will. Sell it off, if you like. You wouldn't have to tell your family the truth about where it came from. Although you're awfully honest, Gerard; maybe you already have.

All my best, Gerard. I hope you have had all the happiness in the world.

Eve

55

KATE

The freight ferry was a one-man operation. Robert Skelly was a tall, thin man with a shock of white hair who accepted their presence with unruffled calm. He even produced lollipops for the children.

'What's the rush to get to the island?' he asked Kate, once the ferry was on the loch. They were all huddled in their coats in the cabin. 'Staying there for Christmas?'

'We're just visiting someone.' Kate dug into her rucksack for the postcard she had brought with her. 'Do you know this cottage?'

He looked at it. 'Aye, Shingle Cottage. It's a bookshop now,' he said. 'Used to be run by an English lady. Nice wee place, people love it there.'

Kate and Alice exchanged a quick look. 'Do you know the English lady's name?' Kate asked.

'Eve something or other. She died a while back though. It's stood empty all this time, I think some Edinburgh lady was going to buy it. A yoga retreat. Is that where you're going?'

'I think so,' said Kate, putting the postcard carefully back into her rucksack.

'You might be stuck there for a while,' Robert said, with a bark of a laugh. 'Not seen snow like this in years.'

Alice groaned. '*This* was your great plan? Trapped on an island in a snowstorm in the house that belonged to our father's mistress?'

Robert's eyes widened and he faced ahead.

'Sorry,' whispered Kate. 'I didn't realise the snow was going to get so bad.'

Alice shot Kate a dirty look, then turned to Matthias. 'I thought you were sensible, but now I think you're as bad as she is.'

He smiled at her. Olivier was snuggled in the crook of his arm. 'I'm just along for the ride,' he said comfortably.

Alice groaned. 'You're both insane,' she muttered.

'It's an adventure, Ally,' Kate said.

'It's a nightmare, is what it is.'

'Could go either way, I'd say,' said Robert Skelly, his eyes on the horizon. 'Could go either way.'

56

JEAN

Jean could imagine how it had gone, that day in September.

Gerard, standing in a house in Kensington Square, feet planted squarely in the thick pile. Broad back, hands stuck in the pockets of his jeans.

'My wife had the baby,' he had said. He looked awful tired, dark circles under the eyes, pallor to the skin. Babies did that to you.

'Congratulations,' said Eve.

'I left her a note.' Gerard rubbed his forehead. 'I said I had to go away for a while.'

'You left her alone with a baby and a note. Is that meant to make me think anything of you?'

'No.' He pushed the toe of his shoe into the thick carpet. 'I don't think anything of myself.'

Eve made a decision. 'Let's go then,' she said. 'Quickly, before my parents get back.'

And so, they went.

They went to Raasay, because he had gone there as a boy. They had walked along the beach and eaten fried food, cockles sour with vinegar from a van. The owner of the cottage was a dour woman who glanced at Eve's bare left hand and tightened her lips.

And then, one morning, Eve had sent him home.

Jean looked at the photograph on the wall of the elegant older woman. Her gaze was cool and challenging, but not unkind. She thought of Gerard that day, expression anguished.

I want you, Jeanie, you and the baby. I always have and I always will.

'I know,' Jean said to herself. And she did.

Jean stood and walked to the window, stared half unseeing at the road, half obscured by the bare hedge. A car drove past, and then a van.

Anyone hearing the story would see only black and white. Gerard was the villain and she was the abandoned wife and Eve the other woman. It wasn't as simple as that, though.

There were decades of marriage in between then and now, years of sleepless nights and sitting by hospital beds, little hands held in big ones, and piggybacks and wiping noses and parents' evenings and anniversaries and yelling and doors slamming. Money worries and laughter in the dark. In sickness and in health. That was what they had signed up for on their wedding day, Jean thought, and she supposed that it didn't necessarily end with death.

The van was back again, reversing slowly down the road. Jean lifted the curtain to look properly.

Her family had come to find her.

57

KATE

Matthias pulled up onto the verge. Max woke up from his sleep with a start. 'Where are we?' he asked.

'The end of the world,' said Rory. He pointed at a sign through the window. 'Says so.'

The Bookshop at the End of the World.

Alice was asleep, a lock of shining dark hair falling over one flushed cheek. Olivier and Emmie were also sleeping, heads thrown back. Matthias turned to look at Kate.

'Ready?' he said. His eyes were very kind. Kate nodded.

She forced the van door open and climbed out into knee-deep snow. As far as she could see, everything was white, dazzling in the sunshine. A little white cottage with a red roof. She tramped over to it and ran her fingers over the sign. Her heart was beating fast in her chest and the tips of her fingers were cold inside her gloves.

The path to the cottage was clear. At the end, Kate saw that the door was open, and her mother was standing there waiting for her.

After the exclamations and the hugs and the cups of tea, after Alice had taken charge and said since they were staying the night she would unpack, and Jean had rung the solicitor to find them some food and they had lit the fire, Kate left them all behind and went for a walk.

The world felt new. The sky was vast, streaked violet and crimson, the sea huge and glassy. Calm.

The snow had stopped for now. Who knew how long they might be trapped here? And the funny thing was, Kate couldn't have cared less.

Now, she saw Matthias walking towards her. Dropping down onto the jetty, stretching out his long legs. Familiar, she thought, for all that he was so new.

'So,' she said, shifting along for him. 'You met my mum at last. Under unusual circumstances. What did you think?'

'She is lovely,' he said.

'Everyone says that about her,' said Kate, squinting out at the dark sea.

'You have her eyes,' said Matthias. He touched a finger to the side of her face and she turned. 'Smiling eyes.' He considered her. 'Now they are grey I think.'

'I always thought my parents had the perfect marriage,' Kate said. 'It was a lie.'

Matthias pulled her against him and she rested her head against his chest. 'They were happy, no?' he said into her hair. 'That part wasn't a lie.'

'Very happy,' Kate said. 'I'm sure of it.'

'Then it wasn't a lie.' His arms tightened around her. 'What do you want, Kate?'

Rainbows, thought Kate, *and the blue bitter smoke of wood.*

'There's something I have to tell you,' she said, pulling back slightly. 'Adam and I had agreed to get a divorce. Then he died.' His expression was unreadable. 'It doesn't mean I don't miss him. I do, so much, every day.'

'Of course,' he said.

'It just makes things complicated.' She risked another

glance at him. 'Well, even more complicated. Single mum, two kids. I guess you knew that going in. I'm probably not the sensible choice for you.'

He stretched out an arm and pulled her towards him again. 'I don't think we always want the sensible thing.'

'I don't want to rush anything,' she said into his coat. 'The children have been through so much.'

'Of course not,' he said, soothingly.

'Are you humouring me?' she asked.

He laced his big hand through hers and his lips brushed her hair. 'I want you,' he said quietly, in her ear. 'That's all. We can take our time getting there.'

She laughed a bit weepily. 'I can't tell if that's annoyingly vague or super functional.'

Matthias lifted his face to the sky. 'We should go in,' he said. 'It's Christmas Eve, and in Belgium, that's when we really celebrate.'

'I'm sorry,' said Kate. 'Sorry I dragged you to the end of the world, to have Christmas with my family.'

He stood and held out a hand to her. 'Nowhere else I'd rather be,' he said.

CHRISTMAS DAY

58

KATE

It wasn't the perfect Christmas.

For a start, they didn't have any presents or stockings or a turkey.

On Christmas Eve, they had the Belgium celebration. The solicitor and his wife came round with a bag full of shopping, tutting and exclaiming over their predicament. They had sausages and bread and butter, which Matthias assured them was a traditional Belgian feast.

After the children had gone to bed, he and Kate pilfered the bookshelves for children's books and filled his and Rory's socks with them for stockings. Jean also produced a bundle of hand-knitted scarves.

'I did these at knitting group,' she explained. 'I'll finish them up for the kids tonight.'

'Were you really going to all those groups, Mum?' Kate asked. 'Or were you sneaking off to meet Rory?'

Jean flushed. 'A bit of both,' she admitted. 'I only played golf once. It turns out it really is a lot of walking.'

'What are we going to do, Mum!' Kate said, looking around. 'It's Christmas and there's no presents or lunch! I wanted this to be perfect.'

Jean squeezed her arm. 'Perfection is overrated,' she said.

There were some tins in the larder that were perfectly good. Mr Scott had given them a cold chicken and a ham, a stew and a loaf of bread, and a Christmas pudding.

'A good thing my wife always makes a spare. You're all mad!' he said, his eyes creasing in mirth. 'Have a good one, though. Happy Christmas!'

Kate slept late on Christmas Day, still exhausted from her stomach bug. She followed the sound of clatter downstairs and came into the breakfast room to find them all dressed and eating kippers and brown bread and butter. To her surprise, Max was on Rory's knee and they were reading a book.

Jean and Matthias collaborated on lunch and they did jigsaw puzzles and ate chocolate in front of the fire, went for a walk on the beach when the snow stopped, drank whisky. The children performed a reprise of THE SEASICK PIRATE'S CHRISTMAS, which Kate had to admit was improved on by a glass of single malt.

Throughout the house, she kept seeing clues as to the woman who had owned it. Muddy boots in the boot cupboard, expensive bath oils in the bathroom, stacks of worn playing cards, a silk dressing gown on the back of a door. The children built an army of snowmen in the garden. Jean was quiet, but not, Kate thought, sad or angry. More thoughtful.

In the evening, the children curled up in front of the fire on cushions with Matthias and Rory to play cards, while Alice chatted on the phone to Mark.

'Fancy a walk, Mum?' said Kate and Jean nodded.

Max tugged on her leg as she stood up. 'Mum,' he whispered. She crouched down next to him.

'What is it, baby?' she asked.

'I just realised.' His face was flushed and sleepy. 'We had two bad Christmases. And now we've had two really good ones – one last night and one today!'

She ruffled his hair. 'That's right,' she said. 'Our luck must be changing.'

She and Jean walked onto the beach and breathed in the clean evening air.

'How about it Mum?' said Kate. 'You owning the house where Dad came with her. Tell me I'm not the only one who thinks it's weird.'

Jean giggled. 'Weird is one word for it. I never would have thought Ger was the type. It makes a funny kind of sense, though, you know. Your father always did the right thing, worked hard, got ahead. He was so scared of ending up like his parents he never put a foot wrong. Of course he would have a moment of madness. Eighteen and a wife, a baby, a job. A mortgage. Away in Edinburgh with those theatre people, it must have seemed like another world. I think he got it out of his system and never looked back. I'd like to think of it like that, anyway.'

'He *was* happy with us,' said Kate firmly. 'We didn't imagine all of that.'

Jean slipped an arm through hers. They turned and looked up at the little cottage, smoke from the wordburner drifting up into the air.

'I'm sorry I dragged you all up here,' Jean said. 'I had to come here before Christmas. For the solicitors, but also to draw a line under it, somehow, if I was ever going to start again.'

'You mean, start again with Rory,' said Kate.

Jean smiled shyly. 'I'm sorry you found out about Rory the way you did. I thought you would come to grief group for a few months and get to know him and realise how dear and kind he is, and then when I told you, you'd be pleased.'

'I understand,' said Kate. 'We're getting to know him now.'

'No more secrets, I promise,' said Jean. 'From either of us. Deal?'

'No more secrets,' promised Kate.

The moon broke through the clouds then, turning the landscape glittering white. 'This feels like a dream,' said Jean. 'What a beautiful place.'

'Shame we have to go back to real life,' said Kate.

Jean turned to her and smiled. In the moonlight she looked very young.

'Real life isn't so bad,' she said. 'And, for what it's worth, I think it's going to be a really good year.'

The snow began to fall again. Standing there on the beach, pebbles beneath her feet and woodsmoke in the air, fat flakes of snow drifting down and the laughter of children carrying in the still air, Kate could almost let herself believe her mother was right.

Not the perfect Christmas. But a good one, all the same.

AFTER CHRISTMAS

59

KATE

On Boxing Day, the snow had cleared enough to travel. Alice, Jean and Rory got a lift to the mainland with Robert Skelly to embark on the long journey home – Mark had driven up to meet them. Kate and Matthias had decided to stay on with the kids for a few days.

'We might as well,' said Kate. 'Things can't get any weirder.'

They set off fireworks on the beach on New Years' Eve and Kate and Matthias drank whisky. They walked with the children along the beach and ate more sausages. Played cards and laughed until Kate felt sick. It all felt allowed, because it was a holiday. The children stayed up late. At midnight, the children summoned Kate into the sitting room.

'What's going on?' she asked suspiciously.

Matthias was laughing. 'At the new year, it is customary for children to write a letter to their parents. They can tell them what they really think of them. Max and Emmie wanted to write one for you. We thought they could read it now.'

'Oh,' said Kate. 'Er. It's all good, right?'

'I'm going to read it because Max can't read yet,' said Emmie. She cleared her throat importantly. 'Ready?'

'Ready,' said Kate, sitting to attention.

Dear Mummy,

    This letter is to tell you what we really think of you.

    First, we think you should try not to worry so much. We miss Grandpa and Daddy and Hamish but there's nothing you can do about that. We like fish fingers. We like it when Fergus picks us up from school.

    Second, we wanted to tell you to try and be brave. Because it's all a big adventure and if you're going to have an adventure, you have to be brave.

    You're the best mummy in all the world, the universe.

    Love, Emmie and Max

On 2nd January, they drove back to the ferry and the city, with the children sleeping in the back. And real life began again. The same, only different.

The relaunch of Caffe Firenze was in early June. Kate took Jean as her plus one for the opening.

'It's beautiful, darling,' said Jean. She trailed her fingers with pleasure over the polished wooden surface of the bar. 'This reminds me of my parents' place.'

'You don't mess with the original when it's as good at this.' Kate grinned at Marco. 'I finally realised that.'

Marco threw an arm around her shoulders. 'She's done a great job, hasn't she?' He looked around, beaming. 'Not too wanky. And that lad's kept our specials on the menu, so the regulars should be pleased.'

The chef had returned to his roots, with a Michelin star to his name, with a menu that encompassed Scottish-Italian comfort food including macaroni cheese and a knickerbocker glory. The early reviews were all raves. Some of them even mentioned the exquisite interior design, the restoration of the traditional Edinburgh Scottish-Italian caffe in all its glory and Kate got a spread in the *Herald*. Marco's father Beppo even clapped Kate on the shoulder and told her she'd done all right.

Kate had been busy ever since. She was suddenly the go-to interior designer. A few weeks later, she met with Madeleine for a drink.

'Two things,' she said. 'Firstly, thank you for putting in a good word for me with Marco. And secondly, I want to come back to Domus.'

'But darling, why?' Madeleine exclaimed. 'You're doing brilliantly. All everyone is talking about is Whyte Designs. Strike while the iron is hot.'

Kate shook her head. 'I thought I was ready to go it alone,' she said. 'I'm not. I miss Domus. I miss colleagues and the office. I miss my amazing mentor.'

'Perhaps there's a compromise,' Madeleine said slowly. 'How does Domus-Whyte Designs sound to you?' She smiled. 'Let's face it, we'll be better off as allies than rivals. I don't think either of us have the killer instinct.'

Jean, Kate and Alice spent hours discussing what to do with the cottage.

'We should just sell it, for goodness' sake,' said Jean. 'It's too strange, a place like that, with all those memories. And which of us have the energy to run a bookshop?'

'I would,' said Alice, surprising them. 'Mark loves it up there. Think how many chickens we could have.'

'The kids did love it there,' said Kate. 'How nice would it be, going there for the holidays. I know it must be weird for you, Mum . . .'

Jean sighed. 'Maybe there is a place in the Whyte family for the bookshop at the end of the world. What about all that money she left though?'

'We'll do something good with it,' said Kate. 'I always

thought I'd make a good philanthropist. But I don't need any of it. I'm doing all right now.'

And she realised, with a glow of pride, that it was true.

School started again, and again things were at once different and the same. Veronica took the news that her wellness retreat actually belonged to Kate's mum with equanimity. She and Craig had spent Christmas together with the kids and were having marriage counselling.

'God knows whether we'll make it or not,' Veronica told Kate and Nat one afternoon at yoga, as they dropped into downward dog. 'But I'm learning a lot about myself. The therapist thinks I might have control issues.'

'No,' said Kate, grinning. 'I don't believe it.'

'I'm going back to business school,' Veronica said. 'I think maybe I got a bit bored. If I'm going to start my wellness empire I want to know what I'm doing.'

Veronica also resigned as head of the PTA. In a surprise move, Euan made a bid for leadership, and beat Tamara in the polls. He told Kate that he was aiming for a fairer, more democratic PTA, with Veronica as his right-hand woman.

'That woman knows her stuff,' he said. 'Everyone deserves a second chance. Will you stay on? You really do have creative flair, you know, she wasn't just blowing smoke.'

'Hell, yes,' Kate said cheerfully. 'The next big event is Easter, right? We'll give Lyndoch Primary an Easter egg hunt to remember. Hopefully without any dramatics.'

With the new year, the old resentments in the class seemed to have died away. Toxic Lydia got into football over Christmas and Emmie started playing with other kids. Doing pickup one day, Kate watched Lydia playing football with a group of boys and girls, shrieking with laughter. Emmie was in another part of the playground, playing tig with Olivier and some other kids. Toxic Lydia had never been toxic, Kate realised; the friendship had been bad for both of them.

Max, emboldened by his cross-country adventure, began speaking up in class more and made some friends.

It was common knowledge that Dan and Lois were getting divorced. On the first day of the spring term, Dan had cornered Kate. 'I'm seeing a therapist,' he explained. 'She seems to think I should start by apologising to people. So, here I am.'

'Is this your apology?' Kate asked coldly. 'Because I didn't hear the word "sorry."'

'Sorry,' he muttered.

'Fine. Accepted,' she said, turning to leave. Then she stopped. 'Oh, and Dan? Stay away from the PTA.'

Lois and Veronica made tentative reparations. Lois stayed on at the PTA but, in her own words, grew a spine. They had all gone for a glass of wine the other week after a yoga class, and, as Kate had told Fergus afterwards, she had been surprised by how much she had enjoyed it.

'They're really nice,' she said. 'You were right, none of them are that scary.'

Fergus had laughed. 'Told you so. Hey, did Nat tell you, we're getting a rescue dog. You can finally pay me back for all those school pickups by walking it once a week.'

Kate and Alice spent time with Rory. They got to know his dry sense of humour and slow smile. He did maths homework with Max and Emmie and talked to laconic Mark about engineering. He clearly worshipped Jean. They were planning a Christmas wedding and Kate realised she was happy about it. He wasn't *Dad*, but he didn't seem to want to be.

'Will he move in with you?' she asked Jean one day, as

they shopped for wedding shoes. 'I can't imagine him in our house.'

'I know,' said Jean, holding a pair of green silk pumps to the light. 'But I think I'll give it a shot. Awful quiet there on my own, you know? And I miss having someone to cook for.'

Grief group carried on. Kate didn't go every Thursday, but she came most weeks. She found she missed the stuffy little room and the bad coffee, Ada and Frances and Maggie.

She was learning that grief was not a box to be ticked or a fence to be hurdled. It was like the sea. Sometimes the sea was calm and she could walk in up to her waist. Then a wave would come and knock her off her feet, pushing her under with so much force that she could barely breathe. Those waves came out of nowhere. But she knew now that they didn't last forever.

It had taken six months, and a determined estate agent, to sell the flat. Kate had barely broken even. They had exchanged smoothly, and she had found them a little two-bedroom place around the corner to rent.

On the day she was due to sign the lease, they were at Matthias's flat. It was Sunday and he had cooked lunch. The children were playing in the other room and Kate was at the sink. She had finally been permitted to do the washing up. She put down the cloth and turned to look at Matthias.

He was chopping an onion in half to add to the pot that had the chicken carcass in it. She watched as he dropped in a bay leaf, a sprinkling of peppercorns. She loved him, she realised. Simple as that.

Without turning around, he said, 'You're staring at me.'

'I'm not,' she said, turning quickly back to the sink.

'I could feel your eyes on my back.'

'I . . .' She swallowed. She couldn't imagine how Matthias would handle an overblown declaration of love. He would probably nod and go back to his stock.

She felt him come and stand behind her. He dropped a kiss onto the nape of her neck and she shivered.

'Kate,' he said quietly, against her neck. 'Are you freaking out?'

'No,' she said, staring at the plates in the sink. 'Maybe a little bit. The thing is . . .'

'Yes?' he said encouragingly.

'I think I'm in love with you,' she wailed to the dishes.

There was silence. Then he pushed her thick hair aside and pressed his mouth against the back of her neck again. They stayed there for a long moment, leaning against each other, and then he said, 'Good. Because I love you too.'

'You do?' she said. 'Why didn't you say anything?'

He shrugged. 'I was worried about *this*. I thought you'd panic.'

'I *am* panicking. This is way too soon.'

He turned her around to face him. 'Do you really want to move into a flat around the corner, when I have this big flat with all this room?'

'No,' she said miserably. 'I want to stay here in your lovely flat and unpack the kids' stuff properly. I want to live here with you and Olivier and be a family. I want to wake up with you every morning and I want you to make us roast chicken every weekend. But nothing is that easy. I can't do this to the children unless I know it's forever and how can anyone know that?'

'How can anyone know anything?' he said.

'Stop being so philosophical,' she whispered.

'Okay,' he said, tilting her head up. 'In that case, I loved you from the minute I saw you, in that miserable playground.'

'Now you're just being ridiculous.' A tear trickled down one cheek. 'You have to tell me that this will categorically, no question, work out.'

He wiped her cheeks. 'How about I tell you this,' he said. 'I love you, Kate Whyte, and I love your kids, and I think you should move in with us and be happy because there's every chance we will be.' He smiled. 'Does that inspire more confidence?'

'A bit,' she said.

They stood there, in the kitchen, for a while, Kate leaning against his chest, his arms around her. Drowsy afternoon summer light filled the room. The chatter of children drifted through from the other room.

If you're going to have an adventure, then you have to be brave.

This is my favourite place, thought Kate. *I could stay here forever.* And maybe, she thought, that was exactly what she would do.

ACKNOWLEDGEMENTS

This book was written in the blur that was early 2020, in lockdown, amidst work deadlines, to a soundtrack of CBeebies and Joe Wicks. A huge thank you to my husband, Alex, for looking after us all so well during that time and going above and beyond with childcare. Thank you also to everyone who helped us during that weird time – grandparents who read stories over Zoom, teachers who kept classes going, school pals who organised WhatsApp groups, friends and neighbours who sent treats.

A huge thank you to everyone who helped with and worked on this book. The brilliant team at Hodder – Melissa Cox, Morgan Springett, Natalie Chen, Claudette Morris, Kate Keehan. Jim Caunter for the copyedit and Susie Wright for such a beautiful cover. My agent Jane Finigan; Louise Lamont for all the Edinburgh inspiration – and the city itself for providing such a fine setting for a wintry romance. Michelle Scott and Fiona Gillespie for the very helpful name inspo and crucial caffeine delivery.

And thanks finally to Florence and Theodore, for being such complete stars this year.